crush

control

crush

JENNIFER JABALEY

control

razor
bill

An Imprint of Penguin Group (USA) Inc.

Crush Control

RAZORBILL

Published by the Penguin Group
Penguin Young Readers Group
345 Hudson Street, New York, New York 10014, U.S.A.
Penguin Group (USA) Inc., 375 Hudson Street, New York, New York 10014, U.S.A.
Penguin Group (Canada), 90 Eglinton Avenue East, Suite 700,
Toronto, Ontario, Canada M4P 2Y3 (a division of Pearson Penguin Canada Inc.)
Penguin Books Ltd, 80 Strand, London WC2R 0RL, England
Penguin Ireland, 25 St Stephen's Green, Dublin 2, Ireland
(a division of Penguin Books Ltd)
Penguin Group (Australia), 250 Camberwell Road, Camberwell, Victoria 3124, Australia
(a division of Pearson Australia Group Pty Ltd)
Penguin Books India Pvt Ltd, 11 Community Centre,
Panchsheel Park, New Delhi – 110 017, India
Penguin Group (NZ), 67 Apollo Drive, Mairangi Bay, Auckland 1311, New Zealand
(a division of Pearson New Zealand Ltd)
Penguin Books (South Africa) (Pty) Ltd, 24 Sturdee Avenue,
Rosebank, Johannesburg 2196, South Africa

Penguin Books Ltd, Registered Offices: 80 Strand, London WC2R 0RL, England

10 9 8 7 6 5 4 3 2 1

ISBN: 978-1-59514-424-9

Library of Congress Cataloging-in-Publication Data is available

Printed in the United States of America

For Chris,

who hypnotized me the old fashioned way—

with his charm.

prologue

Once upon a time there was a boy. His hair was the color of coal, his eyes the color of faded denim. His smile, carefree and inviting, was the one thing that made me brave. He lived in a white-shingled house at the end of a cul-de-sac where we rode our bikes and played kickball. He taught me how to climb trees and how to build drums from an old oatmeal box, paper, and glue. Every adventure, every moment of childhood mischief, was because of him. Max Montgomery was his name.

Then, the summer I was nine my mother dropped the bomb of ultimate betrayal: "We're moving!" She beamed. "To Vegas!" She sparkled like the neon casino lights that would soon become as familiar to me as Max's soft blue eyes.

"Vegas?" I panicked. Sure, I had seen the real estate brochures scattered around the house. I had noticed Mom's growing fascination with the shows on the Vegas Strip. I had endured watching the How-to-Hypnotize-Someone video series with her. But I thought it was a phase. Now we were moving? Seriously? "Mom, I can't leave my friends!" I whined.

"You'll make new friends."

But I could never replace Max.

Later, when I told Max about our plans to move, he reassured me. "We'll always stay friends."

"Best friends," I corrected as we rode our bikes into the entrance of Poplinger Park. We jumped off and parked the bicycles against an old oak tree.

"Best friends," Max agreed. "I promise."

I nodded in confirmation. It was a heartfelt declaration filled with the conviction only a nine-year-old could feel when leaving her best friend.

Max reached up and began to climb the tree. In the distance, a green car came into view. "Shoot." He froze. "Is that my mom?"

"Uh oh," I groaned. "Quick, help me up." Max was supposed to be cleaning out his garage. But he decided he couldn't spend one of our final days together doing chores. So we snuck away.

Max reached down and hoisted me up into the tree. I positioned myself onto a grainy limb and huddled close to him. Below us, the car turned into the bank across the street and we both sighed with relief.

I smiled at him. "Who are you going to have these adventures with once I'm gone, huh?"

"Well," Max said, resting against the thick trunk of the tree. "Trent and I are thinking about starting a band."

What? The correct response should have been: *No one can ever replace you, Willow.*

"A band? Does Trent even play an instrument?" I asked, a little too snappish.

"He just started guitar lessons at the same place I take drum lessons," Max answered.

Well, isn't that nice. I'm not even gone and you already have a replacement friend. I tried to blink fast so my eyes wouldn't well up. I grabbed a higher tree limb and pulled myself away from him but he quickly followed and finagled into a position next to me.

"Mom said I could go up on stage with her," I lied. "Be part of the hypnosis show." *There, I have plans for life without you, too.*

Max burst out laughing.

"What? You don't think I could actually do the hypnosis?" I asked, hurt. "She's had that How-to-Hypnotize video on twenty-four hours a day. It's not that hard."

Max rolled his eyes.

"I'll show you right now! I'll hypnotize you!"

"Fine," he said. "Go ahead. Let's see."

"Fine!" I said, sitting up straighter. "Close your eyes."

He gripped the tree limb for support, and shut his eyes.

"You're feeling very relaxed," I said in a low, serious tone.

Max started to laugh. "What's with that voice?"

"HUSH!" I commanded, glad his eyes were shut and that he couldn't see my cheeks flush. I was just trying to sound like the lady on the video. I readopted my own tone. "I'm going to guide you through to deep relaxation. Take a breath."

Max inhaled then slowly let his breath out.

"From this point on, you will hear what I say, feel what I ask you to feel, see what I ask you to see." I continued through the entire sequence. I wasn't sure what I was expecting, or if it was really going to work. Then, suddenly, Max's head flopped over to the side, resting on the tree trunk. I sat there for a minute with my heart racing. *Had I done it? Was Max really hypnotized?* I looked at his mouth hanging slightly open and his chest softly rising with each breath.

I thought about what my life would be like in a few days—a new city, a new school, Mom's new crazy job. What part of my life would remain unchanged other than my friendship with Max? But now even that was slipping away . . .

I looked at the small amount of drool collecting in the corner of his mouth. If Max was really hypnotized, that meant he was under my influence. "Max Montgomery," I said with a flutter of excitement. "For as long as we live, you and I will be best friends. Even though my mom will drag me two thousand miles away to live in the desert, we will remain friends forever. We'll talk on the phone, e-mail, and when my mom finally gives in and buys me a cell phone, we can text message all the time. Even if you become some big famous rock star and *Trent* is your awesome guitarist and you have a million groupies, still you'll think, *Willow Grey is my best friend.*"

Max's grip had loosened on the tree limb and his elbow had bent in relaxation. On the street below a green Honda Accord drove up to the curb. *Oh no.* The car door opened and Mrs. Montgomery climbed out. *Shoot.* I pulled up my dangling legs and tried to nestle my body into a bunch of leaves.

"Max!" I whispered. "Max!" But he kept on breathing heavily, the stream of drool dripping down his chin now. I tried to lean closer to him. "When I clap my hands you're going to wake up," I said quickly. "You're going to feel refreshed and relaxed, like you just had a long nap." I tried to clap my hands, but I didn't want to release my grip on the tree limb.

Below us, Mrs. Montgomery looked around the grassy area by the picnic tables. "Max?" she called, looking around. She walked over to a lady pushing her son on a yellow swing and asked her something. The lady shook her head and Max's mom turned back around.

"Max!" I whispered. "Wake up!" I used one hand to smack the trunk of the tree and Max's eyes popped open and his shoulders retracted in surprise. His hands flailed wildly and he fell backward, his knees hooking around the tree limb like those of a gymnast on the uneven bars. But he missed his dismount, plunged through the air, and crashed to the ground.

"MAX!" I cried.

He yelled in pain as I quickly shimmied down the side of the tree and hovered over him. "Are you okay?" I panted. I looked over and saw his mom scurrying toward us. "Quick," I whispered. "Do you think you can make a break for it into those bushes?"

"I think I broke my arm," he said.

"Shoot," I said under my breath, just as Mrs. Montgomery's shadow fell over us.

A week later we moved to Las Vegas, and I only saw Max occasionally after that. He was, and continued to be, my best friend. Not a day went by when we didn't call or email. Sometimes I would wonder, was it because we were such good friends or had that attempt at hypnosis in the tree actually worked? And even though I never really knew if I had successfully hypnotized Max or not, that's when my life split in two: before and after the taste of total control.

If I had known I was going to meet anyone of significance that steamy August day, I would not have worn my old cotton shorts and a flimsy white T-shirt with two dancing M&M's on the front. Because first impressions are everything and I'm not all long-limbed and silky like my name, Willow, might suggest. I'm not nimble and flexible like the Cirque du Soleil girls I grew up around in Vegas, and I'm certainly not exotic and alluring like my mom, the Hip Hypnotist ("The hottest show on the strip," according to the posters). If I even attempted to act sexy, raising my eyebrows and purring at a guy, he'd probably call animal control.

I'm just an average-looking girl who tries my best to play the hand I was dealt. And trust me, wearing a T-shirt that highlighted a Halloween staple was definitely not stacking the cards in my favor. The only mention of melt-in-your-mouth chocolate should have been the hot guy's gorgeous, soulful eyes as I stared at him from across the basketball court—not the dancing, hard-shelled candy ironed across my chest.

But the movers hadn't arrived yet and the duffel bag filled with my more acceptable clothing was still jammed somewhere in the trunk of our Toyota, which was parked in our new driveway and overheated after the torturous twenty-nine hour trip. So it really wasn't a matter of choice as much as availability. Nonetheless, at that moment, standing in the park watching this beautiful boy, I could feel a spotlight shining down from the cloudless summer sky, highlighting me in my M&M T-shirt and announcing: *Alert! Alert! Dork approaching!*

For a moment, I stood there behind the safety of an oversize shrub and watched him. He was tall and lanky, shooting hoops by himself and animatedly narrating his three-point shot like he was an NBA announcer.

"The audience waits in anticipation for his legendary half-court three-pointer," he said, stopping to dribble the ball at the half-court mark. "He pauses, taking a moment to hear them cheer his name. Then he takes a step forward and a hush falls on the crowd. He shoots. . . ." He tossed the basketball up toward the goal. His wrist flexed in midair as the ball hit the backboard and swooshed through the net. "He makes it! The crowd goes wild! He just might be the most highly recruited high school senior the NBA has ever seen!" The hot guy turned toward his pretend audience and bowed. "Thank you! Thank you," he said.

He walked over to the picnic table and took a swig from his Gatorade bottle. Then he used the back of his hand to toss his tousled golden brown hair off his forehead. He looked like he could climb onto a surfboard and ride the waves in a California-cute kind of way. Only he was landlocked, stuck playing basketball in this small, sweltering Georgia town, three hundred miles from the nearest ocean. He was completely gorgeous. Completely out of my league.

As he turned toward the shrub, I ducked. This hot guy might not give me a second glance, but I couldn't take the chance of him seeing me like this and forever thinking of me as the M&M girl. I turned to go—I had to dig my duffel bag out of the car and change before I could cause any real damage to my image—but as I did, there was an abrupt tug on the dog leash I was holding in my right hand.

"Sshh!" I said, squatting down to pet my Boston terrier, Oompa. He looked up at me with an irritated expression, the same one he'd worn since my mom and I deposited him into the backseat of our car two and a half days ago. Oompa turned his head in the direction of the hot guy and his ears stood up like two isosceles triangles.

"I know," I whispered. "He's beautiful, right?"

Oompa eyed me and scrunched his face up, looking maybe a smidge jealous at seeing my attention directed elsewhere. Then, all at once, he bolted like a streak of lightning, yanking the leash out of my hand as he darted from our dirt path, across the small patch of grass, and onto the steaming cement basketball court—right towards the hot guy.

"Oompa, come back!" I whispered loudly. But I could do nothing but watch, panicking, as my dog began jumping up onto Hot Guy's leg. Hot Guy dropped the bottle of Gatorade in surprise. Neon yellow liquid pooled on the cement around his feet. "What the . . .?" he floundered. He looked down at Oompa and shook his leg gently.

Then, as I stood there, still hidden behind the large shrub, I watched in complete horror as Oompa velcroed his body to Hot Guy's leg—and began to bounce against it. My dog looked back at me with a smirk across his little dog face as if to say, *How dare you stick me in the car for two days, then lavish attention on someone else?*

Oh my God, my dog is humping the leg of the hottest guy I've ever seen! What do I do? I contemplated running away. But Oompa would never be able to find his way back to our new house. I would have to come out of hiding and coax my stupid dog off his leg. *I can't believe I worried about a stupid M&M T-shirt—because a dog humping your leg is absolutely the worst first impression ever! Ever!*

Hot Guy shook his leg again and laughed. "Wrong gender, dude," he said. "Wrong *species*." He looked around in embarrassment to make sure no one was watching.

When the twenty-seven-pound barnacle didn't dislodge, he reached down and tried to manually break free. But Hot Guy's leg tripped on Oompa's leash that was tangled around his ankle. His Reebok slid in the pool of lemon-lime Gatorade, and all at once Hot Guy and Oompa skidded up into the air. They crashed onto the hard cement with a sickening thud.

"Oh no!" I darted from the safety of the bushes. "Are you okay?" I offered my hand to help him up. "I'm *so* sorry."

He didn't take my hand but eased himself up off the ground, looking perplexed.

Oompa licked the excess Gatorade off his fur then looked up at me with provoking eyes as if to say, *I'm homesick, I'm carsick, and I'm very angry with you.*

"Is that your dog?" Hot Guy asked sounding a little pissed.

"Um . . ." I looked down at Oompa. "Would you believe me if I said *no*?"

Hot Guy smiled a small smile and my stomach relaxed a bit. He shook his head. "Not likely."

I laughed a little. "I am so sorry. He's all crazy." I pointed to my temple and twirled my finger in a circle. "We just moved here. Like today. We've been in the car for an eternity and he's just a little disoriented." *And please don't judge me by my M&M T-shirt and my humping dog.*

"Oh yeah?" he asked, brushing his hair away from his eyes again. "Where did you move from?"

But before I could answer, my mouth gaped open. "Um, ah . . ." I pointed awkwardly toward his hip, where the waistband of his nylon shorts had a darkened red spot. "I think you're bleeding."

He looked down and lifted up his shirt to reveal a scrape. "Oh," he said. He walked back over to the picnic table and rummaged through a small backpack. He found a pocket-size package of Kleenex and pulled out a tissue. He began to wipe up the blood, clumsily reaching around his waist to clean the cut. But it was at the small of his back and hard for him to reach.

I stood there awkwardly. *Should I leave? Offer to help?* I watched him struggle. "Um, do you need some help?" I finally asked.

He looked at me then looked over his shoulder toward the cut as if assessing the probability of reaching it on his own. "Yeah, okay. Thanks," he said. "There are tissues in my backpack." He nodded over to his bag on the picnic table.

As I walked over and reached into his bag, I couldn't help but notice the contents: an iPod, two spiral-bound notebooks, a bottle of Germ-X, a PowerBar, and two bags of M&M's. I looked down at my T-shirt and smiled. Of course he was gorgeous; that was obvious. But how could I not be further enamored of a guy who had the forethought to pack tissues and Germ-X as well as chocolate? Preparation was a priority for me so to see a boy—a hot boy—who obviously valued this as well? *Swoon.*

I walked toward him. He raised his shirt higher and bent slightly forward. I used the tissue to dab at his cut, trying hard not to burst into a fit of giggles because *oh my God, I'm like two inches from his butt! And who knew a back could be so sexy?* In all my seventeen years I'd never seen such a beautiful back.

"Thanks," Hot Guy said as I continued to clean up the blood.

From a few feet away, Oompa let out a low growl. He watched my adoration with a snarl on his face; then he cocked his head, pinned his ears back, and smiled. He pushed off his hind legs and raced toward Hot Guy. He sprang through the air like a grasshopper and fastened himself onto Hot Guy's leg. AGAIN! Then he started to hump the poor guy, even faster this time.

I cannot believe this.

"Oompa!" I scolded. "Get down!" I dropped the tissue and wrapped my hands around Oompa's fat belly and tried to pry him off. "I'm so sorry," I apologized again. "He's all confused and upset by the move." I attempted to loosen the viselike grip of his paws and kept talking, nervously. "When he got out of the car and didn't see his usual fire hydrant, he, like, *freaked out*. He ran in circles and refused to pee. I need to find a vet—get him a dose of Prozac or something. He's not like some sex-crazed dog or anything. He's just mad at me." *I did not just say* sex-crazed *to this hot guy!*

So much for first impressions. I had to get out of there.

Hot Guy looked down at Oompa humping his calf. "I'm not sure I believe you," he said, smiling uncomfortably as he shook his leg again. "Are you sure you don't have a small stash of dog-Prozac on you?" He looked a little desperate.

But Prozac was not what Oompa wanted. I knew that.

"Oompa!" I scolded, wanting to die. Oompa gave me a toothy

snarl and kept right on going. And I knew I had no other choice. I knew there was only one way to get the dog to cooperate. And it wouldn't be pretty. It was even more humiliating than the M&M T-shirt—worse than a humping dog or wiping blood inches from a perfectly sculpted butt. But I had no other choice.

"Fine!" I growled back at the dog. I squatted down closer to him—and hopefully out of Hot Guy's earshot. I adopted my best throaty Cher voice and whisper-sang, "*Do you be-lieve in life after love?*"

Oompa stopped humping but remained attached to Hot Guy's leg. He cocked his head as if to say, *Louder, please.*

I should have never even ventured into this park, I thought miserably. *I should have let the dog roam the streets by himself.* I raised my voice an octave. "*I can feel something inside me say I really don't think you're strong enough, now.*"

And just like that, Oompa hopped down from Hot Guy's leg, walked over to the grass, and plopped down.

Hot Guy's forehead crinkled in confusion. He looked down at his leg then back and forth from me to Oompa in the grass, his head bobbing like he was watching a tennis match. "What just happened?"

Now I'm not, by nature, a liar. And *technically*, the words that came out next weren't entirely untrue. It was more like I concocted an imaginary bridge to steer the conversation. Because I knew that Hot Guy was either going to remember me as the dorky girl in an M&M T-shirt with a Cher-obsessed humping dog, or I could make a more worthy impression. I decided for the latter. So, rather than admit the truth—that Oompa was simply homesick for our Vegas apartment where our eccentric neighbor played a constant sound track of Cher—I chose a slightly more exciting version of reality.

"Oh," I said, shooing my hand toward Oompa. "Back in Vegas,

whenever Cher came to do a show, her dressing room was always next to mine." I rolled my eyes as if to say, *The dog just loved to listen to her sing.* I casually shrugged and waited for his follow-up question. It came quickly.

"Did you *perform* in Vegas?" Hot Guy asked, intrigued. "Like, in a show?" His eyebrows raised high in anticipation.

"Yeah," I said. "My mom and I had a hypnosis show—*The Hip Hypnotist.*" And this part wasn't a lie. Maybe I'd never met Cher, but I had helped my mom entertain Vegas tourists with hypnosis for the last six years.

"Wow," Hot Guy said, sounding impressed. He smiled a relaxed, natural smile now that my dog was no longer accosting him. "That's cool."

"Thanks," I said, thinking that maybe this move could be my chance to finally stand out from the shadow of my beautiful mother— to finally have my own story to tell, not just be her sidekick.

Plus, now that we were back in Georgia, I could be around Max again. "I used to live here," I said to the hot guy. "Like a million years ago. I'm still really good friends with Max Montgomery?" Mom insisted that everyone knew everyone in this town, but that was hard for me to remember or even imagine after living in a place where people were as transient as the wind.

But Hot Guy nodded with recognition. "I know Max," he said. "He's cool. A black belt in karate and a kick-ass drummer."

I smiled and nodded too. "Max and I have kept in touch since I moved eight years ago. It'll be nice to hear the drums banging in person instead of over the phone. I haven't even called him yet because"—I gestured to my two-straight-days-in-the-car outfit— "we *just* got here."

Hot Guy nodded. His golden hair fell over his eyes. He casually swept it to the side in one quick motion. "So, are you a senior, then? Will you be at Worthington High on Monday?"

I nodded. "Yup. Mom's grand plans to reinvent her life couldn't wait one more year to let me graduate with my friends." I tried to sound irritated, like I just left the best life. I couldn't admit the reality—that I kind of embraced the opportunity to reinvent myself. Of course, my reinvention plan never included a first impression like this.

Oompa waddled over and rubbed his head against my leg in an attempt to apologize. I bent down and picked him up. "It's okay," I said, kissing his head. "It's a big change."

Hot Guy walked closer to me and stroked Oompa's head. Then he looked up at my eyes. "Whoa," he said, and I knew what would come next. "Your eyes—they're wicked."

Hmmm. *Wicked* was new. Usually it was *weird* or *strange* or *funky* or, if it was an adult and they were trying to be polite, they'd say, *Oh, how unique*, but I hadn't heard *wicked*. The color of my eyes is just plain hazel, but my pupils aren't round like those of a normal person, they have a strange keyhole shape. I was born with them that way, and my mother always tries to say it's special and distinctive, but if you look it up on the Internet it says it's an *abnormality*, and, let's face it, who wants to be unique if it's abnormal? It's so unfair.

"My name is Quinton," Hot Guy said, moving past my eyes.

"Willow," I said, and we stood there awkwardly for a minute. *Should I shake his hand? I mean, it seems kind of past routine introductions—after all, my hand was just practically massaging his butt.* But the awkwardness continued, so I extended my hand. "Nice to meet you," I said.

Quinton looked down at his right hand, but he was still holding a wad of bloodstained tissues.

I glanced over at the tissue I had tossed to the ground when I pried Oompa off his leg. *He's going to think I litter—on top of everything else.* Quickly I scampered over and snatched up the tissue, which now had soaked up some yellow Gatorade and was a sopping mess. "Let me just clean this up," I said, desperately searching around for a garbage can. When I didn't see one, I shoved the sticky, drenched tissue wad into the pocket of my cotton shorts, shuddering slightly. *Exit now!* "Well, I guess I better get going and take off this T-shirt before these M&M's melt." *No, I did NOT just say that! This day cannot get any worse.*

Quinton looked at me like I was a little deranged. "Okay," he said tentatively. "See you on Monday."

"Not unless I see you first." I pointed at him. *What was wrong with me?*

Quinton smiled at me, but I couldn't quite decipher if it was a smile of sweet Southern charm or if inside he was mocking me. I grabbed Oompa's leash and darted back through the shrubs and down the winding dirt trail. I was disappointed that I'd made such a disaster of a first impression—something that had seemed so enticing to me as we drove cross-country just hours before. When I left Vegas, that was all I wanted—an opportunity to start over, to stand out in a crowd, to throw away the years of blending in and become someone special. Someone extraordinary.

My first chance at reinvention was not at all how I had planned it, but it was memorable nonetheless.

By the time I walked the half mile down the road to our new house, long trails of sweat trickled down my back and my hair was damp at the nape of my neck. We'd left 106-degree heat in the desert, but here, though it was a full fourteen degrees cooler, I felt like I had just walked into a steam room. The air hung on me like a stifling, soggy sweater.

Our house was one story and white, with black shutters and a wraparound porch that seemed to beg for rocking chairs and potted flowers. A Mayflower movers' truck was parked by the curb, nestled between our mailbox and the huge cherry tree that shaded half of our front yard. The back metal doors of the truck were propped open, revealing an array of boxes and furniture stuffed inside. At the house next door, a woman wearing a straw sun hat was bent down pruning the drying periwinkle blossoms off a large hydrangea bush. She looked up and waved a gloved hand in my direction. "Welcome to the neighborhood," she said warmly.

I smiled and waved back. Oompa and I climbed the porch steps and walked into the house, where I saw my mom standing barefoot in her aqua blue halter top and white shorts, directing the moving men to put the kitchen table next to a bank of oversize windows. It's a wonder they didn't crash into the wall since clearly neither of them opted to look where they were walking for fear of breaking eye contact with my mother. She was entrancing that way. I guess that's what made her such a good hypnotist. She wasn't just beautiful, although that was undeniable; she was alluring in an indefinable way that just made people, both men and women, gravitate toward her energy. I noticed the men didn't even glance in my direction once.

That right there summed up how my life had been in Vegas. I had been invisible. Not just when I was with Mom, but at school, too. Everyone knew my Mom was the Hip Hypnotist. It's not like I could conceal it—there were twenty-foot billboards broadcasting her face across town. But I was partly to blame for my invisibility, too. Because the more Mom's show and notoriety blossomed, the more I shrunk back into myself—never even trying to compete for attention. Somewhere along the way I lost the courage to be adventurous. I fell into the role of the responsible one—keeping things organized and running smoothly, while Mom was the star.

You'd think that even if I'd become less adventurous, at least I could still be flirtatious. After all, I lived with the perfect teacher. But the truth was, I never liked to risk the possibility of humiliation. Who would notice me in her shadow? It might have been easy to resent her had she not been so lovable. But that was the thing—for all the reasons everyone was drawn to her—her adorable charm, her contagious laughter, her romantic ideology—I was drawn to her, too.

But now that we had moved across the country, we were both

ready to try on new lives. She wanted to leave the eccentric lifestyle behind, and I secretly wanted to inject a little spice into my own.

"A little to the left," Mom said now, jostling her hand in that direction, and the moving men set the rectangular table down with a thud against the wooden floor.

I looked at the table and thought of all the late nights back in Vegas where I'd sat at one end with my textbooks open, doing homework while I watched Mom and her cluster of friends drinking coffee and eating leftover fried chicken from the casino buffet. They would talk about life and love and movies. Maybe, I thought, this time the table would be surrounded with my new friends instead of Mom's. Maybe instead of sitting around watching *Glee* like Becca, Lauren, and I used to do in Vegas, here in Georgia I'd rent a karaoke machine and all my new friends and I would sing along to the *Glee* sound track. Maybe they'd tell me I could be a star. Mom would be next door talking with the new neighbor about gardening and pruning shrubs instead of drinking coffee with the sequined-leotard-wearing, Cher-loving neighbor from Vegas.

The moving men walked back outside and I pulled one of the kitchen chairs over to the table and sat down. Mom brought two bottles of Aquafina water over from the fridge and slid one across the kitchen table toward me like she was a casino bartender. I wondered if she realized that even though she was two thousand miles away, the lifestyle was still embedded in her simplest actions.

I looked out the window at the lush green landscape—the clusters of leaves grouping together to enclose and canopy the yard. "I don't remember it being this hot."

She nodded. "Ah, the sticky, Southern summer air. It feels like someone hosed you down with hot honey."

I laughed. "Exactly."

The movers came back in, one holding an armload of boxes and the other holding my black Panasonic stereo with the front piece broken off and dangling by a cluster of thin wires. "Looks like this got damaged." The mover grimaced. "You got the moving insurance, right?"

Mom sighed and shook her head.

"Oh," the mover said, looking down at the mangled equipment. "Maybe it's fixable?"

"Just leave it on the table," I said. "I'll take a look at it."

The mover looked startled. Was it because he didn't think a girl could fix electronics or simply that he hadn't noticed I was there? He placed the stereo down on the table in front of me.

Mom instructed them to take the boxes to her bedroom and pointed down the hall. The men lingered for a second, listening to the soft jingle of her thick silver bangle bracelets. I thought back to Hot Guy Quinton from the park and wished he had watched me with that soft longing in his eyes. Instead, he'd just looked a little baffled by me.

"So," I said, after the movers finally walked away. "When are we going over to see Grandma and Grandpa?"

Mom's back stiffened and she pursed her lips ever so slightly. She looked around the house as if suddenly realizing that yes, we had moved back to Georgia, back to the small town she had escaped from eight years ago. "I don't know," she answered nonchalantly.

"What do you mean, you don't know?" When Mom decided to move us back to Georgia everything seemed so urgent. Grandpa had a stroke; time seemed of the essence. We needed to get back home and mend fences before it was too late. So now why the dispassion?

"You said you were ready to reconcile with Grandma and Grandpa. Don't back down, Mom," I said encouragingly, selfishly, because I didn't like having a family divided.

Mom didn't respond. She just looked over at Oompa. He had propped his ear against the wall in a desperate attempt to hear the soft reverberation of Cher's throaty voice. When no lyrics sounded, Oompa moved away from the wall, climbed onto the couch, and burped like a human with indigestion.

Mom got up and stared at the wall like she was mentally planning where to hang her *Casablanca* movie poster. "When we moved to Vegas it was, I don't know, rebellion I guess. I was tired of Grandma trying to mold me into a mini-version of herself." She sighed. "And Vegas is the exact opposite of their quiet, conventional life." She turned and smiled at me. "But I'm thirty-three years old and it's time to grow up, get a real job and live a more normal life."

I stared at her. We could live a more normal life anywhere. We came back to Worthington, Georgia because she wanted to reunite with her parents.

Mom made a big production of looking at her watch. "We've been here for fifty-three minutes and I just drove for two days. Cut me some slack! I'll call Grandma and Grandpa. Just let me rest a little."

I wanted to tell her not to be nervous. We'd be one big, happy family again.

I put my arm around her and we continued to stare at the blank wall. "I never thought I'd say this, but I kind of miss Cher right now."

Oompa buried his nose under his paws and sighed.

From the kitchen table my cell phone buzzed that I had a message. I picked it up and saw that Max had texted. *U here yet?* I smiled. *Max.*

Technically, the first time I met Max, I was still in the womb. My mother had sat next to Max's mom when they were both in Dr. Wendall's waiting room, both nine months pregnant with bulging bellies and swollen ankles, both facing huge opposition from their families. My mother, the daughter of the Worthington, Georgia, town judge and his garden club president wife, was pregnant at sixteen—a scandalous shame for such a reputable family. Max's mother, Maria, was ten years older and married, but her family was unhappy that she had chosen to marry outside their culture. *Not Latino! Not Catholic! Didn't speak a word of Spanish! Didn't know the difference between a tortilla and a gorilla!* Never mind the fact that Max's father was a hardworking and honest man; Maria's family was old school in their customs and very unforgiving. So Mom and Maria bonded in their parents' judgment.

When Max was born two weeks before I was, Mom said every time Max cried I kicked inside her like I was just dying to get out and meet my playmate. And when I did arrive, all squirmy and screaming, I was a colicky mess, crying nonstop until one day Maria came over and placed Max on the couch next to me and miraculously I stopped. Whether it was the warmth of his body or the comfort of his fast-ticking heartbeat so close to mine, we'll never know, but anytime Max was around I was happy. And so was he.

Every story of my childhood somehow involved Max. Every preschool picture I drew included him. Mom saved all the notes from our preschool teachers: *Max and Willow play so nicely together!* Notes from the day care: *Max and Willow love to play Legos together and they only fight when Willow keeps insisting on kissing him!* Notes from our elementary teachers: *Could you please ask Max and Willow to refrain from passing notes during class? It's quite distracting.* Notes from Principal Wells: *It has come to my attention that Max and Willow have each forged a doctor's note and left school early today.* That was Max's brilliant idea—the day we dodged out of fourth grade to go home and build a teepee in his backyard from tree branches and a canvas tarp. Only the tree limbs I selected, entwined with such pretty shiny leaves, were actually covered in poison ivy. That night, while Mom and Maria dabbed pink splatters of calamine lotion all over our bodies, they told us that our discomfort was our punishment. They tried to hide it, but they were laughing a little, because that's just how Max and I were—always together, always adventurous, and always having fun.

But after we moved to Vegas, things changed. I changed. I was no longer the fizzy, fun-loving girl that I had been. I was like when a bottle of old Coke turned stale. No fizz, no excitement. I was the same person, sure, just like Coke is still Coke, but due to time and circumstances, I'd become stagnant. Definitely not the best version of myself. I was in need of a big boost to shake my life back up, and I hoped Max would be the one thing that could do that.

All these years, Max and I stayed in touch. There was just some undeniable connection that came from growing up together. Day after day, we shared stories and jokes and the details of our ordinary lives—until one night the fall of my eighth grade year, when something extraordinary happened.

I was tucked in bed, the comforter pulled high over the cornflower blue gown that I hadn't yet taken off. "Logan dumped me," I garbled to Max on the phone. "Right there, in the middle of Becca's bat mitzvah, right in front of everyone. He said I was boring and that I studied too much." I sniffled. "And he called me a prude. Then he made out with Macy Hollister in the middle of the dance floor. In front of everyone—in front of everyone's parents." Tears spilled down my cheeks and dampened my pillow.

What happened next forever changed the course of our friendship.

"If that guy is too blind to see how incredible you are," Max said, "if he can't see how smart and capable and fun and beautiful you are, then he's so not worth it."

I was stunned into silence. Max, maybe a little embarrassed, changed the subject to some new song he was learning to play on the drums. Eventually, when I was no longer weepy, we hung up. I lay there for hours while the tears dried, the realization dawned on me. Even though I wasn't the most popular girl or the smartest girl or even close to the prettiest girl—even though I had weird, unfixable eyes and a boring, forgettable face and no real talent at all—Max still thought I was beautiful. Incredible. Despite all of it. Or maybe because of it.

And from that day on, I no longer viewed Max as my best friend from Georgia. Suddenly he became so much more. I spent hours imagining how after high school we'd reunite and navigate our way from friends to something more. When we were in person, our real story would unfold. Max would take me in his arms and sing, *I could write the preface on how we met; so the world would never forget. . . . Then the world discovers as my book ends; how to make two lovers of friends.* Of course Max didn't listen to a lot of Harry Connick Jr. In fact, he often made fun of me for my music preferences, but whatever—he'd sing *something* that would propel us from friendship into the whirlwind romance that destiny had in store for us. So maybe our destiny was to start now in high school at seventeen in Georgia. That thought exhilarated me.

Now, in our new home, I grabbed my phone off the kitchen table and texted Max that we were here and he should come over. Seven minutes later I heard the rumble of a loud muffler motoring up our driveway. I flung open the door and stood on our new front porch wondering exactly what to do. I hadn't seen him in five years—the last time we visited—but now he was here, in my driveway, and strangely, I felt a little panicked. It was so much easier to type the letters on a keypad than to say things in person. *Should I hug him? Is he going to high-five me like a buddy? How will I know if he feels the same way I do? Should I just cut to the chase and take him in my arms and kiss him?*

The door of the black truck swung open and Max climbed out, grinning as he closed the door behind him. His black hair was shorter than I remembered, almost buzzed. But his blue eyes were sparkling and as familiar to me as the day we parted. He walked toward me and I stood there, glued to the front porch with my heart pounding. I tried to smile back, but I could feel my lips shaking. Why was I so nervous? This was Max!

He climbed the porch steps and stood in front of me. "Are you just going to stand there?" he asked. His mild Southern accent didn't sound as strong in person.

I relaxed a little and leaned over to hug him. He pulled me in close and I noted that all his years of karate were doing wonders for his chest and arms.

He pulled back and looked at me with a teasing expression on his face. "So," he said, "have you been Photoshopping those pictures on Facebook or what?"

For an awful minute I wondered if he had figured out my little secret—the one where I kind of portrayed to him that my life in Vegas was filled with endless fun. That Mom's hypnosis gig was just the tiniest part of the huge awesome life I had. A stone dropped into my gut as I worried that Max was saying, *You didn't Photoshop pictures—you Photoshopped your whole life.* He was looking at me—analyzing me, actually; then a whole new fear overtook me. "Do you think I'm not as pretty in person?" My voice caught on the words. It had only been five years since he'd last seen me. Could I have deteriorated that much?

"What?" Max reached over and gently put his hand on my cheek. For some reason his touch made me want to cry. He was here, in person, my love, my destiny, but what if . . .

"I *meant* your *hair* looks different," he said, smiling.

The knot in my stomach eased a bit. "Oh," I said, reaching up and patting my hair into submission. "It's this humidity. It's making my hair all frizzy. It wasn't like this in Vegas. Plus I've been in the car all day. Does it look that bad?"

"I like it," he said. "It's kind of crazy—like your eyes." He ran his fingers through a long strand of my hair, just grazing the side of my jaw and neck. A jolt of tingles shot down my spine. Did he feel that, too? He was staring at me. We were so close—just inches away from each other. For a moment, neither of us said anything. There was an undeniable tension building in the air. I wanted him to say something, do something. When he just kept looking at me, I couldn't stand it any longer. I backed away slightly and began to joke.

"Yeah, well, you haven't posted any pictures of you all cue ball. When did you shave your head?" I asked nervously. Max looked away briefly, and whatever was happening between us—the almost-kiss—evaporated. The moment was lost. I silently cursed myself.

He looked back at me. "You like?" he asked, running his hand over his scalp, where his once thick, messy black hair was now chopped into a clean buzz-cut.

Watching that simple gesture gave me another dose of the tingles. "Yeah," I said, sounding flustered. "It makes your eyes look all . . ." I wanted to say *amazing* because they were—ice blue from his fair father against the olive complexion he'd inherited from his mother. His eyes looked like blue jeans—comfortable, and familiar. My heart started to pound harder. "You know, your eyes look all . . . big."

He shook his head and laughed a little.

Again, another silence surrounded us. My hands began to sweat. I suddenly grabbed the doorknob and opened the front door. "My mom is dying to see you," I said randomly. *Who cares about Mom? I just screwed up another opportunity!*

Max walked through the open door, and once he was inside, Mom ran over to him.

"MAX!" she shouted and wrapped her arms around him with all the ease of reconciliation that I wished I had. "Little Max, my God, look at you! You're all grown up!"

Max hugged her back. "It's good to see you, too, Vicki," he said. "My mom said to tell you she's on for dinner this week."

"Great," Mom said, nodding, her eyes roaming to the boxes piled against the wall. "Great. Everything's going to be great." She said, clenching her hands nervously.

I looked from Max to the blank wall. A fresh canvas. A new start. I would no longer have to Photoshop my life. I could create the world I wanted. And it all started here with Max. I needed to stop being afraid and start taking chances. Everything could have been different out there on the porch if I hadn't chickened out. Now was the time to start the reinvention.

I gazed at Max's faded blue eyes and thought, *Yes, maybe everything is going to be great.*

3

The three of us stood in the living room, not quite sure where to pick up the conversation.

"So," Mom said, breaking the awkward silence. "Maybe I'll run to the store and get some peanut butter, bananas, and honey. Do you still eat peanut butter, banana, and honey sandwiches?" she asked Max.

Max cast a glance my way. "I haven't had that in ages." He smiled. "This is going to be just like old times."

Only better, I thought, unable to take my eyes away from Max's suddenly chiseled arms. I had an uncontrollable desire to reach out and touch him . . . take him into another hug . . . give him another opportunity to kiss me. This time I wouldn't ruin the moment.

Mom reached for her purse and keys on the kitchen counter. She swung the key chain on her index finger, winked at us, and walked out. Max and I stood there in the living room amidst the piles of boxes, not sure what to do. It wasn't like we could climb trees and make mud forts anymore. *Kiss me. Sing to me. Tell me I'm all you think about.*

"Hey, look," Max said, walking across the wooden floor, an echo thumping from his flip-flops. He pointed to Oompa, who was curled up into a ball, snoring loudly. "It's Oompa!"

At the sound of Max's voice, Oompa lifted one wrinkled eyelid. Upon seeing Max, Oompa sprang up off the ground and ran to him, circling his ankles like a windup toy gone mad. As Max reached down and picked him up, Oompa nestled his head against the crook of Max's elbow and smiled. "It's like he remembers me," Max said, petting his short fur.

"Of course he remembers you," I said. "How could he forget the guy who rescued him?"

Eight years ago, a few weeks before I moved to Vegas, Max and I had boarded our bikes and ridden down the street to Poplinger Park. After we propped our bikes on the bike rack, we headed over to the pond to feed the ducks. We passed a college-age guy with a box full of Boston terrier puppies and a FOR SALE sign. As we sat down at the edge of the pond and pulled out a bag of bread, we heard something rustle in the bushes. Moments later, the ugliest little puppy emerged, his limbs all gangly and knobby, his body scrawny and his face all smashed like he'd been jammed up against the inside of his mama's womb and his face just froze that way. The puppy scurried over to us and sniffed the bread.

Max scooped up the puppy in his arms and walked back a hundred yards to the college guy and his litter of puppies. "Excuse me," Max said, holding the puppy out. "I think this puppy escaped."

The college guy's face reddened. "Oh yeah," he said unconvincingly. "He must have."

Max and I looked at the box full of fat, adorable terriers and back at the squished runt. "You know what?" Max said suddenly. "I'll buy him. How much is he?"

College Guy waved his hand in the air. "Nah, man, you take him. No charge. Enjoy."

Max let me hold the squirmy dog as he walked our two bikes to his house, where he went inside and begged his mom to let him keep the puppy. She agreed. Max loved that puppy. He took him everywhere with him.

Two weeks later, when Mom and I loaded up the car, ready to take off for Vegas, Max came over and handed me the dog. "I want you to take him," he said. "I named him Oompa." Max sniffled. It was unclear whether he was emotional about giving up the dog or me moving. Maybe both. "I think he kind of looks like the Oompa-Loompas from *Charlie and the Chocolate Factory*."

For the next eight years, every time I looked at Oompa's squished-up face or petted his round belly, I remembered Max. I knew that there was a boy who could find the runt of the litter, look past its imperfect façade, and still find a reason to love.

Oompa hadn't seen Max since our last visit five years ago, but I guess he never forget who rescued him.

Max continued to cradle Oompa in his arms and sat down on the couch, propping his feet on the coffee table. "Where's the TV?" he asked, swiveling his head around.

"Oh, the TV's still in the box." I pointed over toward a large flat box near the wall. "I haven't hooked anything up yet. You know Mom's not good with all those wires and cables and five different remotes so I have to do it. But I've been trying to fix my stereo. It broke in the moving truck."

Max looked over at the stereo on the kitchen table, with the front end cracked open and wires poking out. He got up and put Oompa down on the couch. Oompa let out a loud, wet *phrumph*. Max walked over to the table and began to fiddle with the wires.

I leaned over his shoulder. "Yeah, I tried that."

"Hmm," he grunted and used the pliers to yank at something else.

I had heard that familiar *hmm* many times on the phone while Max tightened wires on his guitar or examined his truck engine. It was different, though, to see the facial expression that accompanied it—the slight furrow of his forehead, the small wrinkle of concentration between his brows. It startled me to think there were pieces of him that were unknown to me.

I sat down next to him, smelling the clean smell of soap on his skin, wondering what else I didn't know. *When he told me I was incredible and beautiful back in eighth grade, did he mean beautiful as a sister? Incredible as a friend? Or were his feelings the same as mine? The lingering stare and silence on the porch felt like an impending kiss but could I have misunderstood? Could all the romantic tension I felt lurking beneath the surface of our late-night conversations just have been a misinterpretation stemming from my own desires?*

Max plugged the cord into the wall and pressed the power button. The stereo remained quiet. "Sorry." He shrugged. "I think it's a goner."

I nodded. "That's what I figured."

He walked over to the large box against the wall and unpacked the flat-screen TV. He picked it up and placed it on the media console. He plugged cords into the wall and hit buttons on the remote to power everything up. "At least this is working." He smiled as the TV scrolled through the channels, linking the remote appropriately. He looked over at me and smiled, squaring his shoulders with pride.

"Thanks," I said. "So, you weren't lying about your handyman capabilities." I tried to lift my voice a notch and adopt a flirtatious tone. "You know, we could use—"

"Uh-oh," Max said, pointing out the window and interrupting my painful attempts to seduce him.

"What?" I looked out the window. Outside, Mom stood at the front of the Toyota, where white clouds of steam poured out the seams of the hood. She stared at the car with a long, thin tree branch in her hand like she was about to use the stick to pry open the hood.

"No!" Max yelled, banging on the window.

She looked up at us and threw up her hands in a helpless, clueless gesture.

Max tore out of the living room and down the front porch steps. "Wait!" he said, a little breathlessly. "There's a latch." He opened the driver's side door, reached inside, and pulled a lever.

As I raced down the steps and stood by my mom, we heard a little *click*, and the hood popped up. Max came over, lifted the hood, and used a long metal bar to prop it open.

"Huh," Mom said. "What about that."

Max closed his eyes and shook his head a little. "Look, if you're going to drive, especially across the country, you need to know some basic car maintenance." He pulled out the dipstick, wiped it off with a tissue, replaced it then pulled it out again. "Jesus, Vicki," he said to my mother. "Please tell me you didn't drive two thousand miles without a decent amount of oil in this car."

Mom laughed nervously.

He shook his head and took my hand. "Come on, Willow, let's go to the auto-body store."

I looked down at our clasped fingers, my heart bursting.

Mom looked like she was going to cry. "You've really grown up nicely, Max," she said.

MOM! I shot her a look. *Don't embarrass me!*

But Max didn't seem to notice. He opened the passenger side door for me. Max drove an old black Ford 150. The paint was chipped in places, and the oversize wheels had mud caked in their treads. But as I climbed inside, I thought, *This truck is a lot like Max: a little messy, hardworking, and powerful.*

He climbed into the driver's side and cranked the engine. He reversed down the driveway fast then sped down our quiet road toward town. I had never seen Max drive, and it gave me a thrill to be in the intimate space of his truck. I felt like I knew Max so well—his thoughts, his likes and dislikes—but it had been so many years since I'd been privy to his actual space and all the things he surrounded himself with. I took in the mound of CD cases piled in his back seat, drumsticks, stray papers with music notes scrawled on them, a pair of running shoes, the white top to his karate uniform (but no bottoms in sight). The rugs and fabric seats could have used a good vacuuming and shampoo.

"What?" Max asked, catching me swipe a few crumbs off the center console.

"Nothing," I said. "Well, maybe we can swing through the car wash after the auto-body store."

Max snorted and rolled his eyes. "I'm not afraid of a few germs."

"Germs?" I countered, trying to readopt a flirtatious tone. "You have a biology experiment growing in this cup holder."

Max laughed and I felt a surge of victory.

"And why is your truck so *loud*?" I continued to tease him. "If you're so handy . . ."

"Hey, I rebuilt this entire engine," he said defensively. "It may not be perfect, but it's mine."

A swell of emotion caught inside me. *I may not be perfect either.*

Max drove one handed and fast, no surprise to me, using his free hand to spin the dial across the radio stations, searching for the perfect driving music. He stopped on something loud and thumping, turned the volume way up and, rather than gripping the wheel, used that hand to drum out the beat on the console between us. We came to a stop sign and turned right onto Main Street. As he turned the corner, he reached over and lowered the radio volume and smiled. He pointed to the two-hundred-year-old oak tree that shaded the entrance to Poplinger Park.

"Remember how we used to climb up to that top branch?" He pointed up to the treetop, and I resisted the urge to place his hand on the steering wheel, arrange his hands in a safe ten-and-two position. "Remember," he continued, "how we used to hang upside down from our knees like monkeys?"

I looked up to the thick, curving branches and remembered the days of playing monkeys. And the day we sat in that tree and I tried to hypnotize him.

He laughed and used his hand to search the radio dial again. "Man, we had some laughs." He turned and looked at me. "You were never afraid to have fun."

I wondered how I had drifted so far away from that fun-loving girl to where I was now—afraid to take any chances. Afraid to let Max know how I really felt. I had spent too many nights hidden behind the black velvet curtain on Mom's stage.

He started banging out the music rhythm again. He pulled into Larry's Auto Body, kept the car running, and said, "Be right back."

After he disappeared, I considered opening the glove compartment or sneaking a peek inside his backpack. I had never snooped before, but curiosity overtook me. Did I really know Max as well now as I did when we were young? Before I could act on my impulse, he climbed back into the car and reversed out of the lot at lightning speed. Max tossed the motor oil onto the floorboard of the car and turned the volume of the radio back up.

As we turned off Main Street and sped down Erwin Drive, my stomach knotted. I had to take a chance. This was my new life. My reinvention. If I kept hiding behind the curtain, another ten years could pass me by and I'd never get my chance to shine. So I took a deep breath and steadied my voice. "So," I said, casually running my hand through my frizzy hair. "Do you want to catch a matinee tomorrow?" *Boom, boom*, my heart raced.

"Don't you need to unpack?" he asked, turning his head to look at me, and even though I could have gazed into his soft eyes for an eternity, I kind of wanted him to watch where he was driving.

"Um, pothole," I said, pointing ahead of us.

He veered around it. "You start school on Monday, right?" he asked. "Don't you kind of need things . . . out of their boxes?"

I was about to suggest that he could come over and help me unpack, but before I could, he shrugged. "I've got plans," he said. "Sorry. I thought you'd be totally swamped."

I nodded. "Yeah," I said, trying not to look hurt. *Did we ever spend a day apart when we were kids?* For a moment I panicked that I wasn't so important to him anymore. But then he pulled into our driveway and proceeded to take out a long metal toolbox from his backseat, fished out an old dirty rag, and propped himself under my mom's car for hours. I sat on the hot, black driveway and ate a banana, peanut butter, and honey sandwich while he worked. This was Max's way of telling me he cared, right?

When he wriggled his way back to a sitting position, dirt sprinkled over his olive face, he pointed at me. "You're not driving this car to school until we get a few more parts."

I shook my head. "Mom's taking the car to her new job. I'll ride the bus."

His eyes widened. "Seniors don't ride the bus." He wiped his hands on his shorts. "I'll pick you up. Monday morning at 7:45 a.m."

I reached over and wiped a black smudge of motor oil off his cheek. And standing there in the sweltering heat, in the driveway of my new home, it felt intimate and special—like he was taking me under his wing and caring for me.

He smiled. "Don't be late."

I smiled back. "I'll be ready and waiting for you." *Like I have been for years.*

4

My bed was hidden under piles of clothes neatly laid out in color-coordinated ensembles. I looked at the khaki cotton skirt and lavender short-sleeve sweater set. I had been told purple was a good color for me—that it brought out a rosy flush in my skin. But staring at it now strewn across my bed, the whole outfit seemed so dull. I reached over and put on the black shorts with a black and white striped top. I stared in the mirror. Blah. How could I be who I wanted to be—dazzling and memorable—with a wardrobe of forgettable clothes?

I got an idea. I crept across the living room and tapped softly on Mom's door. I stuck my head in. "Mom?" I called, hearing the soft drum of the shower from her bathroom. "Mom, it's 7:30 a.m. You better hurry up."

"I know, I know," she answered, turning off the faucet. "I'm not used to early mornings. Willow?" she called from behind the bathroom door.

"Yeah?" I answered as I peered into her closet.

"Will you turn on the coffee pot, hon?"

"Already did," I answered, snatching her tall black leather boots.

"Thanks," she said.

I raced out of her room before she could see me with them. Not that she wouldn't let me wear them—she would—but I didn't want to explain my sudden interest in her wardrobe.

Back in my room, I pulled the soft high-heeled boots up, zipping them over my calves. I closed my door and modeled them in front of my full-length mirror. I put my hand on my hip and walked across the carpet. "Well, hi Max," I practiced with a smile. I had to show Max I was still fun and a little wild.

Under my desk, Oompa groaned and shook his head.

"What?" I asked the dog. "Do I look that ridiculous? Is it so impossible to think I could be sexy?" I turned back to the mirror, cocked my hip, and winked at my reflection. I turned on the heel and promptly crashed onto the carpet.

Oompa looked at me apologetically, then buried his nose.

"Fine," I muttered, unzipping the boots and stashing them under my bed. I would return them later. I left the black shorts on but changed the top to my lavender short-sleeve V-neck and matching button-up cardigan. I stood in front of the mirror and unbuttoned the top two buttons. *There, I'll show a little skin. A little cleavage.*

I looked in the mirror. I hated that no amount of make-up could fix my unfixable eyes. It was so unfair. One of my friends in Vegas, Becca, had terrible acne. But one trip to the dermatologist, a prescription cream and suddenly her skin was transformed. I begged the eye doctor for some magic fix. But no, my eyes were destined to stay the way they were. Imperfect.

I looked at my hair, all frizzy and mangled. Well, at least hair was pliable. I attempted one more squirt of hair spray to tame my hair with little success. I couldn't understand what was happening to it—my hair had never given me this much trouble. It was never glamorous. It was a very average dishwater blonde, shoulder length and straight. Becca always said it could be pretty—an asset, even— with just a few highlights. But I was a little freaked out about the idea of someone putting chemicals and foils on my head. What if they messed up? What if they miscalculated the amount of bleach? So I left it alone. But now, with this sudden dose of humidity, it was like the strands were refusing to hang down my back. They acted like they'd ingested some helium and were levitating ever so slightly into the air—just enough to give my hair a strange poofy triangle shape.

I sighed and pulled it back into a low ponytail. This would have to do.

The car horn beeped at exactly 7:45 a.m., but it wasn't like I couldn't hear the engine rumbling up the street five minutes before. I hopped down the porch steps and got into the passenger's side.

"You look nice," Max said.

"Thanks," I said, suddenly nervous again. I swiped my hand over the seat, but the crumbs were gone. I wondered if Max had cleaned up for me. A jittery, tingly feeling of excitement coursed through me and I felt my cheeks flush. I looked over at him while he drove, spotting the little unexpected details that emerged over the years we had been physically separated—the way he had lost his baby fat and now his body looked so much leaner; the way his face was so much more angular. The way a dark shadow of stubble sprouted around his jawline and under his nose.

I wondered what evidence of womanhood he noticed about me.

The curve of my hips? The angle of my cheekbones? The emergence of breasts that were not as voluptuous as the full C cup Mom had but still decent? I suddenly felt too exposed. I nervously reached up and re-buttoned my top two sweater buttons, glad I'd decided against the boots.

Max pulled into the student parking lot and I followed him over a footbridge that crossed a bubbling stream and into my new high school. He paused in front of the glass window of the principal's office and indicated with a thrust of his chin that I needed to go inside.

The secretary greeted me with pleasantries, handed me a class schedule, a locker number, a map of the school, and pamphlets on the school's policy for attendance, dress code, and behavior. When I emerged from the office five minutes later, Max was still waiting for me, drumming his fingers to a fast beat against the wall. He was talking to some guy who wore a white T-shirt with a flaming guitar painted across the chest.

"Willow," Max said as I approached. He paused his finger-drumming. "Do you remember Trent? I know it's been a long time."

"Hi," I said.

Trent nodded at me. "Hey. Max talks a lot about you."

My insides fluttered. "Max tells me you're the best guitar player around."

Trent smiled. "Damn right." He laughed.

Max rolled his eyes.

Trent nodded at me. "Later," he said then turned to Max. "Four thirty p.m. at my house, okay? Will you tell Conner?"

Max nodded. "Will do."

Trent disappeared down the hallway.

Max and I began to walk. The hall was more crowded now, with students headed to their lockers. Occasionally I would recognize a face from so many years ago, but there were so many new people I didn't know—kids from several different schools that had merged into this one high school. I felt a flutter of excitement. I was the new girl.

Max stopped in front of a tall metal locker and spun the combination. "Where's your locker?" he asked, and I told him the number. "Oh, that's just right down there." He pointed down the long hallway. He grabbed a few books then kicked the metal door shut with his foot. He turned like he was ready to escort me when a tall, curvy girl with thick, shiny black hair came up to us.

"Hi," she said to Max a little breathlessly. She had plump lips with no lipstick, just a smear of clear gloss.

"Hey, you," Max said, smiling at her. He reached over and took her hand. My heart froze. *Why is Max holding this girl's hand?* "This is Minnie," he said. "My girlfriend."

What? My breath caught.

"And this is Willow," he continued.

I blinked my eyes. He wasn't holding her hand anymore. *Maybe I imagined it,* I thought desperately.

"Nice to meet you!" Minnie smiled genuinely, flashing a big grin in my direction. "Max talks so much about you."

It was the same thing Trent had said. *Max talks a lot about me.* That had to mean something, right? "He talks about you a lot, too," I lied. Why didn't Max tell me he had a girlfriend? And what about the way he looked at me on the porch? That was not the look of a guy who had a girlfriend.

"Wow, your eyes! So . . . interesting!" Minnie said.

Max made a face. "Interesting?" he teased. "More like *crazy!*" He distorted his face into a wacky expression.

I tried not to tense. Max didn't know how much my eyes bothered me. How it was my one unfixable flaw. I smoothed my hand over my hair, taming any stray frizz. He was, after all, teasing me. *Or is it flirting?* Suddenly, everything felt so confusing.

"No," Minnie said, "seriously, your eyes are fascinating . . . captivating, really."

It was hard not to like Minnie. I looked at her flowered short skirt, white T-shirt, and makeup-free face. She had an innocence about her that made me think of her running through a grassy meadow barefoot, picking daisies and plucking each petal while chanting, *He loves me, he loves me not.* She seemed nice. Sweet. Like someone I would want to be friends with. *Maybe we* could *be friends,* I thought, *except, oh my God, she's KISSING MY MAX!*

What just happened? Sweet, innocent, daisy-picking Minnie just leaned over, pressed her ample bosom into Max's chest, and sucked face with him RIGHT IN FRONT OF ME! My heart pounded, kickboxed my ribs. My mind raced around like a rat running through a wooden maze. *What just happened? What's going on?*

I put my hand on the cold locker door to steady myself. The bell rang. Minnie released her grip on Max and waved casually to me as if she hadn't just shattered my world.

"Have a great first day!" she called. Why did she have to be so friendly? I wanted her to be mean. I wanted her to be a bitch, but she was just waving at me like I was her best friend.

"See you!" Max called to Minnie then returned his gaze toward me. He stared at me, waiting for some reaction, maybe?

I steadied my breathing and prayed he couldn't hear the crazy thumping of my heart. He just kept looking at me. I felt the back of my throat burn. *I thought I was incredible. Smart. Capable. Beautiful.*

Quickly, I looked away. Someone slammed a locker next to me, breaking the awkward silence.

"So," Max said. "Your locker is right down there and"—he glanced at the schedule in my hand, all wrinkled and hot from my tension-filled grip—"your first class is one building over. Just tell the teacher it's your first day. They won't be mad if you're late. But I've got to run." He looked at me one more time, waiting for me to say something.

But I couldn't. I knew if I opened my mouth I would start to cry. So I nodded and gave a forced smile. "Thanks," I squeaked out.

He looked at me for another long second then darted off toward his classroom.

And I stood there, watching him go, his words rattling in my distressed mind. As if he thought instructions to class would somehow make everything okay.

I looked down at my class schedule. My first class was calculus. *I can't go to calculus*, I thought frantically. *I can't think about derivatives and quadratic equations while my whole life is falling apart!* But what could I do? It wasn't like I could just skip class—that was something I only reminisced about doing with Max back in the day when I was carefree—before I analyzed and planned each day. Before GPA and college admission were a daily consideration.

The late bell rang, and I stood there in a panic. I couldn't start the first class at my new school all frazzled like this. I had already botched a chance at a great first impression with Quinton at the park. I couldn't risk another catastrophe. I scanned up and down the hallway, feeling completely unglued and without a plan.

Quickly I found the nearest bathroom, crawled into a stall, and had a complete meltdown. The tears plummeted down my face in a full-on deluge. I looked around the cold, blue stall of the girls' bathroom. I was such an idiot! I had thought this move would be a great opportunity. I'd thought it would be fun—finally, an adventure in my boring life. I'd thought Max and I would be together and suddenly I'd transform into the person I wanted to be. *How stupid I was to place all my emotions, all my happiness with one person! A person who chose a girl named after a mouse over ME!!!* I felt a wave of loneliness wash over me—a sudden vacuum of emptiness. I missed Lauren and Becca. I missed our row of three desks in the corner of the library, and I missed our favorite diner, Café Tango. I missed having them around to comfort me.

I would have to find new friends, I thought miserably. I'd have to go through the whole process of breaking the ice, cultivating interests, working my way into a circle of girls who already had private jokes and experiences. Ugh! I felt so unhinged—so out of control. This was not at all how I planned my new life to unfold.

Just as I sighed at the weight of it all, I heard someone knock on the stall door.

"Um, are you, like, okay?" a high-pitched voice called. When I didn't answer, a mop of tight black curls appeared under the door. Their owner turned her head and looked up at me.

"Um, hello?!" I said, just a little snippy at the invasion. Thankfully I wasn't actually *going* to the bathroom.

"Oh, thank God, you're alive!" she said dramatically.

"Of course I'm alive," I said. "I'm crying, aren't I?"

"Sure, but crying in the bathroom at school—it can't be good." The curly-haired girl backed out and let me open the door. "Let me guess," she said. "Depression? Regret? Shame?" I walked out of the tight stall. She took one look at me and pointed her finger. "Heartbreak," she declared, shaking her head sadly. "It's always heartbreak."

I nodded silently.

"So what happened, did he cheat?"

I shook my head.

"Tell you he's gay?"

"No."

"Say he's just not that into you?"

"No."

"Thinks of you more like a friend?"

"I guess that's it," I garbled, fighting the urge to cry again.

"Oh, *just friends*. That's a tough one."

I sniffled, wiping my eyes. "Are you like some relationship expert or something?"

She shrugged. "I watch a lot of TV. A *lot* of it."

"Oh," I said, and for some reason, I found myself explaining to the strange, curly-haired girl all about me and Max. "It's not like I think I'm desirable enough that a guy would actually want to date me," I said. "But for once," I sniffed, "I was hoping I was."

"Oh, that's awful," she said and handed me a tissue.

I wiped the smudgy pools of mascara from my face.

"Who's the guy?" she asked.

I told her it was Max.

"Max Montgomery," she mused, twining a tight curl around her finger. "Yes, I think I know which one he is. Shaved head. Nice arms. Blue, blue eyes."

I nodded miserably.

"Yes, Max Montgomery. He orbits in a different stratosphere from all the petty immature high school guys around here. He belongs in the solar system of *men*. Pity to lose that one."

I burst into a fresh swell of tears.

"Sorry, sorry," she said and rubbed my back with compassion. "Well, if this isn't just like when Bruno led on Ava for years only to wind up marrying Francesca in season five of *Rhapsody in Rio*—the most heart-wrenching story line of all time, in my opinion."

I looked at her like she was speaking Arabic and she quickly explained.

"*Rhapsody in Rio*! It's the number one all-time highest rated Spanish soap opera! They dub it into English and play it every night at 9 p.m. on SOAPnet."

"Oh," I said. "You weren't kidding about TV, huh?"

She laughed. "Someday I'm going to act on a soap opera." She beamed. "Or at least be a writer for a TV show," she said, breaking her confident stride slightly. "My name is Georgia. I just moved here this summer from Philadelphia."

"Your name is Georgia and you moved to Georgia?" I asked.

She rolled her eyes. "Don't get me started." We walked over to the mirrors and I dabbed at my puffy eyes with a cold, damp paper towel. Georgia told me she'd started at this school two weeks ago, when the school year officially began.

"Yeah," I said. "We intended to get here a few weeks ago. I told Mom about the first day of school and I even got the bank to move up the closing on the new house, but . . ." I sighed and ran my hand under the cold water. I used my wet fingers to smooth my flyaway strands back into the ponytail. "Well, Mom's not one to stick to a schedule."

Georgia shook her head in sympathy. "Parents." She looked at my schedule and told me that we had third period English together. Then, in a move that erased just a fraction of my pain and gave me a sliver of hope, Georgia offered to skip her next class, hang with me in the bathroom, and tutor me on everything she had observed in her first two weeks at our new high school. I hesitated for a moment. After all, skipping one class because of an emotional disaster was one thing, but skipping a second? But, I reasoned, I wasn't skipping without a plan. Georgia was offering valuable assistance to aid my transition. So I nodded in agreement.

She tossed the wooden hall pass into the garbage bin with a casual shrug and proclaimed, "I'll tell them I got lost." She pulled a trifolded paper towel from the dispenser and smoothed it out. She grabbed a pen from my messenger bag, sat on the floor, and drew a huge triangle onto the white cloth, the black gel ink bleeding into little stray lines.

"So, from what I can make of it, the complex hierarchy of social order here is just like at any other high school." She took the pen and scribbled some names at the apex of the pyramid. "In ancient Egypt, the gods sat atop the pyramid and here, the gods of Worthington High are Mia Palmer and Jake Gordon. The power couple—king and queen—yada yada yada. You get the drift. Jake is your average football-player jock meathead and Mia is of course the top cheerleader on the squad."

I sat down on the hard concrete floor of the bathroom and looked on with interest.

Georgia started adding lines and words to the pyramid. "Football players and basketball players outrank soccer players and wrestlers. Student government fits in here." She drew an arrow. "Band, here . . ."

Another arrow. "Mathletes, foreign language clubs, speech team, and the like go here. Theater—here—which just makes no sense. I mean, we all worship actors and actresses, right?"

I nodded. "Sure."

"But most actors and actresses were in drama club in high school. So why is drama not more toward the top of the pyramid?" She sounded a bit defensive.

"Are you in drama?" It seemed like a logical assumption.

She nodded. "Well, I was, in Pennsylvania. I'm trying out for the spring play, that's for sure. I've heard that Abigail Vorhees gets the lead every year, but I intend to break her reign. Seventeen years of dedication to television and romance novels is bound to pay off. What about you?" she asked, scrutinizing me. "What do you do?" She looked over at my bag. "I don't see any instruments. There's no paint or charcoal or any signs of creative art on your hands." She looked at my color-coordinated notebook sticking out of my bag. "You look organized—you could be in student government—but you also look somewhat athletic. You're not bulky enough for softball, not glam enough for cheerleading. Tennis? I'm thinking you're a student government officer who plays tennis."

I sat there thinking that I had never had someone ask me that point-blank, *What do you do?* I was always just "the daughter of the Hip Hypnotist." I thought back to when we first moved to Vegas, when I joined the Girl Scouts. I loved the perfectly starched uniforms and the idea of earning each little badge and lining them up in a row on a sash. We met on Thursday nights at 6 p.m. Mom would drop me off, and I would go home with Lauren until Mom could pick me up after her show was over. Lauren's mom was more than accommodating but

I felt like such a burden—hanging out on the couch with Mr. and Mrs. Clemmons long after Lauren and her sister had gone upstairs to bed. So eventually I said I'd rather go hang out at the hypnosis show and I let myself become a fixture in my mother's life. And as I got older, I carved out a purpose there—running the audio onstage and managing our finances at home. But now, if you strip those things away—no more show and Mom's newfound desire to be the responsible one—who was I, really? A girl who hung out with her friends at the library and movies? It sounded pathetic. All the more reason for reinvention.

"No," I answered. "No tennis or student government." I pointed back at the densely diagrammed paper towel, shifting the focus away from myself. "So where's Max in all this?"

Georgia drew a wide circle around the pyramid. "Best I can tell, Max orbits. He's friends with everyone."

Not surprising, but I was his *best* friend, right? I looked at the wide black circle encompassing everyone and wondered if that was still true.

The bell rang and moments later the bathroom was infiltrated with girls fixing their hair at the mirrors, re-applying make up, and texting. Georgia and I pulled ourselves up off the floor. I grabbed the paper towel and shoved it into my bag for further dissection later. I followed Georgia down the long hallway and out onto a covered walkway, watching the streams of people pass by as the sticky heat enveloped me.

We walked into the next building over and were hit with a welcome blast of air-conditioning. Georgia gestured to the first door and I walked into English class, put my bag down in the first empty seat, and went up to introduce myself to the teacher. When I turned around and walked back to my desk, Georgia had taken the seat behind me.

A petite blonde walked through the door. She glided over to the chair adjacent to mine and sat. Her long straight hair was the perfect shade of blonde—not as light as Playboy Bunny processed platinum, but not dull and dingy like the dishwater blonde I was. Her hair was soft and shimmering—classy and polished, like a long plate of glass. It caught the twinkle of the fluorescent lights from above. Not a strand was out of place. Not a fraction of frizz. I smoothed my hand over my head, a sliver of envy creeping into my insecurity.

Georgia nudged me from behind. I looked back at her. She nodded over toward the beautiful blonde and steepled her hands into a pyramid. *Mia*, she mouthed. *Queen bee.*

Just then, in walked the hot guy from the park, Quinton, with his hair all tousled and gorgeous.

He patted Mia's desktop two sharp times as a hello, and then, out of the corner of his eye, he saw me. He stopped his stride and turned in my direction.

Just like in the park, I became flustered. Even though I knew I wasn't, I instinctively looked down to make sure I wasn't wearing my M&M T-shirt. I nervously unbuttoned then re-buttoned the top two buttons of my sweater.

A small smile crept across Quinton's face. He pointed at me. "*Do you be-lieve in life after love?*" he sang. He laughed then walked toward the back of the room.

I felt everyone staring at me, wondering who I was. My hands felt hot and sticky.

"Oh. My. God." Georgia's hot breath streamed into the back of my hair. "Quinton Dillinger is gorgeous. Gorgeous! THE QUARTER-BACK! If not the god at the top of the ancient Egyptian pyramid scheme, definitely whatever comes next—a pharaoh? A noble? A priest?"

"I highly doubt he's a priest," I mumbled back as Mrs. Stabile stood up to start the lesson.

"If this is your first day here, how do you know Quinton?" Georgia was hyperventilating.

I waited until the teacher looked down at her book, then turned and talked out of the side of my mouth like a ventriloquist. "My dog humped his leg at the park on Saturday."

"Ah!" Georgia gasped. "Memorable! Just like on *Rhapsody in Rio* when Eva met Juan for the first time because she caused his toilet to overflow. Awkward at first, sure, but eventually, in season six, it became the focal point of the speech at their wedding!"

We both turned and looked back at Quinton, who was running his fingers through his golden brown hair.

I smiled and nudged Georgia. "Did he just sing Cher to me? I didn't, like, hallucinate that, did I?"

Georgia shook her head. "One microphone away from karaoke."

I turned back toward the front of the room and tried to calm my racing heart. Quinton just sang to me. And not in a mocking way, but rather in a *we've got a private joke* kind of a way. A warm heat coursed through me. Hot Guy Quinton, Grand Pharaoh of the Pyramid of Greatness at this school, not only remembered me but maybe—just maybe—was a little bit amused by me. Maybe I wasn't a tennis player or a student government officer, and I didn't have perfectly glossy hair, but maybe without even realizing it, I'd already started the reinvention.

"This could be the perfect way to get your mind off Max," Georgia whispered as class began.

Hmm, I wondered. *Get my mind off him . . . or make him realize exactly what he's missing?*

5

I walked the two miles home from school in the sizzling heat, with each step my hair levitating upward with frizz until I looked like a puffy dandelion. I climbed the front porch steps and entered the house, so quiet, still so empty. It was much bigger than our apartment in Vegas, and my mom thought this was fantastic—*you can get so much more for your money here!* But Mom failed to realize that extra space meant we would need more furniture to fill in the gaps, more rugs to stop the echoes, and since Mom wasn't the best with budgeting, I suspected we'd be hearing echoes for quite a while. Since Mom had now officially taken over the checkbook, we were probably late on the mortgage the minute we crossed the threshold.

No, I reprimanded myself. If I was capable of transformation, so was she.

I tossed my canvas bag onto the kitchen counter, grabbed a Twinkie from the wicker basket of snacks, and plopped on the couch. Oompa waddled out from my bedroom, shook his head as if to say, *This place is so quiet, with only the rustle and tap of the maple tree branches against the window, and that, my dear, does not compare to Cher.*

"I know," I agreed and patted the cushion next to me. Oompa backed up, giving himself an ample runway, then heaved himself up onto the couch with a thud. I scratched his ear, thinking how for so many years I'd assumed Max's feeling for me were deeper than friendship. He gave me his dog, after all. "When you saw Max yesterday, could you smell that girl on his clothes?" I asked Oompa. "Did you know he had a girlfriend?" Oompa snorted and buried his nose behind a pillow, looking guilty. "You could have warned me." I sighed and propped my feet up on the old, scratched coffee table.

I flipped on the TV and quickly got frustrated that I couldn't find my favorite stations on the never-ending list of channels on the menu guide. Everything felt so weird. Mom was supposed to be here, eating Twinkies with me, asking me how my day was and watching *Dr. Oz.* She'd make her weekly promise to eat healthier, then get ready for her show. Instead, it was just me and Oompa and TV stations that were all wrong. I decided to pick a movie from the towering stack of romantic comedies that Mom had collected over the years. Feeling full of self-pity, I popped in *My Best Friend's Wedding* and watched Julia Roberts concoct manipulative plans to steal her best friend back from the clutches of the wrong woman. If only I had a gay friend to masquerade as my boyfriend and make Max jealous, I thought. *Would Max be jealous?*

The front door opened and Mom walked in. I was startled at the sight of her. She looked completely unchanged. She was wearing a short, eggplant-colored dress with a rhinestone-studded belt wrapped around her waist. Her legs were bare except for the thin diamond anklet sparkling against her tanned skin. Her matching purple leather heels were four inches, and her voluminous hair added another inch to her height. Her eyes were rimmed in charcoal liner.

"What?" she asked, all frazzled and breathless, dumping a pile of books next to mine, kicking off heels, and grabbing a Twinkie. She unwrapped it from the crinkly cellophane and joined me on the couch. Oompa grumbled at the unexpected shift in his cushion. She propped her feet next to mine and exhaled loudly. "Who knew nine to five was so . . . long." She looked over at the TV. "Ooh, I love this part," she said, and proceeded to laugh at the antics onscreen. She turned back toward me with a quizzical look on her face. "What?" she asked again, eating the last gobble of Twinkie. "Why are you making that face?"

"Your clothes," I said. "I thought you were working at a doctor's office?" I asked, although I knew she was. "I just thought—"

"What?" She turned toward me.

"You're dressed like you're going to do a Vegas show." I tried to keep my voice calm. "I thought you said you wanted to change, to have a more normal life. . . ." *Normal moms don't wear four-inch purple heels,* I wanted to say. *Normal moms don't get catcalls and whistles from the road.* I blinked my eyes so I wouldn't cry. "How are the patients going to take you seriously if you're dressed like that?"

Mom turned her lower lip in and chewed on it for a few seconds. "People will take me seriously because I know what I'm doing. I'm going to help them. And"—she pointed to the stack of books on the table—"I'm really going to work hard to be the best hypnotherapist I can be." She bit her lip again. "I'm not going to let anyone down, most of all Charlie." *Her new boss.* "He took a chance on me, and I'm going to prove to everyone that I can do it."

"I know you will, Mom," I said. "I just think that here, especially in a small Southern town, maybe your appearance might be . . . a distraction. You say you want to be taken seriously, but maybe someone might be too blinded by the rhinestones to even give you a chance."

"My appearance shouldn't dictate my value." They were words I'd heard before—every time Mom and Grandma fought.

Mom relaxed her shoulders. "If I told you I wore a lab coat, would that make you feel better?"

I smiled. "Maybe."

She smiled back and got up.

I followed her into the kitchen.

She randomly opened the cabinets and stared at the boxes and cans. She pulled out a box of Kraft mac 'n' cheese and shrugged. I understood the dilemma. Our schedule was so out of whack. We were accustomed to eating a snack after I came home from the library, then eating a bigger meal after the show. Mom didn't like to feel weighed down onstage, so we'd wait until the last person in the audience had departed; then we'd raid the casino buffet and traipse home with white Styrofoam boxes filled with an assortment of fried, greasy foods. It had been ages since we'd actually prepared a meal.

I took out a pot and filled it with water and turned on the stove. I looked over at the purple leather heels resting on the ground. This perplexed me—the shoes. The outfit. I just wasn't expecting it.

There had been a long-standing battle between Mom and Grandma about Mom's lifestyle and choices. After an especially large battle, they had stopped speaking, and our visits to Georgia had ceased. I found letters from Grandma begging for reconciliation crumpled in the trash, and Mom always argued that Grandma wanted to reconcile but on her own terms. Grandma wanted Mom to lead a more conventional life—to have a more acceptable job with a daytime schedule, a more conventional wardrobe, a steady relationship—all the things that she thought would give me a more normal life. But Mom wanted her mother to accept her regardless of her choices. She wanted Grandma to admit that, even though Mom's life was the complete opposite of Grandma's, she was still a good mother, a good person.

It was sad, because even though, essentially, they were arguing about what was best for me, they failed to realize that their stubbornness carved a chasm in my life. I wanted my family to be together. I missed my grandmother, but I hated that she was so judgmental. I felt loyal to Mom because despite the craziness of our lives, she was still an awesome mom, but I resented her for fracturing my relationship with my grandparents.

So I did what I always do—I tried my best to control the situation. When I talked to Grandma and Grandpa on Sundays, I did it in private where Mom wouldn't hear. And when Grandma asked probing questions about Mom's job or boyfriend of the month, I simply deflected the conversation to a less controversial topic. And for years that's how it was. I maintained both relationships with a delicate balance.

Then, quite unexpectedly last spring, Mom began casually mentioning her parents.

"You know, your grandmother does that exact same thing," she commented, noting how I lined up the Easter egg dyes according to the color spectrum: red, orange, yellow, green, blue, indigo, violet.

Or, "Funny, last night I watched *Driving Miss Daisy*, and that stuffy old woman sort of reminded me of Grandma."

Then, "Last night that creep in the front row was so obnoxious and I just got to thinking what it would be like to have a different job."

And that's when the tingle of anticipation crept inside me—the possibility of a new future seemed within reach. A future where I could have a mother who looked like other teenage girls' mothers and had a normal job and I'd be the one bringing new boyfriends to the house. We could have family dinners on Sunday nights instead of phone calls in private.

Then, a few weeks after Mom began talking about her parents and a new job, she met Charlie. It was an accidental fleeting encounter—one of those crazy scenarios where she was racing for the elevator, he held the doors, and they rode up twelve floors together. And in that time she told him she was a hypnotist; he told her he was a doctor; and apparently they had some lightning-bolt connection. Not romantic, she insisted, but some crazy energy passed between them. Mom suggested an idea—a way to help his patients deal with their pain through hypnosis. He came to her show. She impressed him, naturally. Then he told her she was smart. Not beautiful, not sexy. Not intriguing, enticing, entertaining, or any of the zillion other compliments she heard on a routine basis. He said smart.

Then he said too bad he lived so far away or he'd give her a job. He pulled out a card and handed it to her, saying, "If you ever move east, give me a call." And when she looked at the card, the NORTHWEST ATLANTA HEADACHE CLINIC was located, unbelievably, twenty minutes away from her hometown of Worthington, Georgia.

Two weeks later, Grandpa had a stroke. Grandma called, and for the first time in five years she spoke to Mom. She told her that Grandpa was asking for us. *That's too many coincidences,* Mom said, *too many signs pointing us back to Georgia.* Mom was a big believer in signs. And suddenly we were packing our bags, leaving our show, changing our life like it was the most natural direction for us to take.

So what I couldn't understand was . . . if she was ready to quit Vegas and reconcile with her parents, why was she still wearing the purple shoes? And why had we not gone to see Grandma and Grandpa yet?

"Willow," Mom said softly. "Change has more to do with what's happening inside the heart than with what someone's wearing on her feet."

A lump formed in my throat. I knew she was right, but what did that leave for me and my transformation? If change happened within, how could I control the way Max viewed me?

I sighed a little too loudly as I rummaged through a box for a colander.

Mom poured the hard macaroni noodles into the boiling water and stirred it with a knife because we hadn't unpacked the wooden spoons yet. "What?" Mom asked. "Why the dramatic exhale?" She pulled out a package of hot dogs from the fridge. "Shoot, I forgot to buy buns."

I tried to change my expression to mask how devastated I was. "Max has a girlfriend," I said, shrugging a little. "I guess I just thought we'd be . . ."

"Together all the time," Mom finished for me. "Like before?"

"Uh-huh." I nodded. "But now it's like he has to divide his time between me and *Minnie.*"

"Minnie?" Mom screwed up her face. "What kind of name is that?"

"I know, right? Hello Minnie Mouse."

"Does she have big ears?" Mom asked, smiling devilishly.

I laughed, and I loved her for indulging me instead of scolding me for being petty. "No," I said. "Her ears are small, inconspicuous. Perfect."

"What's she like?" Mom asked.

"She's fresh, not showy . . . She seemed . . . nice."

"Ah," Mom nodded, draining the noodles. "You like her. Well, I would expect Max to have good taste."

I didn't answer, because how could I like someone who'd stomped on my dreams? But I had only met her for a few minutes. I held onto the hope that she had flaws. Major ones.

Mom turned and looked at me with the steam wafting around her dark hair. "Listen, Willow, take it from me: Girlfriends and boyfriends come and go. The good times had with them are easily forgotten. But best friends stay in your heart forever." She put her hand over her heart and smiled. "Minnie will never replace that special bond you two have." She poured the noodles back in the pot and added the butter, milk, and cheese. "And Max is a good guy. He'll make time for you."

But would it be enough? Could I go back in my mind to thinking of Max as just a friend?

After we ate our macaroni and cheese and hot dogs, I retreated to my bedroom, cracked open my history book, and settled into the chapter on Korea. I heard a crash at my window, the sound of something solid pelting the glass pane. I froze in my seat. I sat perfectly still as my heart ticked a little faster. Again, a smack shook the window. With a tingle of nerves, I slid off my seat and eased over toward the window. Cautiously I took the long cord of the blinds and slowly pulled it up, one lever at a time. And there was Max with his hands pressed against the clear pane of the window.

I tried not to smile and instead threw on a quick expression of surprise. "What are you doing?" I unlocked the window and pulled it up.

"Where the heck were you?" he asked as he negotiated his way through the window like this was completely normal behavior.

"Um, I do have a front door."

Max looked at me like I was clueless. "It's almost 10 p.m."

"So."

"So doesn't your mom . . ."

"No," I said, taken aback for a minute because Max should know that my mom wouldn't care. I never had curfews—our lifestyle didn't roll that way.

"Oh," he said, and his face told me that obviously Minnie's mom did care. I shook the image of him crawling through her window from my mind.

Max pulled the screen down behind him then sat on my bed, taking in my newly decorated room.

"What?" I asked, following his eyes.

"It's more . . . pink than I would have thought."

I looked at the rose-colored bedspread and the framed pictures of pink and purple irises.

"You just don't seem like a pink kind of girl."

I wasn't entirely sure what to make of that. Did he not think of me as a *girl*, just a buddy? Or was it that, of course I'm a girl, just not the frilly variety? But before I could press for details he interrupted my thoughts.

"I waited by your locker for twenty minutes. I was late to teach karate and the six-year-olds were restless. I tried to call you and text you like a billion times and you never answered. Then I had drum lessons and dinner and all day I was worried that you were like, stuck at school or worse, took the bus and had to ride with all the underclassmen."

"I walked." I sat back on my bed. "No big deal."

"Walked? It's like a hundred degrees." His face contorted. "Why?"

"Well, I don't know, we hadn't nailed down any plans and I thought maybe you'd be driving Minnie." I tried not to sound so juvenile. So hurt. So transparent.

"When have we ever *nailed down plans*? I've talked to you every day for the last seventeen years and suddenly we have to *nail down plans*?"

"Well, I didn't know," I said sounding defensive. "I mean, your car's not exactly huge, and with all the crap in the backseat—what if Minnie needed a ride?"

"Minnie has a car," he said, the edges of his lips curling into the beginning of a smile. "Are you jealous, Willow Grey?"

"What? No!" I sprang up off the bed as if standing made me more believable. "Like you're going to boot a seventeen-year friend-ship? Please!" I faked confidence. "I wasn't *jealous*—just, you know, surprised. Why didn't you tell me you were dating her?"

He shrugged. "I've talked to you about Minnie."

"Yeah, but anytime you talked about her it never sounded like you were a couple. You always made her sound like a little bit of a ditz."

He smiled. "She *is* a little bit of a ditz. Reminds me of when we used to watch *I Love Lucy* reruns with your mom, remember that? Minnie's kind of dingbatty sometimes. Naive." You could tell by the way he talked he thought it was cute. Endearing. My heart plummeted. Because if ever there was a word that didn't describe me, it was *ditz*. I wasn't beautiful. I wasn't enticing, intriguing, sexy, or sultry but I did have a decent amount of brains, and I was not flaky or ditzy or dingbatty at all. I liked to be in control of situations as best I could. That's how Mom convinced the stage manager to let me be her assistant at such a young age. I was responsible. Dependable. If Max thought ditzy was cute, well, what future could we have?

"What kind of name is Minnie, anyway?" I didn't mean to sound so judgmental. After all, my name was Willow, and that wasn't exactly normal.

"She's named after her grandmother!" he said protectively. "Minta—it's Greek. Her parents own that little Greek restaurant in town—the Olive Tavern. I'll take you there next weekend. The food is amazing."

Max taking me to his girlfriend's parents' restaurant? It was too painful.

Suddenly Max stood up, crossed the beige carpet of my new room, and pulled me into a tight hug. "God, it's so good to have you here," he said.

I smelled the fresh soap fragrance on his neck—clean and wonderful.

He pulled back and looked at me. "There are just so many things I can't wait to show you."

And as he wrapped his arms tightly around me, I let myself dream and hope that maybe Minnie was around only because I hadn't been. And that once he started showing me all the things that were important to him, he'd realize that Minnie was no longer necessary because now I was here and that was all he wanted.

6

A tall girl with mahogany hair hovered next to Mia's desk at the start of English class the next day. As the students all bustled around, taking out notebooks and gossiping, Mia and the dark-haired girl discussed the cheerleading fund-raiser they were in charge of. They both wore the tight white T-shirts that said SAVE THE TA-TAS. These were the shirts they were selling to raise money for breast cancer awareness. Mia had a calculator out and was tabulating their current profits.

"Even after the proceeds that go to the breast cancer society," Mia said, "we should still have enough profits to buy new uniforms."

"Uh-huh," the mahogany-haired girl said, sounding bored.

Mia continued to tap the calculator buttons.

"So," Mahogany-Haired Girl said. "Riley is refusing to cheer at next week's competition unless we change the music."

Mia snapped her head up from her calculator and running tally. "Why?"

"Apparently"—Mahogany-Haired Girl rolled her eyes—"she's taking a stand against any musician whose lyrics are violent or disparaging to women. You know, *ho, bitch, slut . . .*"

Mia held up her hand to stop the girl. She reached down into her backpack and pulled out another notebook and a four-color pen. She flipped open the notebook to the red tab marked CHEERLEADING and clicked her pen to red. I watched with fascination as she began to write in perfect block letters.

"Okay," Mia said, unaware of my curious stare. "Let's come up with a list of politically correct musicians and songs we can use." She began to construct a bullet-point list.

Mrs. Stabile rose from behind her desk. "Let's get started. Sadie?" she called over to Mahogany-Haired Girl. "What are you doing in this class?"

"Sorry." Sadie smiled. "Just conducting a little business." She waved good-bye to Mia and darted out of the classroom.

Mia clicked her pen over to blue, shut her extracurricular activities notebook, and returned to her English notes.

Mrs. Stabile announced that she was dividing us into groups to discuss different topics from *A Midsummer Night's Dream*. She began sectioning off the class. Slowly she worked her way toward the far left of the room, where I was sitting. She pointed her chubby finger at Mia, Georgia, and me. "You three," she said, "can compile a one-page report on the images of love and marriage in the play versus how they've evolved through history."

Mia quickly jotted down the assignment in blue block letters. We stood up and turned our desks so we faced one another. Georgia rummaged through her backpack for her copy of *A Midsummer Night's Dream*. Mia already had her copy out on the desk. Several

Post-it notes stuck out from the pages, with words like *characterization* and *key plot point* and *symbolism* marked.

I looked up and caught Mia eyeing me. "Um, I . . ." I stammered because it wasn't like I could say to the queen bee, *Wow, I really admire you.* Didn't she hear that on a regular basis? For different reasons, I'm sure, but still. "Uh, I'm just a little panicked," I improvised, "because I've never read *A Midsummer's Night Dream* and it seems like I'm going to be pretty behind." At least that was true.

Georgia popped up from her backpack and tossed her book onto the desk. It was dog-eared and wrinkled and looked like she had spilled some nail polish on the cover. "I can bring you up to speed," she offered.

"That'd be great," I said. "Do you mind?" I found myself asking for Mia's permission. She just sort of commanded the room that way.

"No, of course not," she said and folded her hands on top of the desk. She seemed interested to hear Georgia's explanation.

Georgia began her summary. "Hermia loves Lysander but her wicked father insists that she marry Demetrius." Georgia pulled out a sheet of white lined paper and began to diagram the love triangle. "Hey, do you mind if I borrow that?" She reached for Mia's pen and began to color code the diagram. "So Hermia and Lysander escape to the woods, but Demetrius follows because he totally digs Hermia. Then Helena follows Demetrius into the woods because she totally digs *him*. It's a complicated mess." And from the circles and arrows on the page, I could see it was.

"That was good," Mia said, her arms propped on the desk, totally immersed in the description. She looked over at Georgia's mangled book, perhaps a little surprised that someone could fully comprehend a reading assignment without detailed notes. "But then in the woods," Mia added, "a fairy uses the juice from a magical flower to put a love spell on Lysander to make him fall in love with Helena."

"A love spell?" I asked, intrigued.

They nodded in unison.

Just then, the classroom door opened and in walked Quinton, all flushed and glowing like he'd just ridden a wave to class. "Sorry I'm late," he said, handing the teacher a note.

Mrs. Stabile glanced down at the paper then scanned the class-room. She pointed over at our group. "Join them; they only have three."

Quinton sauntered over. He grabbed an empty desk and chair then picked them up into the air with no signs of strain, like he was lifting a Kleenex off the floor instead of a hunk of steel and wood. He placed them down into our mix. "Hey," he said to Mia, not really even noticing me or Georgia.

"Where've you been?" Mia asked. "You weren't in history."

Quinton shook his head slightly, like he was disgusted with him-self. "I know, man. And we have a test on Friday. Can I borrow your notes?"

Mia nodded. "What happened?"

Quinton let out a long breath. "I woke up at my neighbor's house this morning—sleeping on their couch."

"Sounds like a story there," Mia said.

"Damn sleepwalking," Quinton said. "It's getting worse. I've never left the house before."

"You sleepwalked to your neighbor's?" Mia asked, wide-eyed. "How did you get inside the house?"

He shrugged. "Who knows?"

I laughed and he turned toward me, noticing I was there finally.

"Hey, it's the hypnotist girl," he said.

I smiled at him, a small tingle coursing through my veins because he remembered a detail about me other than the humping dog, the M&M T-shirt, or Cher lyrics.

"Hypnotist?" Mia and Georgia asked at the same time.

Mia started to click the four different colors of her pen. *Click, click, click.*

"She's the Hip Hypnotist," Quinton said, flashing a sparkly grin. "From Vegas."

Another detail. My cheeks flushed. Suddenly I had this image in my head of me and Quinton and Mia huddled on the green chenille couch in my new house. Me with the top-of-the-pyramid people. A video of our hypnosis show would be on. They would be amazed at the volunteers, slumped in their chairs, heads fallen to the sides, performing like puppets on a string. They would laugh at all the shenanigans, ask if it was real, inquire how we got that stodgy old woman to kick her legs like a Rockette showgirl. But then I imagined what would happen next—Quinton's eyes would bulge and his mouth would drop open slightly. *That's your mother?* he'd drool as she walked around the stage in her tight black mini-dress with her long cascading locks of dark hair that framed her face. *She's so young.* And then Mia's forehead would crease as she realized that really it was Mom who was doing the hypnosis. I was just the sidekick, the girl next to the curtain, controlling the audio, moving the chairs, helping if any of the volunteers got too uncensored.

And then I'd be right back in familiar territory. New place, new school, new friends . . . exact same scenario: falling into the background. Always the sideline girl. I was tired of it. *New canvas,* I thought. *Blank slate. Reinvention.*

So I closed *A Midsummer Night's Dream* and tucked it under my hands. I leaned forward on the desk and spoke in a hushed tone, like I was letting them in on a secret. "You know, some people think hypnosis is a crock—that it's fake—that we paid the audience members to act. But I can tell you with 100 percent honesty—it's real."

Georgia inhaled a small gasp of excitement, and Mia and Quinton were fixed on my every word.

"When people think of hypnosis, they think of a zombie—someone compelled to obey no matter what's being asked. But that's not at all correct. Actually, when we hypnotize our volunteers, they're not asleep—they're alert the whole time. They're just deeply relaxed. When they're that relaxed, they tend to be highly suggestible. If someone tells them to do something, they embrace it wholeheartedly. Fear and embarrassment just . . . evaporate."

A devilish grin played on Quinton's lips. "So you could make people do, like, whatever you wanted."

I loved the sound of that—such control. I never really thought of it that way before, maybe because it was always Mom throwing out the commands. But I didn't tell them that. I smiled and enjoyed the spotlight. "Within reason," I said.

"Awesome," he said, and Mia and Georgia nodded in agreement.

Mrs. Stabile clapped her hands together in a sharp smack, interrupting my moment in the limelight, and told everyone that class was about over and that each group was to write a one-page homework assignment on what we discussed. The bell rang and everyone quickly gathered up their things.

Mia picked up the colorfully diagrammed paper and inserted it into the pocket of her notebook. She stacked her books into her bag.

"I'll e-mail you the history notes after I type them tonight," she said to Quinton.

"Thanks," he said.

"I'll call you tonight," Georgia offered to me. "We can work on the assignment together."

"Thanks," I said, still not knowing much more about *A Midsummer Night's Dream* than the complicated love triangle.

"So when are you going to show us some of this hypnosis?" Quinton asked, startling me. He tossed a backpack onto his broad, football-sculpted shoulders.

"Oh, I don't know," I said. "It's not like I could do anything here at school."

"What about this weekend at Jake's?" Quinton suggested, looking at Mia.

"What?" Mia asked, clearly taken aback.

I recalled Georgia's pyramid, with Mia and Jake at the top.

"It could be fun," Quinton said. "Different, at least."

Mia just stood there frozen as swarms of other students passed us on their way out of the room.

"No, no," I said, waving my hand at the suggestion. "I don't want to crash."

Georgia eyed me curiously, standing just ahead of us, pretending to walk toward the door but obviously eavesdropping.

"Plus, what if I did hypnosis and someone got mad at me because they were embarrassed?"

"*Or*," Quinton interjected, "it could be really funny. Because as I recall, outrageous antics sort of follow you around." He gave me a crooked smile. He was so persuasive in a charming, cocky sort of way.

"I guess . . ." Mia squinted at me a little then looked over at

Quinton, clearly not knowing the story of our encounter at the park. She started to move toward the door, maybe indicating that the conversation was over.

"Well, either way," Quinton said to me, sounding like he was losing interest. He started to follow Mia toward the door.

And I knew I had to act now. If I hesitated, like I had on the porch with Max, the moment would be lost. I could lose a key opportunity to redefine myself. Instead of being the sideline girl, I could be invited to a top-of-the-pyramid party where I could have a chance at the spotlight for real.

"Okay," I said, following behind them quickly. "I'd love to go to the party."

"Cool," Quinton said.

Mia smiled tightly. "Well, great."

We walked into the hallway and the three of us went our separate ways. As I walked on to my next class, the realization hit me. I had done it. I had taken a chance. A surge of happiness floated up my spine. I was on my way.

When I got home, I flung my bag onto the counter and immediately dove into the stacks of DVDs lined up in the media cabinet. My heart pulsed because somewhere around sixth period I had realized my fatal error. Sure, excluding Mom from the stories today at school was exhilarating but now—the idea that they wanted me to do a hypnosis show was sobering because I had never actually done the hypnosis. Well, there was the one time when I attempted to hypnotize Max but he fell out of the tree before I could actually tell if he was truly under.

I had been onstage for five shows a week for years—I knew the routine, I knew the sequence of events . . . but could I do it? It felt like the first time I took Mom's car and drove on my own. I had been to my favorite Chinese restaurant a billion times, but had I ever really paid attention to how we got there? Could I make all the correct turns and find the right streets when it was just me behind the wheel?

I found a copy of one of our recorded performances and popped it into the DVD player with a notebook in front of me, pen poised to take notes. I watched my mother stand in front of the volunteers with confidence and control. "You're going to think it's not work-ing," Mom said with a little smile. "You're going to think you're not hypnotized." She walked closer to them. "Close your eyes. Breathe in and out. Relax."

I watched onscreen as the volunteers obeyed her every com-mand. Such power. I wondered if anyone would ever follow instruc-tions from me.

I had just propped Oompa on the coffee table and was improvis-ing a trial run when the front door swung open. Mom walked in and stopped, frozen in the foyer.

"What are you doing?" she asked. She walked over and looked at herself on TV. She seemed lost in thought for a moment; then she turned the TV off. "Why are you watching that?"

I stood there like a thief caught red-handed.

She looked at Oompa sitting erect on the table, wide-eyed and a little dazed.

"Were you . . ." She bent over and snatched the fat dog into her arms. "Were you trying to *hypnotize* Oompa?"

"No, no," I lied. "He was just so . . . homesick and I was trying to, um, make him feel better. Thought I'd let him watch the show and bring back some old memories."

Mom's mouth cocked into a doubtful expression. "Oompa never saw any of the shows, Willow."

I dramatically hit the side of my head with my hand. "Right! Silly me."

Mom said something into Oompa's ear then put him back on the ground, and he ambled away, zigzagging across the carpet like he was confused. "Willow," she said seriously, "what's going on? You're not going to show people this? Try and impress people or, God forbid, try and *perform*, are you?"

I threw on a big shocked expression. "What? No!" I waved my hand through the air as if to say, *How ridiculous.* "I've already made friends—no need to impress anyone. There's this other new girl, Georgia—she's really nice and she's calling me tonight to help with homework. And there's this guy, Quinton, and he invited me to a party this weekend."

Mom seemed somewhat satisfied by this. "And Max? You two are all right? Even with Minnie in the picture?"

I nodded. "He picked me up and dropped me home from school. So maybe you were right—he will make time for me."

She nodded. "Tell him I got that filter thing replaced in the car. Good thing he spotted it—the repairman said it was ready to go." She kicked off her heels—black stilettos today—and wandered over to the wicker basket on the kitchen counter. She pulled out a bag of Otis Spunkmeyer cookies and tore it open, still looking at me suspiciously. She took a bite of a small cookie and swallowed, her gaze never leaving me. "I just really want to leave that life behind, okay? It was fun, sure, but like I said, it's time to grow up, use my potential, do something respectable. I don't want anyone around here to know about us performing in Vegas. Last thing I need is for one of

Grandma's snobby friends from the garden club finding out." She ate another cookie and looked a little sad.

I knew that Grandma had kept Mom's hypnosis show a secret. It had always made Mom upset that Grandma was embarrassed of her. I saw a small hint of red work its way across her cheeks. She examined the cookie wrapper as though she'd developed a sudden interest in the caloric content.

"Mom," I said softly, "even if the show in Vegas wasn't something that Grandma liked, still, it's nothing to be ashamed of. People loved it. They loved you."

She shook her head. "I don't need a pep talk, Willow. I just want you to promise me that performance hypnosis is a thing of the past. The only hypnosis in our lives now is the more respectable kind that I use at work for therapy."

I looked at her soft, honey-colored eyes lined in ebony, and wondered if she was rehearsing for when we would see Grandma and Grandpa. I nodded. "Okay," I said. "No hypnosis."

And I wondered who I was going to disappoint: her, my new friends . . . or myself.

Saturday evening, I stood in my bathroom in my jeans and black top. I added another layer of black liquid liner to the rim of my eyelids, but all it did was make my pupils look darker, more bizarre. So I soaked a Q-tip in makeup remover and washed it away. Instead I asked Mom if I could borrow one of her necklaces.

"Sure, honey," she said and rummaged through the pile of chains and beads on her dresser. She held up a thick silver chain with a round, heavy charm. She laid it against my chest.

I cringed. "It's kind of big and heavy."

"Geez," Mom teased. "Take a little fashion risk for once." She put the necklace down and picked up another.

But I spotted a different chain with a small turtle charm. I clasped it around my neck. "I'll wear this one." The shell had little green stones that sparkled when they caught the light.

"It's so small." Mom scrunched up her nose. "And it blends right into your dark shirt."

But I didn't care. I liked that the turtle's head was just barely poking out of its shell. That's what I was going to do tonight. Emerge.

"So what time is Max picking you up?" Mom asked.

"Any minute." I had casually mentioned to him that Quinton and Mia had invited me to Jake's party. If he was surprised that top-of-the-pyramid people had befriended me, he made no indication. He said he planned on going to the party, and if I'd feel more comfortable going with him than showing up alone, he'd love to pick me up.

"Max is here!" Mom called as the sound of his truck filled the house.

I grabbed my bag and waved good-bye.

"Have fun!" she called as I flew out the front door.

I sank into the passenger's seat and buckled my seat belt.

"You look great," Max said and smiled. He looked great too. Better than great, in his khaki shorts and white T-shirt that made his skin look so tan. He backed down our driveway and cranked the radio. I was feeling great; I was excited about the night, I was sitting here with Max, and the song on the radio was fun. I started moving my head along to the beat. Max looked at me slyly.

"You like this song?" he asked.

"Uh, yeah" I said. Max was so into music, there was no way I was admitting I'd never heard it before in my life.

"You actually *know* this song?" he teased. "I thought all you listened to was Cher."

"Hey!" I pushed him lightly. "Not by choice."

I don't think he bought it. I was a Top 40 pop queen and it would take him hours—no, days—to deprogram my brain and introduce me to some of his music choices.

"I'm going to make our car rides all about music education for you," he said. "I'm going to whip up a mix CD this weekend of decent music—some old school like Nirvana, Chili Peppers, maybe throw in a little Oasis and Pumpkins." Max was all excited, nodding his head and smiling. "Weezer, the Killers, 311, the White Stripes . . ."

I smiled and laughed. My heart swelled with the possibility that I had been right—that Minnie had been a distraction for him, a placeholder until I arrived.

He jerked the truck to the right and pulled up a driveway.

I looked around. "Where are all the cars?" I asked. "We're not the first people here, are we?"

"No, this isn't Jake's. I told Minnie we'd swing by and pick her up."

"Oh," I said, trying not to visibly deflate. *What the hell? He was just flirting with me—wasn't he?* Suddenly, I felt awkward, like a total third wheel. *I guess I was wrong.* I was just his friend. Minnie was his girlfriend. "I didn't mean to intrude."

"Hey, I offered to take you. I *want* to take you." He smiled.

Why? I wanted to ask. *Because you love me and want to be near me? Or because I'm new in town and you wanted to help out a friend?* I was so confused.

Minnie floated down her front steps, her short skirt bouncing up around her thighs as she skipped (skipped!) across the driveway. She seemed so light and effervescent—like a glass of champagne, and all at once I felt very unfeminine. Sure, I was a good companion, like milk is for cookies, but I didn't make your nose tingle. No wonder Max was surprised at the pink in my room. I made a mental note to wear more skirts.

Max got out of the truck to greet her, so I got out of the car too, and I stood pathetically against the car door while they kissed. I turned my back and stared at the puffy white clouds in the sky start-ing to turn a pale shade of petal pink as the sun set. *A pink sunset. How romantic. Let me go vomit.*

Minnie came over to my side of the truck. "Hi!" She beamed. "Love those jeans. So flattering!"

"Thanks," I muttered. *Did she have to be so darn nice?* I opened the door and started to climb toward the backseat.

"No, no," Minnie said. "You should sit up front. You were here first—you have automatic shotgun!"

"No, it's fine," I said. "You have a skirt on—you don't need to be climbing all over the place. I'll be fine back here."

"Well . . ." She hesitated for a moment. "Okay," she relented.

I climbed into the backseat. "Do you have enough room back there?" she called over her shoulder as Max started the truck. "He's such a slob! There's junk everywhere!" She reached over and play-fully rubbed his head and I felt the palm of my hand burn. I wished I could feel his soft scalp under my hand.

"Willow," Max called over the thumping bass. "Minnie's taste in music is just as bad as yours. Maybe worse! She likes"—he looked over at her and used his free hand to pat her knee affectionately—"*country* music."

"It's not that bad," she said, laughing, "if you'd just give it a try."

"*All my exes live in Texas,*" Max sang in a thick, put-on drawl.

Minnie laughed and I counted all the ways that sitting in the backseat, nestled between a mountain of CDs and a dumbbell, watching my best friend, my soul mate, touch and laugh and flirt with the most adorable girl I'd ever seen, was pure torture.

Max jammed on his brakes and my head flung forward and knocked against the back of Minnie's seat.

"Sorry!" Minnie said, as if she was the one who drove recklessly.

"Are you okay?" Max turned to look at me.

I pointed to the windshield. "Could you please keep your eyes on the road?"

"We're here," he said, throwing the truck into park.

I looked out the window and gawked. It's not like I never went to parties back in Vegas—of course I did. I lived for my friend Lauren's annual Halloween party. But the parties were small, intimate—twenty or so of us crammed into an apartment, filtering out onto a balcony into the desert heat.

But here it was like the entire school had taken over—not just the two-story expansive brick home of Jake Gordon, but the partiers had spilled out into the entire neighborhood. Cars haphazardly lined the driveway—some half-parked on the grass—and snaked down the curb of the street as far as the eye could see. The girls wore skirts and tank tops and the guys wore shorts and T-shirts. People overflowed out of the house, littering the lawn with their red plastic cups.

Max came over to the passenger side of the car and offered a hand to help me out of the backseat, and I noticed with utter inferiority that Minnie showed no signs of jealousy. There was not even a morsel of concern in her mind that Max could be attracted to me.

We walked side by side, Max cluelessly nestled between two girls who loved him, up the long driveway. Halfway up, Trent bounded over and high-fived Max. Immediately they started talking about music. Another guy, big and sweaty, with flushed cheeks, barreled over and pressed cold red cups into our hands.

"What's up guys?" Sweaty Guy asked and joined the conversation between Max and Trent.

Minnie turned toward me and asked if Worthington was very different from Vegas. But I could barely respond, because panic overtook me when I realized we were staying there—outside—in the sweltering, oppressing humidity. It would only be a matter of minutes—seconds, really—until my hair frizzed up and resembled a rat's nest.

I told Minnie that Worthington was very different from Vegas but that right now the humidity was the change that was causing me the biggest problem. "I can't take this muggy weather," I said, tugging at my hair. "And what was I thinking, wearing jeans?"

She laughed then turned to talk to another girl who'd walked up.

The sweaty, flushed-faced guy looked at me. "So you're the girl from Vegas?"

I nodded. "Uh-huh."

"Quinton Dillinger is, like, telling everyone that you're going to do a hypnosis show tonight," Sweaty Guy said. His name was Conner.

Max craned his neck away from his conversation with Trent and looked toward me. "You are?"

"Are what?" Minnie asked, turning back toward me.

"She's going to do hypnosis tonight," Conner answered excitedly.

"Well, I'm not sure," I said noncommittally. I thought back to my mom's pleading eyes, her emphatic request to leave that life behind.

"Really?" Max asked, a huge grin breaking across his face. He turned toward Conner. "She's hilarious. Hilarious." He told him that he had seen our show when he visited Vegas many years ago. "I promise you," he said enthusiastically, "you guys are in for a treat."

He shook his head affectionately at me. "It's always exciting when you're around, Willow. You know how to have fun, how to throw a little adventure into life."

I couldn't help but notice a small line crease between Minnie's eyebrows as her face shifted into a slight show of concern. And I looked her over, standing there in her bouncy skirt and sandals, and suddenly something occurred to me. Minnie, fresh and feminine, genuinely kind and a little ditzy, might just be a little bit boring. I looked back at Max, still smiling at some recollection of mischief we'd gotten into together. He didn't have to know that I had become a little boring too. He still believed my Photoshopped life. Now I had a chance to make that life a reality. I reached up and felt the turtle charm. Time to emerge. Take a chance.

Minnie was watching Max smile at me.

Then suddenly Minnie grabbed at her eye and called loudly, "Oooh, my eye! I've got something in my contact!"

"Here." The girl beside her reached into her pocket and pulled out some eyedrops. "I've got some solution."

"Oh," Minnie said, sounding both surprised and disappointed. "Well, I . . . I need a mirror." She grabbed Max's hand. "Max, walk me to the bathroom? I can't see!"

He took her hand obediently and gently led her across the grass, weaving between partiers.

What just happened? I watched as Max opened the front door and led her inside. *Something* had happened, that was for sure. And that's when I knew I had found my opportunity. I could show Max everything he'd been missing. Fun. Excitement. Adventure. And I could start by doing a hypnosis show tonight.

"I'm going to do it," I said to no one in particular. I was abandoned, standing alone at a party where I hardly knew a soul.

Conner, the sweaty guy, patted me on the back. "Awesome!"

And I did think briefly about my mother and her sad, beseeching eyes. But Mom was a romantic. She would understand that I was just taking the necessary steps to open the door to true love.

8

"You're going to do it?" Quinton asked.

"Sure," I said nonchalantly, as if I wasn't defying my mother in every way. My heart played bumper cars in my chest, slamming back and forth into various organs as I tried to calm my nerves, tell myself I could do it. No big deal. I'd channel my mother and everything would be fine. Better than fine, because I'd be reminding Max of my adventurous spirit—something maybe, just maybe, he was missing.

"What will you need?" Mia asked, very businesslike. I half expected her to whip out her four-color pen and create a list.

"Um, a stage?" The sound of the words made me shiver. *A stage. My stage.*

She nodded and began to walk up the driveway and around the house.

The mahogany-haired girl, Sadie, walked over to Mia. I recognized her from the previous day in English class. "Hey girl," she said to Mia.

"Hi." Mia adopted a much lighter tone than the one she had used with me.

"Love your skirt," Sadie said.

"Thanks." Mia smoothed the sides of her painted-on, metal-embellished black skirt. "Did you tell Riley about the new song?"

Sadie nodded. "Total approval."

"Whew." Mia smiled. "Thanks." She started to walk again, and I followed, feeling a little bit like a dog. I couldn't quite get a handle on Mia. She wasn't mean to me, and I didn't exactly feel invisible, but she seemed very wary of me for some reason.

"So," she said, turning toward me. "How exactly is it that you became friends with Quinton?"

"We sort of . . . bumped into each other at the park."

She looked me over with an intrigued expression, like she wondered if *bumped into each other* was code for *bumping and grinding*. I almost jumped in to correct her, but then I decided to let Mia wonder if I was the kind of girl Quinton would go for. It was thrilling to even pretend of the possibility. This was my reinvention, after all. I followed her behind the house to the backyard, where there was a large brick patio—perfect for a stage. Several people stood around a stone fire pit where an actual fire was sizzling—a fire! In this heat! Insanity! But the flickering yellow and orange flames sent waves of amber light into the darkening sky, and it did set a nice mood.

Mia scanned the area in planning mode when a burly guy, tall and gorgeous—looking a little like Taylor Lautner—walked over. His eyes were semi-closed under thick black eyebrows and he wore an expression like maybe the English language was too hard to muster right now.

"Hey sweetie!" Mia cooed, reaching up to stroke his mammoth bicep. "Are you having fun? Do you need another drink?"

I realized this must be Jake—Mia's boyfriend.

He shook his head.

"Your party is *great*." Mia tilted her chin up at him—maybe waiting for a kiss, or maybe just trying to close the gap in their height difference. "I mean, like, *everyone* is here. Everyone!"

He looked over at me and Mia followed his gaze. "Are you that chick who's doing a hypnosis show?" Jake asked, shocking me that he could, indeed, speak. "Quinton said you had weird eyes."

I didn't know whether to be happy that Quinton was talking about me or upset because he'd called my eyes weird. At the park he'd said *wicked*. *Wicked* was much better than *weird*.

"Yes," Mia answered for me with a pinched look on her face. "Her name is Willow."

Jake lumbered in the direction of the patio door. "I'll go tell Quinton. He'll be psyched."

Quinton will be psyched. I replayed the words in my head and for a moment, contemplated, could Quinton—beautiful, tousled, almost-top-of-the-pyramid Quinton—like me? I quickly squashed that thought and reasoned that he was just excited about seeing his classmates do something funny.

Jake opened the glass French doors and started to walk inside. He paused momentarily, halfway into the threshold, and I wanted to tell him to shut the door or all these softball-size bugs would enter the house, but I kept my mouth shut. He looked back over at me. "You need anything?" he asked.

"Could you get me a drink?" Mia asked sweetly.

"I meant for the show," he said.

"Oh," Mia said softly.

I felt uneasy, like I was caught in some kind of a quiet, passive lovers' quarrel. I looked at Jake. "Um, some chairs?" I suggested.

He gestured with his chin toward a collection of wicker patio furniture. "I'll get some folding chairs too."

"And my drink?" Mia asked, slightly desperate.

He disappeared into the house without answering.

I began to lug the heavy, cushioned love seat out onto the patio area when suddenly two large floodlights, anchored at the corners of the roof, turned on and illuminated the area with crisp white light. Word spread quickly, because in a matter of minutes, the backyard filled up with hordes of people, all sort of staring in my direction, and without much preparation, everything felt very real. I was going to do it. This was my chance to have eyes on me, the spotlight, everything I never had but always wanted.

Jake and Quinton came through the French doors, stacks of folding chairs shoved under their thick arms, and quickly assembled them into a straight line across the patio as I instructed them to. More people spilled from inside the house and began seating themselves on the plush green lawn, looking in my direction. As others followed suit, the mass of partiers quickly became an organized, seated lot— an audience, huge and interested. Quinton stepped off the patio and squeezed himself onto the grass close to the stage.

Mia held her thin, sculpted arms into the air, taking charge, and the crowd immediately hushed, listening eagerly. "I'm not sure," Mia said, raising her soft voice as loud as it would go, "if you've met Willow. She's new at our school—just moved from Vegas, where she had a real hypnosis show! And she said she would do a little performance for us tonight!" She sounded so excited, so different than just moments earlier. I recalled how Mom could put on a stage voice and create a presence. I realized that was exactly what Mia was doing.

The crowd burst into a rowdy applause and I felt a tingle work its way up my spine. Fear. Insecurity. Doubt. I was going to humiliate myself. I wouldn't be able to do it the way Mom did. I wouldn't even sound as good as Mia. Just then, the patio door behind me creaked open and I saw Max, holding Minnie's hand, slither around the perimeter of the patio and squeeze into the seated crowd. Max smiled broadly at me. Minnie's eyes looked weak, a little red, and I wondered if it was from a true contact lens emergency or if she had been crying. I felt a twinge of guilt. I didn't want to cause them to fight.

But then Max touched his index finger to his temple—a sign from our youth when we would signal to each other, *If you think you can do it, you can do it*, and something inside me snapped. I could do this. I would do this. And it would open the doors of Max's heart to me. He would see my spunk, my energy, my adventure—all those things that I had lost over the years. And of course I would channel my mother and be sexy and confident and alluring, and if Max liked that too, well, fabulous. And if Max happened to realize that he was with the wrong girl, then that wasn't really my fault—Max would be making that decision.

And really, it would be doing Minnie a favor, because if they weren't meant to be—if they weren't true soul mates like Max and I were—wouldn't I just be saving her future heartache?

So I smiled and adopted Mom's low, sultry stage voice. "I'm Willow Grey and we're going to have some fun tonight."

I saw Max giggle at my put-on voice and I remembered how he laughed so many years ago when we were in the tree and I used the same voice. But the crowd went nuts. Maybe it was the heat or maybe it was all the red plastic cups of beer consumed that made them so enthusiastic, but maybe, I thought with hope, maybe it was just me.

"I need some volunteers," I said, and arms shot up everywhere. Mom always took fifteen but she had me to help her so I decided to just pick five people from the audience. I randomly pointed to five people, and they ran across the grass to the patio. I motioned for them to sit on the chairs. They high-fived one another and made victory fist pumps into the air.

I asked the audience to be very still, very quiet; then I had the volunteers close their eyes. I took a deep breath. I knew the words. I knew the sequence. I didn't have the audio of the soft ocean waves to play, but I prayed it would work anyway. "I want you to take a deep breath, focus on my voice, and I'll guide you through," I said calmly.

For the next three minutes, with complete silence behind me, I found myself just falling into the routine, saying the words I heard my mom say so many times before. I didn't have time to be nervous anymore. I was invested in the process. "From this point on you will hear what I say, feel what I ask you to feel, visualize what I ask you to visualize." The five volunteers slumped in the chairs, heads limp to the side, some resting on the shoulder of the person next to them.

I turned back around to the audience and smiled. "Ready?" I asked. "You can make noise now."

And they did.

"Okay!" I said, imagining how in our show the pulsing music would start to play. I had the volunteers open their eyes. I walked over to the guy wearing a Georgia Tech Yellow Jackets T-shirt. "Uh-oh," I said to him. "You just got stung by a yellow jacket." For some reason this sent the crowd into a huge uproar. Burly jocks stood up and screamed things about football and rivals. I knew the response wasn't exactly because of me, but still, it gave me a little dose of confidence to know everyone was so enthusiastic. I turned back to the Yellow Jacket guy. "Your tongue is swelling up to twice its normal size. You have no trouble breathing, but it's difficult to talk."

"Oh no." Yellow Jacket Guy grabbed at his mouth. "My thongue!"

There was more hooting and hollering from the crowd. I stared at the Yellow Jacket guy for a moment, watching as he poked his lips with his fingers. I had done it. Hypnotized. Excitement swirled in my stomach.

I turned to a petite girl in a pink sundress. "On the count of three," I told her, "you will become Grammy-winning entertainer of the year, pop sensation Taylor Swift!"

"Woo-hoo!" The crowd applauded.

"One, two, three!"

Pink Sundress Girl popped up off her chair and sashayed toward the edge of the patio, a fake microphone in her hand, and began to sing loudly. The crowd went wild.

I stared into the audience of my new classmates and felt flushed with exhilaration. This was working. I was entertaining them. Then, at the very left side of the crowd, I saw Max and Minnie sitting so close to each other their arms looked zipped together. Minnie leaned over and kissed Max's cheek. And he looked lovingly at her. I was onstage but he was looking at her.

Pink Sundress was singing "Mine," but I had an inspiration. I tapped her on the shoulder. "Hey Taylor," I whispered. "Why don't you sing that song about the girl who secretly loves her best friend."

Pink Sundress nodded eagerly and started to sing "You Belong with Me."

I turned back toward the other volunteers sitting on their chairs. Yellow Jacket guy continued to poke at his mouth. I pointed to a girl with honey-streaked hair. "Can you put your hands in a fist? Good. Perfect. For the remainder of the show, your hands are stuck that way, okay? You can't seem to pull them apart, but just keep trying."

She began to struggle to separate her hands. At the edge of the patio, Pink Sundress sang, "Dreaming of the day when you wake up and find that what you're looking for has been here the whole time."

I looked over my shoulder. Max was looking at me now. My heart rocketed into my ribs. *Keep his attention. Show him how much fun you are. Make him realize he wants to be with you.*

I turned back to the girl with the pretend fused fists. "Oh, and for no apparent reason you've completely forgotten what your name is and any time I ask you your name, you'll get up and sing this line from the song 'That's Not My Name': *'They call me quiet, but I'm a riot . . . Mary, Jo, Lisa, Always the same. But that's not my name.'* Okay? So, tell me, what's your name?"

The pretty girl, trying to pull her hands apart, got a confused look on her face. "I'm not really sure." She giggled. "*They call me quiet, but I'm a riot . . .*"

A huge burst of laughter erupted from the crowds. This feeling was totally new to me—the feeling of deserving that kind of reaction, of owning the stage. Of being the star. Max was smiling, nodding in appreciation. I needed to really amp up the antics—show him how much fun I was. I tried to think of some outrageous things Mom did to really keep a crowd going. There was the bit where Mom had a volunteer think he or she was having sex—something Grandma called particularly crude and cruel. But it sure did get laughs. What if I just had one of my volunteers think he was making out with a Victoria's

Secret model? I looked over at the remaining volunteers. They were both guys. What if they got, like, a boner or something? Sure, it would bring the house down, but I kind of agreed with Grandma—it was cruel and something I couldn't do no matter how much I wanted to prove to Max that I was adventurous. I got a different idea.

"You," I said, pointing to a dark-haired guy wearing a baseball cap. "What's your name?"

"Davis."

"Davis, for the remainder of the show whenever I say your name, you'll get a sudden bout of gas and fart explosively. Okay, Davis?"

Phrrrrrt.

The audience went crazy. Doubled over laughing. I looked at Davis. No boner, so I didn't feel too cruel. The remaining volunteer was a broad-shouldered, good-looking guy, clearly a teammate of Quinton and Jake's. "And what's your name?" I asked. "It's not Davis, right?"

Phrrrrrrrrrt!

Laughter and snorts filled my ears.

"It's Hayden."

I looked over at Max. He was watching me, but I also caught him glancing over at Pink Sundress as she continued to sing: "Been here all along so why can't you see? You belong with me . . ."

Was I imagining it, or did Max have a contemplative look on his face? Like maybe, just maybe, the words of the song were seeping into his brain?

I needed to do something to show Max he could act on his feelings. I turned back to my final volunteer. "People have secret crushes all the time, but sometimes they're just afraid to act on it, you know?" I said.

Hayden nodded, and suddenly the audience got very quiet.

"When I say your name, Hayden," I continued. "I want you to get up and walk toward the girl you've always secretly liked but never told anyone about. When I say your name, I want you to lose that fear and just take a chance, okay?"

He nodded. The audience was very, very still.

"Go for it, Hayden," I said.

Huge applause ripped through the air as all the football players stood up and egged him on. All eyes were on Hayden as he walked toward the edge of the patio. Mia, at the very edge of the brick stage, sat erect and poised. Everyone seemed to cast their eyes toward her, but Hayden walked right past her. Mia's face froze in a plastered smile like the camera shots of losers at the Oscars. Everyone mumbled in surprise and looked on in confusion as Hayden navigated his way through the crowd toward the very back. He walked up to a nondescript mousy girl dressed in jean shorts and a green halter top.

"Hey," Hayden said and smiled at her.

"Oh my God," she whispered in shock.

The crowd, clearly surprised at his choice, looked back and forth from hot Hayden to this mousy, nondescript girl. The mousy girl, overwhelmed, started to cry.

Hayden reached over and wiped her eyes. "I think you're so great."

Then the crowd started to cheer. "Go for it, man!" someone yelled.

"Excuse me," I said to the girl onstage who was still trying to pull her stuck hands apart. "What was your name, again?"

"*They call me quiet, but I'm a riot . . .*"

"Why don't you dance, Davis?" I said.

Phrrrrrrrt! He got up and started to dance.

"Everyone, get up and dance!" I commanded.

The pretty, forgot-her-name girl danced around with her hands in a fist. Yellow Jacket danced around with his swollen tongue hanging out of his mouth, and Hayden danced with the mousy-haired girl at the back of the crowded lawn. And Taylor Swift continued to sing "You Belong with Me."

The performance was a success. I did it. I made it happen by myself. In the crowd, I saw Max, laughing and having a good time and I felt a zing of satisfaction. I had made my mark on this new school and on Max. And finally, I felt like I was emerging from the shadows.

9

The next day, Georgia invited me over to work on our English assignment but also, I think, to get the gossip about Jake's party. Georgia's mom answered the door with a broom in her hand. I followed her inside. The house was immaculate and orderly. They had moved in just three weeks before we did but there wasn't a cardboard box in sight. Pictures were hung on the walls. Knickknacks adorned the shelves; small table lamps and perfectly placed stacks of magazines sat on the end tables.

Georgia's mom shuffled me upstairs to Georgia's room. She opened the bedroom door to reveal a haphazard, cluttered mess. Every inch of wall was covered with posters except the top six-inch border, which was stenciled with movie quotes. In one corner of the room sat a leopard-fur lounge chair, while in the opposite corner a four-foot-tall bust was draped in dozens of costume necklaces, beads, and pearls. There were two TVs—one mounted to the wall and the other resting on top of the dresser. And under the window was a huge knee-high black patent leather boot used as a flowerpot, with an overgrown spider plant crawling down the sides. Lying on her bed in the middle of all the clutter, was Georgia.

"Hey!" Georgia popped her head up off her pillow.

Georgia's mom pulled out a rag from the pocket of her sweatpants and dusted the top of her dresser. "You'd think if you knew you were having company . . ."

"Ma," Georgia said. "I hardly think Willow cares if there's a little dust."

Georgia's mom huffed then closed the door behind her.

I walked over and ran my fingers over the piles of necklaces hung around the fabric-draped bust. "Wow, that's a lot of necklaces."

"Yeah, well, we moved here to take over the Worthington Diamond Center so I have a lot of inventory at my disposal. You can try some on if you want."

"Oh," I said. I looked at the oversize beads and dangling charms. They were definitely more suited for my mom. "It's okay. Thanks, though."

"So," Georgia asked eagerly, "how was the party? I hate that I missed it. I can't believe my mom made me go to my aunt Lynne's birthday party." She huffed. "Was the night a success?"

"I don't know," I said as I pulled my copy of *A Midsummer Night's Dream* out of my bag and placed it on her bed. "I mean, it was obvious that Max liked the show—I saw him laughing and smiling and he gave me our secret signal." I tapped the side of my temple.

"What's that?" She made a face.

"It's a thing we used to do when we were kids. It's special."

Georgia readjusted herself on her bed. "Okay, so he had fun, but then what?"

"Well," I started, but Georgia held up her hand to stop me.

"What?" I asked.

She held her finger to her lips to hush me. *Listen,* she mouthed. Outside the bedroom door we heard heavy breathing. *She's trying to eavesdrop.* "Mom?" Georgia called.

Georgia's mom opened the door with a basket of laundry on her hip. "I've got your laundry," she said cheerily.

Georgia gave me a look that said, *Yeah, right.*

"Need anything?" Georgia's mom asked.

"Nope, we're good," Georgia answered.

Georgia's mom took a few items out of the basket and placed them on top of the dresser. Then she heaved the laundry basket up with a grunt and shuffled away with her slippers skidding across the shiny hardwood floors.

Georgia got up and closed the door after her. She rolled her eyes. "Continue."

I told her about Minnie's contact lens debacle, and I told her about how Max seemed to be smiling right at me through the whole show. "After Hayden acted on his hidden feeling, I *swear* I caught Max staring at me with, I don't know, *longing* in his eyes. But then when he drove us home—me jammed in to the backseat again—it was weird . . . stiff. I don't know. Strained."

"He's confused," Georgia said. "It's a classic love triangle . . . like Peyton, Lucas, and Brooke on *One Tree Hill.* Or Joey, Dawson, and Pacey on *Dawson's Creek.* Even Bella, Edward, and Jacob in *Twilight,* although none of you is a vampire or a werewolf."

We heard Georgia's mom shuffle by the door again. "You watch too much TV!" she called.

"MA! Privacy!" She got up, opened the door, and craned her

neck out into the hallway, but her mom had already disappeared. As Georgia walked back toward the bed, her face twisted up and she shook her head. "Maybe you should just forget about Max."

"Forget about Max?!" I didn't mean to shout. "He's my BEST FRIEND!"

"I don't mean forget about him all together. I just mean—be his best friend. Let him figure out what he wants with Minnie or with you, and if it's meant to be . . ."

I sighed and leaned back against a *Pretty Little Liars* poster. "I'm tired of waiting," I said. "My whole life I've been waiting. Waiting to break out of my mother's shadow. Waiting until Max and I could be together in the same city and,"—my shoulders slumped—"I just never imagined it like this."

Georgia looked sympathetic. "You need a distraction. Hey!" Her eyes lit up. "You should date Quinton! He's so hot."

"Oh my God, he looked so good last night," I said. "But come on—why would a guy like Quinton . . . want me?"

Georgia held up her hand again and I quieted. We heard breathing at the door.

The door inched open and Georgia's mom stuck her head through the crack. "I've got some iced tea?"

"Okay," Georgia said. "Thanks."

Georgia's mom scuffled in, pulled out two napkins, and placed two large glasses of iced tea on the desk. She looked over at us on the bed, two copies of Shakespeare lying between us, unopened. She swallowed, smiled a tight, closed-lipped smile in my direction. "You're a pretty girl," she said. "And I can tell just by listening to you that you're smart. Don't ever let yourself feel second best."

"MA!!!"

Her mom shrugged her broad shoulders and threw her hands up in an innocent gesture. "That's all," she said, turning back toward the door.

"I'm *so* sorry," Georgia said.

"It's okay." I laughed and thought that sure, I was glad that my mom respected my privacy, but it was kind of nice, too, to have someone reassure you with such confidence.

"Okay, sure, Quinton is like . . ." Georgia returned to our conversation.

"Totally out of my league."

Georgia didn't disagree. She got up and brought the glasses of tea over to the bed. "But, he seems really fascinated by you."

"He's fascinated by hypnosis, not me." I took a sip of the sugary sweet tea and thought of something. "At the end of the party he did come over to me. He touched me on the shoulder and said, *You're so funny.*"

"Oh my God!" Georgia popped up. "Was there any squeeze of the shoulder or just hand placement? And how did he say it? Was it like, *You're so funny my abs hurt from laughing and you should have a late-night program on E!* or was it like, *You're so funny and I totally want to practice my football moves and tackle you right now and kiss the crap out of you?*"

I bit my lip. "Maybe somewhere in between."

Georgia gasped. "How could you not tell me this?"

"I don't know. I was too busy trying to figure out the situation with Max."

Georgia giggled. "I don't think Quinton is dating anyone."

"Oh, come on," I said. "This is ridiculous."

"Oh my God," Georgia panted. "Who knows—maybe *Quinton* is

your destiny. Or"—she stuck her finger in the air—"it's the perfect plot twist to make Max jealous."

This made my ears perk up. Would Max be jealous? And would Quinton ever really date me?

"Think about it," Georgia said with a satisfied look on her face. "Ron and Hermione started out as childhood friends in Harry Potter, right? But each time one of them started dating someone else, the other would get jealous. Jealousy is used all the time to bring out that perfect lightning-bolt moment needed for a good plot twist."

"Hmmm," I mused, somehow thinking all of Georgia's character knowledge might be relevant to my life after all.

"Oh yeah. And Ron and Hermione *did* wind up together, you know. I mean, it took seven books, but eventually they got married and had two kids."

I nodded slowly and thought about jealousy. Maybe Max just viewed me as his best friend—the girl from his childhood. But if he saw me date someone, it could be just the lightning-bolt moment he needed . . .

"You could live happily ever after," Georgia said, and I smiled.

"Okay." I picked up *A Midsummer Night's Dream*. "So tell me more about this crazy love triangle."

Monday morning I texted Georgia: *When Max picked me up this morning he was all smiles—totally normal.*

Of course he was. Minnie wasn't there! she texted back.

In English class, Mrs. Stabile announced that we were going to break into our groups again to discuss the themes of love and magic in *A Midsummer Night's Dream*.

Georgia, Mia, Quinton, and I pushed our desks together and pulled out our notebooks.

"So," Mia said, immediately jumping into the assignment. "Lysander immediately falls in love with Helena because he's totally under the influence of the magic love spell."

"Right. So . . ." Georgia turned toward Quinton. "Are you excited for the football game this weekend?"

Mia's forehead crinkled at the departure from academics. Or maybe she was just perplexed that an unknown would talk to a popular football player with such ease.

Quinton smiled a winsome smile. "Sure."

Georgia nodded. "I can't imagine how you balance it all—honors classes, football, girlfriend . . ." She was as subtle as her mother.

He cocked his head to the side. "I'm a hardworking student. I'm a fantastic football player and I'm a freaking awesome boyfriend. But I'm not going to lie to you." His smile widened. "I haven't managed to pull off all three at the same time." He shrugged. "So I know my limits. That's why I have a strict no-dating-during-football-season rule. Don't want to be a boyfriend if I can't be the best. Or maybe"—he leaned in a little—"maybe I just haven't found the right girl who makes me want to make the time."

The three of us just sat there, silently swooning. Then Georgia kicked my shin under the desk.

"But what about you?" he asked me. "How did you manage your schoolwork and do a show like that when you lived in Vegas?"

"Oh, I managed." I tried to adopt a mysterious tone. God forbid they knew about the permanent butt imprint I had created on my favorite seat in the library.

"The show was so funny," Quinton said. "The way you were able to make people just do things."

"Yeah," Mia said. "Like Hayden is *dating* Sarah now. Did you know that?" It wasn't clear who she was asking. Surely not me or Georgia; she'd never really addressed us beyond the schoolwork.

I thought of hot Hayden, all blue eyes and boulder biceps, and the mousy-haired girl in the far corner of the audience. A mismatched couple anywhere, but especially in high school, where social status was so crucial a pyramid could be diagrammed in a matter of minutes.

"He probably never would have asked her out," Mia said. "It's not like she's . . ."

"In his league," Georgia said and kicked me under the desk again.

Mia abruptly turned toward Georgia, shocked, maybe, that she was being so blunt. From under the desk I heard the soft *click click click* of Mia nervously changing the colors on her pen. "You *made* that happen," she said softly, looking at me. "You . . . erased his fear."

I felt a small burst of pride. Really, I was just trying to entertain, to make people laugh and show Max how much fun I could be. I never realized I could potentially change someone's life. It felt pretty amazing. To help mold destiny.

Mrs. Stabile walked by and Georgia spouted something about artificial affection and the power of the love spell. The bell rang and we all gathered our things to go.

In the hallway, Max waved to me. I was about to go over and talk to him but Quinton walked over to Max and asked him something. Max burst out laughing and I felt all jittery inside. Could they possibly be talking about me? I walked behind them, analyzing the way each walked. Quinton: smooth and relaxed, his chin up, arms swinging, hips sauntering with long strides. Max: quick paced and light, with a spring in his step and his broad shoulders squared.

Mia was walking to my right and Sadie ran over toward her. They were both wearing their cheerleading uniforms for a pep rally later that afternoon.

"So," Sadie said. "I heard that next week they're taking nominations for Homecoming Court."

Mia smiled that stage smile I'd seen at Jake's party.

"Why even have a contest, right?" Sadie laughed. "Just give the crowns to you and Jake!"

As if on cue, Jake rounded the corner. Mia turned her stage smile his way. "Hi sweetie!"

"Hey." He leaned down and pecked her on the lips, and she looked like she would levitate with happiness. It looked like they'd resolved whatever argument they were having.

I walked into the bathroom. A few minutes later, I was just about to exit the stall when I heard someone come in and go over to the sink. Then the person began making a big ruckus, struggling with something. Whoever it was fumbled and grunted and huffed in exasperation. I took my hand off the flusher and for some reason, found myself peeking through the crack between the door and wall. To my surprise, it was Mia. She rummaged through her book bag and pulled out a small plastic case, unzipped it, and pulled something slim and shiny out. Oh my God, what was going on? Was she doing drugs? Did the perfect queen bee have a needle?

I flung open the bathroom door. "Stop!" I commanded. "You'll ruin your life!"

"What?" She turned toward me and I saw her face, all flushed and rosy, tears streaming down her porcelain skin. She looked so different—still beautiful—but in a much softer, vulnerable way. Like a Jane Austen heroine who just lost her lover. She was holding a needle—a sewing needle—and a spool of white thread.

Mia quickly patted the puffy areas under her eyes and stood a little straighter.

"Are you okay?" I asked, walking out of the stall.

For a minute she held her all-business facade like she was about to say, *I'm fine, perfect,* but then suddenly she just . . . cracked.

"No," she said. "I'm not fine." She grabbed her skirt. "It caught on my ring and ripped this huge hole." She spread the pleats of the skirt and showed me a three-inch gap of fabric. "I was going to sew it, but I only have white thread and the skirt is gold, and at first I thought it would hide under the pleat, but when I do a high kick"—she frantically started kicking her leg in the air—"it's like totally noticeable. And we have the pep rally this afternoon." She burst into tears.

I stood there completely dumbfounded. I was uncertain what to do. But then I remembered when I was the one crying in the bathroom and Georgia stayed with me and how much I appreciated that. But Mia hadn't exactly indicated that she was interested in a friendship with me. I tentatively took a step toward her. "It'll be okay," I said, but Mia sat on the ground, still crying. "It's just a skirt. And it's fixable."

She looked up at me with her weepy eyes, and I got the distinct feeling it wasn't just about the skirt.

I sat down next to her. "What's wrong?"

The warning bell rang. Mia inhaled sharply. She quickly started to gather her things.

I opened my purse and pulled out a safety pin. I held it toward her. "Maybe you can pin it from the inside just until you get home and can properly hem it?"

She hesitated for a minute, then took the pin and nodded. "That's a good plan."

I smiled a small smile.

"Thanks," she said. She flipped the edge of her skirt, secured the fabric with the safety pin, and turned it back down. "Why are you being so nice to me?" she asked.

"Aren't most people nice to you?"

"I guess . . ." She tensed. "I don't know . . . it's sort of a fake nice." She was quiet for a minute. "It was genuinely nice what you did for Hayden and Sarah," she said softly, her Southern accent echoing against the tiled walls. "I don't think they'd be together if not for you. He might have worried what his friends would say, but you took away his fear. . . ." She looked at me and I saw how clear her green eyes were—lucid, like a transparent stalk of celery. She stared up at the ceiling, looking away from me. "Could you do that for me? Erase my fears?" she whispered.

"Um," I stammered, completely thrown off guard. "I'm not sure what you mean? You have fears? You're the head cheerleader and the most popular girl in school. You're perfect!"

A fresh swell of tears filled her eyes. She scanned around again, looked under the stalls, although clearly no one had entered the bathroom. "That's just it," she said, her voice catching. "Everyone expects me to be perfect. I do most of the complicated tricks in the tumbling routines and on the squad. But they just keep wanting more and more."

"Okay," I said, unsure where she was going.

"Well . . ." She blinked fast, looking increasingly desperate. "The team wants me to do this flip off the top of the pyramid, and I hate heights."

"You're a cheerleader and you hate heights? Isn't that kind of . . . paradoxical?"

She exhaled. "I know. But I need to do this trick if we're going to win the upcoming competition and I don't want to let the team down, let my parents down." She looked at the floor and her eyes got glassy again. "I Googled hypnosis yesterday and found that people use hypnosis to lose weight, to stop smoking, and, I don't know, it worked so well with Hayden's inhibitions I just thought maybe hypnosis could be the answer—to not be afraid of this flip." She was talking very fast. "But I didn't know if I could trust you. I mean, I didn't know anything about you, what your true intentions were, so I decided against it. But now . . ." She fingered the safety pin on her skirt then looked up at me. She spoke very softly. "Could you help me?"

My mind raced. She wanted my help. Me. The most popular girl in school wanted something from me. Something that I could deliver. Couldn't I? I wasn't sure, but if I could, it might change destiny like with Hayden and Sarah. It could change Mia's destiny but also mine. I could be Mia's friend. I could be popular in addition to being memorable. And that felt pretty powerful.

Mia walked over to the mirror and quickly applied some make-up around her eyes. The bell rang. She looked at me expectantly.

There was the tingly feeling of endless possibilities coursing through my veins. So I smiled and said, "Well, I've never done anything like that before. But I'd love to try."

She smiled and opened the door. We walked out together into the hallway and raced off to our next classes.

10

Later that day, after Max dropped me off at home, I snuck into my mom's room in the hope of finding some information I could use to help me with Mia's hypnosis. After all, Mom was working at the Headache Clinic, using hypnosis to help control pain. She had to have some information about how she'd made the leap from performance hypnosis to hypnotherapy. As I opened the bedroom door, I felt a pang of guilt knowing how much Georgia hated that her mom invaded her space. And my mother was so mindful of mine. But we'd always been so close; there had never been anything to hide until now. Now that I was doing exactly what she'd asked me not to do. A sour swell of guilt dropped into the pit of my stomach.

The door creaked open and I crept in quietly, even though the house was empty except for Oompa, who was trailing me with a quizzical look in his eyes. Mom's bed was unmade and a pile of dirty clothes was strewn on the floor. I instinctively picked up the clothes, separated out the delicates, and put the rest in the laundry basket.

On the nightstand, next to the old metal lamp we bought at Pottery Barn, was a stack of textbooks. Hmm. I walked over and picked up the top text, *Basics of Hypnotherapy.* As I flopped onto her bed and cracked open the cover, there was a loud thumping sound followed by a tinny rattle. I looked up, half expecting a cop to be standing there, all uniformed with his silver badge shining, arresting me for trespassing. But I was still alone. Except for Oompa, who had flexed his stumpy legs into his best imitation of guard dog position.

Then I realized the room was filled with silence. More silence than I could remember. Panic sprouted inside of me when I concluded that the gentle hum of the air-conditioning had stopped. I got up and knelt down at the vent. I placed my hand over the grate. Nothing. Instantly it seemed like the room got hotter. I looked out at the smoldering sun, the sizzling beams of light shrouding our house with intense August heat. *Okay, don't panic. It's probably just a fuse.* I got up and started to search for the fuse box.

In a matter of minutes, the air inside the house began to feel stale, suffocating. I could feel the nape of my neck dampen. I decided to go look in the garage for the fuse box when, from down the hall, I heard a commotion in my bedroom. I suddenly feared our house was being robbed. *They turned off the air to suffocate us then they'll rob us blind!* I snatched up Oompa and was darting toward the front door when I heard someone shout my name: "Willow!"

"Ahhh!" I screamed, pulling Oompa in front of my face like a shield. But it was just Max, walking out of my bedroom. "What are you doing?" I asked, all out of breath.

"I tried the front door but it was locked. You left this in my car." He held up my cell phone.

"Oh, oh." I felt myself breathe again. "The air-conditioning went out and then I heard all this racket and I thought someone was attacking me."

"By shutting the AC off?"

"Well, it didn't seem so ridiculous in the heat of the moment. I'm trying to find the fuse box."

"Did you try the garage?"

"I was just heading there."

We walked to the garage, where we located the switches and, much to my dismay, realized the fuse was not the problem. By the time we walked back into the house, the temperature had risen a few degrees. Oompa was plopped on the cool kitchen tiles, with his paws splayed out in an X, a little puddle of drool under his panting tongue.

I called my mom and left a message. Five minutes later she texted back that the repair man couldn't make it until tomorrow.

"You're not staying here!" Max said. He pulled out his phone, called his mom, and the next thing I knew, I was packing a bag to stay over at Max's house.

"Wait," I said before we left. I ran back into Mom's room and put the textbook back on top of the stack on her nightstand to disguise my snooping.

"Why are you reading your mom's books?" Max asked.

And so I made him swear to secrecy; then I told him about Mia's request. Saturday night at Jake's house, Max had been all enthusiastic about me doing hypnosis, but there, standing in my mom's room, he wrinkled his forehead up in concern. "I don't know, Willow," he said. "It's one thing to do fun party tricks, but now you're talking about controlling someone's mind—their thoughts." His face was serious, in such stark contrast to his usual joking demeanor. And I didn't like it. I didn't want him to put a damper on this newfound opportunity I had. So I tried to turn it into a joke.

"Hey, did you know I just read that you can hypnotize someone in ten seconds with just a sharp handshake?" I playfully reached for his hand. "*Max*," I said in a low, put-on voice, "*I will hypnotize you. . . .*"

But he didn't think it was funny. He yanked his hand away. "Quit it, Willow, I'm not kidding. Do you want to mess with someone's mind? Years from now Mia could be off somewhere at college having a good time and suddenly she'll hear *your* voice in her head? Do you want that?" He had a weird look in his eyes—not exactly mad, but not exactly happy, either.

I pulled my hand back to my side. "Geez, take it easy. I was just kidding."

"About Mia?"

"No, not about Mia."

"I just think you're making a mistake."

He started for the door and we were silent as we left my house, which was hot and stuffy now. I followed him out to his truck and climbed in. Oompa jostled his way into the backseat with a loud, disapproving grunt as he teetered atop a messy pile of CD cases. Max laughed at the dog, breaking the silence between us, and reached back to scratch Oompa's ears. And the awkwardness was over—it evaporated and it was just us again.

Max's mom was at the stove, apron on, spatula in hand, with the aroma of spice wafting around her. She hugged me fiercely and said Mom and I were welcome to stay as long as we needed.

"Oh, the AC repair man will be by tomorrow," I said. "But thanks."

A thin, forced smile formed on her lips and I didn't quite understand why she looked so sad. But when Max disappeared to talk to Minnie on the phone, I called Mom and her voice was just as thin and forced as Max's mom's smile.

"What?" I asked her.

She sighed. "The repair man said it was going to be two hundred dollars just to come look at the system, then most likely five hundred dollars or more to fix it if it's a simple problem."

"We'll just have to use the emergency fund," I suggested. She was quiet. I felt a pang of anxiety. I didn't like my new lack of access to the finances. "Did you use the emergency fund?"

"Yes," she answered, not telling me how she'd squandered the money I had diligently hoarded for years. But it wasn't like I could demand answers. It was, after all, her money. "Sorry," she answered sounding guilty, like she was proving Grandma right. "I can't go into it now, but you just have to believe me that I'm doing the best I can." She sounded like she was going to cry.

I couldn't stand the sound of defeat in her voice. "No big deal," I said. "So we'll buy some fans, okay? It'll be fall before we know it." I did my best to sound positive, not thinking that if I had to live in an un-air-conditioned home, I might as well just dye my hair pink and sell it as cotton candy at the homecoming parade, because the frizz would never cease.

She was quiet on the other end except for a small, quivery inhale.

"It'll be fine, Mom. Plus, tonight, we can slumber-party at Max's!"

"Yes," she said, and I could hear the tiniest bit of a smile in her voice. "Yes, we can."

We hung up, and since Max was still in his room on the phone

with Minnie, I found the Montgomerys' couch and chatted with
Max's mom. A few times, when Mrs. Montgomery had her head in
the fridge and we weren't talking, I heard Max's voice through the
wall. It kind of sounded a little irritated and I wondered if they were
fighting. I wondered if they were fighting about me. Was Minnie
jealous that I was there? But fifteen minutes later, he emerged from
his room looking calm and happy, so I concluded I must have been
wrong. I sighed. *She wins, even when I'm in person and she's just a
voice on the phone.*

"Hey, come here," Max said. "I want to show you something."

I followed him into his room. His bed was unmade and the pillows had been tossed to the floor. Over his desk was a framed poster
of dogs playing poker. His iPod was set up in a docking station, and
small box speakers were mounted in all four corners of the ceiling.
In the corner of the room was a huge five-piece drum set in wine red
with two sixteen-inch gold cymbals. I walked toward them, taking
the long wooden drumsticks in my hand. Then I noticed sheet music
resting on the stool. In Max's scratchy handwriting there were music
notes and words scribbled.

"Oh," I said, putting the drumsticks down. "Are you writing a
song?" I started to reach for it but Max raced over and snatched the
sheets off the stool. "Oooooh," I teased. "Is it a *love song* for Minnie?"
I reached around his waist and grabbed for the papers.

"Quit it," he said, angling the music out of my grasp.

"*Oh, I love you soooooo,*" I mocked, reaching around the other
side.

"Stop!" Max said, sounding serious but laughing. He stretched
his hand way out of my reach.

"Oh, it must be really mushy." I climbed onto his chair and reached for his hand but he snatched it away so fast I lost my balance and fell off the chair, pulling him with me.

"Willow," Max cried, dropping the music sheets and reaching for me. The white sheets of paper fluttered through the air as I crashed toward the ground and Max fell on top of me.

I could feel his heart thumping against my chest. I could feel his lungs expanding and contracting with every breath. I could feel the weight of his body pressing against mine. His lips were inches from mine. His breath smelled like Orbitz spearmint gum. He wouldn't stop looking at me.

"Is everything okay in there?" Mrs. Montgomery called. Footsteps approached. Quickly Max scrambled up off of me. I sat up, dizzy from both the fall and the circumstances.

Mrs. Montgomery poked her head in. "You all right?"

"Just took a tumble," I said. "I'm fine."

Max gathered up the sheets of music off the ground and swiftly shoved them into his desk drawer.

"Dinner's ready," Mrs. Montgomery said.

"Great." Max smiled and followed her out like he was eager to get away from me or from the situation. *Away from his feelings.* And again, the moment was lost.

My mom walked in and we all sat around their circular table. Mrs. Montgomery served chicken quesadillas and rice.

Max looked across the table at me and I held his stare. *What just happened?*

"Remember that time," Max's mom said, "when the kids were seven and they got sent home with a note from their teacher for talking too much in class so they decided to run away?"

"And we got a call from Ann Marie Gallagher," Mom interjected. "She had picked them up in front of the BP gas station, all sweaty and exhausted because you two thought that 'running away' meant you had to actually *run*." Mom and Mrs. Montgomery laughed and laughed. Max looked at me again, but this time the smile was different. Less desire, more reminiscent. *Definitely a friend smile.*

"And Willow's backpack," Mom continued, "was all appropriately packed with fresh underwear and toothpaste and a map but the only thing Max had packed to take with him for the rest of his life was his drumsticks and a box of fudge Pop-Tarts!"

We all laughed. I remembered that night well, even without the constant replays. Mom had unpacked my bag and told me that no matter how upset I was, I couldn't run away from my problems—that distance wouldn't solve anything. But less than one year later, Mom packed up our apartment and we took off for Vegas, putting a two-thousand-mile separation between Mom and her problems. *Some example.*

After dinner, we all cleared the table. I was loading silverware into the dishwasher when Max walked into the kitchen holding a stack of plates. He playfully bumped his hip into mine. "Hey," he said. "Watch it."

I bumped him back. "Sorry, tight quarters."

He reached over my arm and dumped the four plates into the dishwasher.

"No," I said. "If you put them this way, there's more room."

"Why do we need more room?" Max asked. "Are you planning on entertaining some gentlemen friends tonight?"

I smiled devilishly. *Jealousy is a great plot twist.* "Never can tell."

Max held my stare for a beat; then he reached down and began rearranging the cups on the top rack. "Well, then, by all means, let's make room."

Mrs. Montgomery walked past us. "You kids," she said breezily, but I caught Mom eyeing our exchange with a touch more scrutiny. I wondered if she could see past my false bravado and see how desperate I was for Max to adore me?

Mom was snuggled under the covers with her textbook, so I crept out into the living room, figuring I'd watch some TV. Max sat on the couch in a pair of loose white karate bottoms and a blank white T-shirt. He looked up and smiled at me.

"Like your jammies," he said.

Suddenly I felt very exposed. I wondered if he could tell I'd taken off my bra. I crossed my arms over my chest and sat next to him. He looked down at my loose cotton shorts. They were periwinkle blue and covered with pastel-colored hearts. I wore the matching short-sleeve top.

"Like the hearts," he said.

"Yeah, well, this is what I like to sleep in."

"So you'll dream of romance?" he teased.

"Maybe," I said and wondered if he's purposefully brought up the topic. Maybe he wondered if I'd purposefully worn the hearts. Had I?

"Look," he said. "The way the shirt wrinkles here, it looks like one of your hearts is broken.

I looked down.

"Have you ever had a broken heart?" he asked seriously. "How come we've talked about everything but I've never really heard about any of your boyfriends?"

Because I've been waiting for you.

I'd liked boys, sure. I'd even dated a few. But it was always pathetic, really. It never lasted long, and mostly we just held hands and made out a little. Nothing special. I never ever felt the way I felt now, with Max.

"So have you?" he asked again. "Had your heart broken? Other than that asshole Logan in eighth grade, of course. He doesn't count."

"Right," I said. "He doesn't count." *Except that's when I realized I loved you.* "Yes," I finally answered. "I have had my heart broken." And it was true. *My heart is breaking right now thinking that you don't love me back.* "What about you?"

He shook his head slightly. "I don't think so. Not really. I mean, I've been dumped—remember Caryn in ninth grade? Whew, that was awkward . . . but crushed? Nah. I don't think so."

"You'd know if you had," I said.

"So why don't you tell me about it?" he asked.

I looked into his blue eyes. *Once upon a time there was a boy. His hair was the color of coal, his eyes the color of faded denim. His smile, carefree and inviting, was the one thing that made me brave.* It was quiet for a moment, just the soft hum of the air-conditioning blowing through the vent above us.

"What happened?" Max asked softly, intently.

"The boy I loved chose someone else."

We stared at each other. In the background, Conan made jokes about a politician. Max reached over and took my hand. I slumped into the couch and pretended to watch TV but all the while I wondered, *Are you holding my hand to console a friend, or have you felt the connection all night, too?*

Early the next morning I was stumbling to the hall bathroom when I heard whispers from the living room. My heart sank at the thought of Max and Minnie sitting on the couch together, holding hands, Minnie the window climber this time—sneaking over sometime in the middle of the night. But when I pressed myself to the wall and snuck a glance, it wasn't them. It was Max's mom and my mom, sharing a large navy blanket and talking.

"I wish I could lend you the money," Mrs. Montgomery said. "If I had it."

"No." Mom shook her head. "Thanks, but I'm just going to call today and see if it's too late to cancel the registration check."

"No, Vicki, you can't. That's too important."

Mom sighed. "Well, maybe I can return that video equipment." Her mouth twisted. "Do you think they'll take it back if I've opened it?"

Max's mom sighed and pulled the blanket up under her chin. "I don't know."

Back in Vegas there were times when money would get tight. I'd have to reel Mom in, tell her the credit cards were steaming, remind her she didn't need another pair of dangling crystal earrings. And she'd watch her spending and we'd be back on track in no time. When we left, I was reluctant to hand over the checkbook, relinquish that control, but she insisted. It was not fair, she said, the way she had dumped that responsibility on me. *But I like it!* I insisted. No, things were going to be different in Georgia.

It was really hard now, after such heartfelt proclamations, to watch her fumble. *How could she have spent the emergency fund?* I felt like a mother watching her child make mistakes, helplessly standing by, cringing, but unable to control the course of fate.

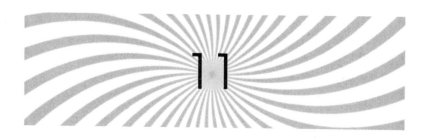

All day I felt out of sorts. I had spent the entire night replaying the scene on the couch with Max and now I couldn't concentrate because I was all jittery with nerves about going over Mia's to try and hypnotize her.

That afternoon I texted Max that I didn't need a ride home since I was going over Mia's house. Max texted back, *I'd think twice before going through with this.*

But I couldn't back out now. Ever since I'd agreed, Mia had asked me to sit with her at lunch, talked to me in the hallway, and smiled her thousand-watt stage smile at me. I'm sure she needed to make a show of friendship so no one would question why I was going to her house—but still, it felt kind of nice.

At the end of the day I met Mia in the student parking lot. She pressed a button on her key chain, and the locks clicked open on a shiny new apple red Lexus IS convertible. It was sleek, pristine, and top of the line—exactly the kind of car I pictured her driving.

"Wow," I said, climbing in the passenger side. "This is such a nice car."

"Thanks," she said, then asked me if it was okay to ride with the top down.

"Sure." I smiled and she backed out of the lot with the wind whipping through our hair. She drove through town and turned left onto an unfamiliar road, driving to the north side of Worthington, close to where I remembered that my grandparents lived. She slowed the car down and pulled into a development where the homes were grand and the yards were sprawling and manicured. We continued down a long driveway and pulled into a huge three-car garage.

The kitchen was practically the size of our entire house. It was bright with sunlight streaming in through oversize windows. Adjacent to the kitchen was a dining area with a crisply ironed pale yellow tablecloth and plates and silverware set for a family of three. I noticed fancy fabric napkins artfully placed inside napkin rings delicately set atop the china plates. I thought of our kitchen table—no tablecloth, no place settings, more often strewn with magazines and DVD cases than plates. Most of our eating was done on the couch while we watched TV. And while I've always loved the easiness of that, for some reason, staring at that table gave me a little pang—at how much thought and preparation was displayed for the family.

Mia walked over to the counter, where there was a plate filled with slices of apples chopped into uniform bite size wedges. A small note was stuck next to the plate. *Have fun today with your friend. The PTA meeting should be over by 7 p.m. Love, Mom.* Mia offered an apple wedge to me and I took a bite.

"At my house," I said, "the only snacks we have are cookies and twinkies."

"Oh my god, I *love* cookies," Mia said. "But I can't eat them." She patted her flat stomach.

I looked at her tiny size-zero frame. "You're kidding, right?"

She sighed. "I have to be careful. Mom told me when she went to college she gained the freshman fifteen—got boobs and hips. She thought it was great until she tried to do a double back tuck and crashed. Her center of gravity was all thrown off. She almost was booted as captain. She had to work really hard to hit her landings again."

"Oh," I said, because I really didn't know what else to say.

Mia grabbed some water from the enormous, stainless steel fridge and indicated for me to walk with her down a long hallway toward her bedroom. On the taupe wall hung an oversize oil painting of Mia and her parents at the beach. It was a beautiful picture. Everything looked so perfect. The pristine white beach. The aqua sea in the background. The cloudless blue sky. But it was more than the setting. The family looked perfect—all three of them dressed in white linen, the breeze blowing the tall sea grass against their legs. They looked so happy. *That's what I want*, I thought. No crazy divided family. No bizarre jobs and clothes. Just . . . the perfect beach photo.

Mia noticed me staring. "My mom *loves* beach pictures," she said with a roll of her eyes. "We have to pose for one every year." She shook her head and I nodded, indulging her as if posing for pictures on the beach was such a pain in the neck. But deep down, I couldn't suppress a tiny ache. What would my family picture look like? No dad, no grandparents. Mom kept saying this move was going to change our lives—be more conventional—but what had changed other than our address? She still dressed like a stage performer; we didn't have dinners at a table set with real plates and fabric napkins;

she wasn't getting involved at my new school and our bank account was overdrawn. She still hadn't gone to visit Grandma and Grandpa. She had made one hasty phone call to check in on Grandpa's health and tell them we had arrived, but that was it. And that was not the reunion I had imagined.

"What's wrong?" Mia asked.

"Oh, nothing." I tried to blow it off, but Mia put her hand on my shoulder—a simple gesture, but one that seemed so unexpected. It wasn't her thousand-watt stage smile, and it wasn't a carefully crafted outline or bullet-point note. It seemed, maybe, a little more genuine than that.

"It's just, I don't know, you're living like the perfect life. Perfect family, perfect house, the hottest boyfriend, captain of the cheerleading team, great grades. You're always happy. You have willpower to not eat junk food and your hair is never frizzy."

Mia sighed. And there, standing in the soft light of the hallway, again she looked more like the broken cherub from the bathroom meltdown than the perfect queen bee. "It's hard," she said.

I had seen her crack over a ripped skirt. "Hard to keep up the facade?" I asked gently.

She nodded and walked to her bedroom. So I followed. She sat on the silky yellow duvet cover on her huge queen-size bed and fiddled with the ends of her corn-silk hair. "Everyone expects me to be perfect. Not just my parents, but *everyone*—teachers, friends, neighbors, my coach. Like with such a perfect life, I have no excuse not to get straight A's and be class secretary and nail that double back tuck."

I looked around her huge room, at all the plaques and trophies and shiny blue and red ribbons that crowded the bookcase shelves above her desk. There were framed photographs of Mia as a toddler, then as a child, dressed in ruffled gowns, sashes across her chest. A pageant child.

"I mean," she continued, "people would just die if I ever admitted, *Hey, I don't think I want to try that flip.* Or *I don't think I can do that flip.* Or what if one day I just failed a calculus test and tried to say I couldn't study because my parents were fighting all night because Mom says Dad works too late and never makes time for us? People would never believe that, would they? And my hair *is* frizzy. I just spend a lot of time and money on products to make it appear like it's not." She looked over at the picture of her and Jake framed on her nightstand. He was decked out in his football uniform, all sweaty and muddy, and she was standing next to him, looking minuscule in her tight cheerleading uniform and sneakers. "Or what if one day I just broke up with Jake and said, *You know, I can't take it anymore. Your idea of romance is pizza and a football game. You gave me a birthday card with a fart joke inside!* But people expect me to date him." She looked down. "Everyone expects something from me," she said quietly.

I felt bad for her. Because while I had no boyfriend, no father, no grand house with a table fully set, my mother never made me feel pressured to do anything other than just be me. And suddenly I had an overwhelming urge to help her, to do for her the one thing that maybe I could do to erase her fears and help her perform that tricky tumbling pass for the cheerleading competition.

"Look," I said, "I've never done this kind of hypnosis before but I read about it, not just like on the Web, but in real textbooks, and I think I can do it."

"Really?" She brightened and sat up straighter. "Willow," she said, looking serious, "I've never told anyone any of this before."

"I won't tell anyone," I said. It felt special that Mia was trusting me with this. Her insecurities and the hypnosis.

She showed me a video clip on the Web of a move called the Arabian that she wanted to do and asked me to give her the ability to calm her panic about the flip.

So I did. I took the same familiar steps of deep breathing and counting to achieve muscle relaxation to put her under hypnosis. I was relieved when I saw the telltale sign of her shoulders slumping and her head dropping. I pulled my handwritten notes out of my pocket and began to speak in a low, calming voice, telling her that she could take her fear out of her mind and place it on a shelf. I held up my hand and rubbed my thumb and forefinger together. "Can you do that?" I asked.

Mia copied the simple gesture.

"Whenever you get scared," I said, "I want you to discreetly rub your fingers together like that and it will remind you to take that fear and remove it. This movement will calm you and put you back in control of your thoughts."

A small smile played on her lips and I felt a zing of hope course through me. I brought her back to a normal state and Mia stretched her arms over her head.

"Wow! I feel amazing!" she said. "So relaxed, like I just had the best nap ever. Thank you!"

"Well, thank me after we know it works," I said.

"Seriously, Willow, thank you." She smiled, and I think we both knew it was about more than just the hypnosis.

Mia dropped me off at home. When I opened the front door, I felt a wave of humid heat envelop me like I had just opened the door to an oven set at five hundred degrees. Only there was no smell of roasting turkey or baking pies—just the smell of thick humidity and possibly the smell of my skin singeing just a little. A large box fan was plugged into an outlet in the family room and spinning on high. Oompa was sprawled on the floor in front of the circulating air, his pointy ears shimmying in the welcome breeze.

I headed into my room to tackle some homework. Just as I sat down at my desk, there was a tapping at my window, followed by the creak of the windowpane sliding up, and Max crawled in, toting my overnight bag on his shoulder.

"Your mom forgot this when she left this morning," he said and hurled it onto the floor. "What do you have in there, a dead body?"

"Anti-frizz products," I said. "They add up. We do have a front door, you know."

He smiled. "Yeah, but this way is more fun." The smile vanished quickly. He looked at my open calculus book on my desk. "Okay, I'll go and let you study." He headed back toward the window. He had acted strange all day. Was this still about his opposition to hypnotizing Mia? Or was it about what happened at his house?

"Geez, it's like a thousand degrees in here," he said. "Do you want to stay over again?"

My heart fluttered at the invitation, but his voice seemed flat. I couldn't read him. Was he offering out of obligation? "Well, Mom said the AC guy would be here tomorrow. . . ."

"Oh, okay. Well, good night then."

Had I said no?

He walked toward the window. His hands were on the windowsill, ready to climb through.

I wanted to cry, *Wait! Beg me to come! Want to spend time with me!*

"Wait!" It slipped out.

He turned and looked at me.

"Um . . ." My heart ticked uncontrollably. I was certain I was having a heart attack. I wanted an opportunity to talk to him more and try and understand what was going on between us. I rifled through my brain for something to say. "Do you ever wonder what it would be like to have our fathers around?" I asked.

He pulled his leg off the windowsill and faced me with his forehead all wrinkled up. "Sometimes." He walked over toward me. "Why?"

I shrugged, willing my mouth not to spout all the feelings that had ricocheted around in my head earlier. I thought about the beach photo—the perfect family. "I don't know. Sometimes I just wonder what it would be like, you know—to have a normal family."

It was real quiet for a minute, and the weight of silence made me fear I was going to crumble. "It's just, you know, Mom said she was going to reconcile with Grandma and Grandpa, but I guess that's not going to happen anytime soon. I really just wanted some semblance of a family."

"You and your mom *are* a family," Max said softly.

My eyes welled. I nodded. He was right. Why was I always trying to fix things?

"When my dad was around, it was always so stressful—he and Mom were always fighting. So I don't know, of course I miss him, sure, but I kind of like having the peace."

I nodded again, agreeing that peace was good. I'd never lived with parents fighting because by the time I was born, they'd already split up. But I remembered what it was like when Mom and Grandma and Grandpa were always at odds.

Max knew the history—my mom pregnant at sixteen; the guy, my father, quickly shipped off to college, his parents handing my mother a check as if a little bit of money would absolve him of his involvement. *It wasn't his decision,* Mom always told me, defending him. *He didn't leave us,* she insisted. *His parents pushed him away. He was seventeen. I don't blame him and you shouldn't either,* she said. Mom was always open about who he was, where he lived, like I could go seek him out and create this beautiful bonding moment. But I kind of always wished that he'd seek me out first.

"It's not really about my dad," I said honestly. It was about Mom, Grandma, and Grandpa, and it was about Max. In my mind I had built up this beach-photo-perfect depiction of how life would be once we moved to Georgia, and so far, things weren't turning out as planned.

Max's legs swung back and forth, draped in front of my desk. "I think it's kind of cool that we both are raised by single, strong, independent mothers," he said.

And I smiled, agreeing with him. Because there it was, another thing that bonded us. And everything else just fell away.

Friday morning I woke up to a rusty grumble from the vent above my bed, followed by a welcome blast of frosty air. I lay there for a few minutes letting the cool wind saturate my sweltering skin. When I emerged, Mom was sitting at the kitchen table with a young guy, probably in his twenties, eating lemon pound cake, drinking coffee, and discussing the tattoo on his left forearm.

"Yeah, so it's a symbol for me," the guy said between bites of the breakfast cake, "of my life before."

"That's so interesting," Mom said with her innate ability to have complete strangers want to open up and divulge their life stories. "I'm doing that too," she added, conspiratorially, like they were on the same team. "I'm starting over too."

The AC repair guy smiled. "Looks like you're doing a great job."

I cleared my throat and they both looked my way, startled.

The AC guy was closer to my age actually than Mom's. "Well, I better get going," he said. "I've got a ton of service calls. This heat wave is doing a number on all the units around town."

Mom thanked him again and closed the door behind him. "Hallelujah, I can breathe again!" she said, gesturing to the blowing vent above her. She sat back down at the table and I joined her. She broke off a sheet from the paper towel roll and passed me the store-bought cake. "So," Mom said. "We're going over to Grandma and Grandpa's tonight for dinner."

"Oh," I said. I looked at her stirring the three teaspoons of sugar into her coffee and wondered if the AC repair had anything to do with our sudden plans—if the money came from somewhere other than our account.

"It's time," Mom said with no mention of money. So I would never know if she called them and asked for help or if she finally just felt ready to face them.

I nodded. "When?"

"Seven."

We both glanced over at the clock.

All along I'd been wishing and waiting for our reconciliation with my grandparents, so now that it was finally happening, why did I feel more nervous than excited?

After school, I asked Max if he could drive me into town to a clothing store.

"Sure," he said. "Where do you want to go?"

"Someplace your mom shops."

"Okay." He hooked an illegal U-turn and pulled up next to the curb in front of a store called Angie's. Max stayed in the car while I walked inside. It was small and intimate, with twenty or so racks of sweaters and pants. A middle-aged woman came over and asked if she could help me.

"Mom and I are going to a nice dinner tonight," I explained. "And she asked me to pick up an outfit for her."

"Oh, how nice," the saleswoman said. Together we picked out a pair of straight-leg black pants and a light blue button-down top. It was fitted, with a little bit of spandex, so Mom couldn't say it was old-ladyish, but it wasn't low-cut or cropped. It didn't have any sequins or rhinestones. It was perfect.

The sales lady rang up the bill, but when she slid the credit card through the reader, she grimaced. "I'm sorry, hon, it's saying the card is declined. Maybe she gave you the wrong one?" she asked kindly.

"Um, yeah. Probably." I backed out quickly and raced toward Max's truck.

"Didn't find anything?" he asked, turning down the volume of the radio.

I shook my head. "Let's just go home."

He nodded and drove away, not asking any more questions. Back at the house, I rummaged through Mom's closet, trying desperately to find something she could wear that would not provoke Grandma. As each minute ticked closer to 7 p.m., my nerves frayed. I didn't know what to expect. After everything with Max, I was learning that words on paper or the computer screen or even the phone didn't always translate into the relationship I'd built up in my mind.

It was hard to know how to feel. My memories of my grandparents were both good and bad. I remembered Grandma taking me to the American Girl doll store, letting me pick out any doll I wanted and buying all the clothes and hair accessories. I remembered

Grandma teaching me how to play chess. I remembered our hour-long Scrabble marathons. I remembered Grandma telling me that her beautiful mother, my great-grandmother, had keyhole-shaped pupils too, and that a key was a symbol of authority. It meant I would have great responsibility in my life. I remembered Grandpa teaching me how to throw a ball, how to cast a fishing line into the river by their house. I remembered how he laughed so easily, so heartily. But I also remembered the tension that filled the air when we visited—the sharp words that passed between them and my mother and the hurt in Mom's eyes whenever we left their enormous farm and returned to our small apartment across town.

Mom came home dressed in a sleeveless polyester beaded dress with a sixties geometric design. She wore large gold-plated hoop earrings, an oversize rhinestone cuff bracelet, and platform wedge shoes. I took a deep breath.

"Do you want to borrow my cardigan?" I asked. "In case, you, um, get chilly?" It was ninety-seven degrees outside. Mom looked at me for a long minute. I tapped my foot nervously and wondered if ever there was a time when Mom redressed me in her mind. If when she pranced around the show lights of Vegas, she wished her daughter wasn't afraid to wear fishnet stockings or zebra print. No, I thought, looking at her. She was nothing but proud of me. Enormous waves of shame crashed over me.

"Ready?" Mom asked.

I nodded. I followed her to our car and we drove the ten minutes across town in silence. We passed the entrance to Mia's subdivision, with clusters of kids riding bikes and Big Wheels in the cul-de-sac, and then turned down Magnolia Drive. The houses grew farther apart, long stretches of green rolling pasture separating them. At the first

sight of the familiar white split-rail fence, Mom took in a sharp breath.
I reached over and put my hand on top of hers on the steering wheel,
trying to calm her. But instead, my touch shocked her, jolted her out of
some long-forgotten memory, and her hand jerked, pulling the steering wheel fast to the right and onto the shoulder of the road.

"Oh Jesus," she said, hitting the brakes. Then she started laughing, the hysterical, maniacal laughing that only nerves can bring. I
laughed too.

After a few minutes we regained our composure. She took a
deep breath and put the car in drive. We pulled up the long, curving driveway to the stately white-columned house on top of the hill.
She parked the car and just sat there for a minute, staring out at the
chestnut-colored horse grazing on some hay.

I elbowed her gently. "Come on, Mom," I said, afraid that she
might sit there in the car all night.

We walked slowly up the stone walkway under the white arching
branches of river birch trees. She pressed the doorbell and everything felt odd—ringing the doorbell at her parents' home, the home
she grew up in. I could never imagine seventeen years from now feeling like I couldn't just barge in on my mom's life.

The heavy double doors opened and there was Grandma, wearing a pale blue striped skirt and an ivory short-sleeved sweater. She
wore pearl earrings, and her platinum hair was coiffed to chic perfection. "Willow!" she exclaimed, taking me into a hug and pressing
me against her soft chest. She smelled sweet like a mixture of powder and flowery perfume. It felt like just yesterday that I had been
in her arms. She pulled back and smiled. "How grown-up you've
become," she said. She held one of my hands then turned toward

Mom. Her glassy hair moved in one shellacked swing. "Victoria," she said tentatively.

"Hi Mom," Mom said.

We stood there on the porch with the soft sound of crickets starting to chirp off in the distant woods. It felt stiff. Like a first date.

"Well, come in," Grandma finally said. She led us through the foyer, closing the doors behind us, and into the formal living room, where overstuffed couches were adorned with matching decorative pillows and beautiful framed photographs artfully decorated the top of a glass table. I noticed all the pictures of my mother as an infant, a child, an adolescent, but none after that. Pictures of me in matching silver frames joined the others, making me feel special, documented. Mom never seemed to be organized enough to print out pictures off her digital camera, let alone frame and display them.

A shiny black grand piano sat adjacent to two sets of French doors. A spread of sheet music rested on the top of the piano as if just last night this room was flooded with joyful music and happily dancing and singing people. A flash of a memory snuck into my mind of me and Grandma and Grandpa, squeezed onto the slippery piano bench, the keys of the player piano automatically strumming Christmas carols as we sang along.

Adjacent to the living room, a large mahogany table was draped with a white linen tablecloth. Four places were neatly set with bone white china, two plates on each side facing each other and a large vase filled with fresh flowers in between. I looked over at Mom, easing herself down onto the couch painfully, as if it were made of needles instead of obviously expensive fabric, and wondered how she could have chosen to leave all this. How could Mom have felt so suffocated and strangled here when I, stepping into such order and tidiness, felt nothing but harmony?

Grandma took a seat on the ivory wing-backed chair and crossed her legs at the ankle. She gestured with a sway of her bony hand to the large, sweating pitcher of iced tea resting on a silver platter between us. "Some tea?" she offered.

"Is it sweetened?" Mom asked.

"No," Grandma said and motioned towards two small ceramic containers. "There's sugar and sweetener if you'd like."

"Yes," Mom said tightly. "You know I like my tea sweet. You know Willow likes her tea sweet. And I know *you* like your tea sweet. You could have just made sweet tea."

My back prickled. Why was Mom getting so irritated?

"But," Grandma responded tensely, "if you make sweet tea, you can't take the sugar out. You can always *add* sugar."

Mom exhaled loudly. "But if you know we all like sweet tea . . ."

I knew this wasn't about the stupid tea. As always, it ran so much deeper. "Okay," I said, clapping my hands. I was feeling a little desperate. We hadn't been there for ten minutes. I reached over and poured three glasses of tea. I handed one to each Mom and Grandma. I added a teaspoon of sugar and took a sip. "Delicious," I said loudly.

Grandma took the glass with a small nod of approval. "Thank you, Willow." Mom gave a forced smile and I was ready to just stand up and say, *Come on guys! You're sorry, she's sorry, everyone's sorry. Let's move past this rift so I can have grandparents again and we can be a normal family.*

Everyone slipped into silence.

"Where's Dad?" Mom asked, craning her neck to look toward the study.

"He's not feeling well," Grandma said, a concerned look falling over her face.

Mom got up and walked toward the study. I followed, stopping beside her at the entrance to the bookshelf-lined room. Propped in a cognac-colored leather club chair, Grandpa snored softly, his reading glasses dangling from his wrinkled hand. He looked like a fraction of the burly linebacker he once was. The Grandpa I remembered had mitts for hands and a fierce grip. He had broad shoulders and a thick neck, eyebrows that looked like bushy caterpillars. But this man was shrunken—shriveled, actually—a pathetic remnant of the man he used to be.

A gasp caught in my throat. Only seeing him now, seeing how sick he looked, made me realize how easily a relationship built on phone calls and letters could disguise the real truth.

Mom turned away, visibly upset by the sight of him and the undeniable evidence of how much time had passed. "He looks terrible," she whispered to Grandma as we found ourselves back on the stiff living room couches. "Has he been in therapy since the stroke?"

Grandma nodded slightly. "Yes, physical therapy. It's helping a little with mobility but doesn't really help much with the pain. The doctors keep trying to pump him full of pills, but you know your father—he doesn't like medicine." She twisted her hands together in her lap.

"You know . . ." Mom seemed to perk up a bit. "I've been—"

"I heard you're working at a doctor's office," Grandma interrupted, sounding pleased. "Word travels." She winked at me. "It must be so nice to have your life on a regular schedule. No late nights, no shows on the weekends. Your mother can be around to attend any of your functions—cheerleading or tennis, whatever you chose to do. And of course I can be there too."

"Willow doesn't *play* tennis or cheerlead," Mom answered, irritating me by interrupting my mental image of Mom and Grandma sitting in the bleachers next to Mia's family. Of course in my mental playbook I've suddenly developed athletic skills.

"Well, I could," I said. "I've never had the time to." Mom looked like I'd just slapped her, but Grandma smiled and nodded approvingly.

"So." She turned toward Mom. "What are you doing at the doctor's office? Filing? Answering phones and making appointments? You know, I heard that you could take an online medical coding class and get certified in under a year. You should look into that, Victoria."

Mom took a deep breath, closed her eyes momentarily then reopened them. "Actually, I'm using a technique called hypnotherapy to help people with chronic headache pain. And so far it really seems to be working. The patients are excited and seeing changes. I bet I could help Dad. . . ."

Grandma stood up and looked shocked. She lowered her voice. "I thought you gave that—that *hypnosis* up," she said, looking on the verge of tears. "It's ridiculous."

"I know you never liked the idea of me doing the shows, but this is different. This is helping people! I have a patient who's had chronic tension headaches for five years and now—"

Grandma sighed. "Just because you moved from the stage to an office doesn't make it any less absurd. How do you think Willow feels when her friends find out about your hocus pocus nonsense?"

"It's not nonsense!" Mom said, raising her voice. "And Willow wouldn't have friends as judgmental as you. You're so rigid and critical that you pushed your only daughter two thousand miles away."

"I didn't force you to leave." Grandma said through a clenched jaw. She reached up and anxiously clutched at her pearl necklace.

"You criticized my clothes, my friends, my interests. You wrote an article for the Junior League on what to do when your daughter doesn't live up to your expectations!"

My eyes bulged out. I never knew about that. I nestled down further into the couch and let their jabs volley over the top of me.

"No," Grandma said, tears filling her eyes. "I asked how to help my daughter make better choices."

"How was that supposed to make me feel, Mom? I'll tell you: like I wasn't the daughter you really wanted."

"That's not true!" Grandma cried.

"Why did you always try to control everything I did?" Mom asked. "Why didn't you have faith in me?" She reached over, grabbed my hand, and pulled me up off the couch. "Come on. We're going. Nothing's changed."

Inside my head I screamed, *No, please, not again. Don't leave.* But I couldn't make my mouth say the words. So I let Mom pull me through the house like a rag doll on a string. As she fumbled with the front door, Grandma took my other hand toward her and I stood there, literally the rope in a tug-of-war.

"You listen to me, Willow," Grandma said to me, standing so close I could see the golden flecks in her brown eyes. "I don't know what your mother has told you, but it was her decision to leave. I never wanted you to go so far away. Now that you're back, if your mother still chooses to banish us from her life, well, I want you to know that it doesn't have to include you. I'm just a phone call away. Just a short car ride away." She reached up and touched my cheek. "I want a chance to be your grandmother. A chance to go to your school events. An opportunity to be there for you—not just in cards and phone calls."

Mom flung the front door open and Grandma released my hand. I didn't know what to do. Part of me wanted to say something to Grandma, to take her up on her offer of a relationship, but the other part of me felt swayed by loyalty to my mom. Just because Mom didn't live her life as carefully constructed as Grandma, it didn't make her a bad person. It didn't make our life a bad life. But, that said, I knew what it felt like to warn Mom about our finances and still watch the credit card get denied.

I followed Mom down the porch steps and into the car without saying a word. I looked over my shoulder once and saw Grandma still standing on the porch, the double doors open behind her.

Mom cranked the ignition and sped down the long driveway, no dreamy lingering stares at the chestnut-colored horse this time.

As we pulled onto the road, Mom shifted into gear, accelerating the car way past the speed limit and mumbling under her breath, "Oh sure, she'll be there for you. As long as it's cheerleading or tennis or something that she approves of."

I gripped the side of the car door and pulled my seat belt a little tighter. I felt bad for Mom, knowing this was not the reunion scene she'd hoped for. But I felt bad for Grandma and myself, too. Because all my future plans of Sunday afternoon chats on the porch swing with Grandma's sweet iced tea and Scrabble games vanished like the white split-rail fence and green rolling pastures that disappeared in the distance behind us.

13

Saturday morning I wandered into the family room. Mom was wrapped up on the couch, drinking a cup of coffee and watching *Dirty Dancing* on TNT. Even though she'd seen the movie a thousand times at least, she couldn't peel her eyes away as she motioned toward the kitchen. "There're muffins on the counter," she said.

I went to the counter and pulled a blueberry muffin from the grocery store bakery box. I wondered if things had gone better last night if we would have been over at Grandma's—maybe sitting out on the veranda for brunch overlooking the grassy fields. But I glanced over and saw Mom, curled into a semi-fetal position, the hurt still visible in her eyes and decided it was okay, I liked blueberry muffins on the couch, too.

"Want to go to a movie today?" Mom asked during a commercial break.

"Oh, actually today I'm going to my friend Mia's cheerleading competition. It's at one."

"You can take the car," Mom said, staring vacantly at the TV. "I don't have any plans."

It was strange. In Vegas, Mom's weekends were filled with dates and activities. But apparently it wasn't as easy to meet available men working at a doctor's office. And now we lived in a quiet neighborhood of families instead of an apartment complex filled with eccentric singles.

"Thanks," I said. "But Max is picking me up."

She smiled. "Okay." She fiddled with the edges of the soft blanket. "Cheerleading competition, eh? Wouldn't Grandma love that?"

I didn't know what to say. I felt somehow disloyal—like there was another thing that Grandma and I had in common. But it wasn't like I could say, *I'm going because I need to see if my hypnosis worked.* Mom would freak if she knew I did that. So I just shrugged. "Yeah, weird, huh? Everyone here is really into school spirit and the sports teams."

"Well, have fun," she said with a smile, and we left it at that.

When Max picked me up, he was looking especially good in a black T-shirt with a white Beatles logo ironed across the chest. His blue eyes popped and his black hair had started to grow in. The whole visual just looked perfect.

"Like your shirt," I said, and he instantly grinned.

"So you *do* know some music outside your Top 40."

"Come on." I laughed. "It's the Beatles. Everyone knows the Beatles."

He gave me a skeptical look. "Hey, all I've ever heard in the background on the phone was Cher."

"Not my fault." I smiled. "And that was only in Vegas."

He nodded and started the truck. "Still, it's nice to know you have some basic knowledge of music legend." He smiled and I got the sneaking suspicion that he had handpicked that shirt to provoke me. It gave me a total thrill. "So," he continued. "I have something for you." He reached into the backseat while barreling down the road, paying no attention to the mailboxes he kept almost skimming. "Here." He tossed a CD case into my lap and re-gripped the steering wheel.

It was a plain silver CD in a clear plastic case—no labels, no markings. "What's this?" I asked.

He accelerated onto Main Street and cranked the radio. "It's something"—he looked over at the CD in my lap—"I . . . made for you. I thought you might like it."

He made me a mix CD, I thought. *Isn't that something you do for someone you're into?* I felt warmth spread through my veins. "Hey," I said, noticing that we were headed toward school. "Aren't we picking up Minnie?"

"Nah, she has to help her parents at the restaurant for lunch. She'll come later."

Just me and Max. Alone on a weekend. A mix CD just for me. This had to be more than just friend behavior. A smile engraved itself across my face.

The auditorium was filled with students, teachers, and families, all chatting excitedly with their eyes trained on the large navy blue mats that covered the hard floors. I was surprised by how many non-students were there, outfitted in the crimson and gold school colors, but Max informed me that our cheerleading squad was really good. They had advanced to the state finals last year. People were always excited to watch them compete.

Max and I crossed the auditorium. We climbed up the bleachers toward the top seats where Trent and Conner waved to Max. Garage band musicians at a cheerleading competition? There really was school spirit here. I quickly spotted Georgia and flagged her over. Her eyes darted from Max to me; then she raised her eyebrows suggestively.

"He made me a mix CD," I whispered, as Max said hi to his friends.

"Oh my God. Thoughtfulness, time, and effort. This means something. What kind of songs? Hard-core, *I want to throw you against the wall and rub my hands all over your hot body*? Or soft and mushy, *I want to shower you with delicate kisses on a pink cloud of love*?"

"Sshh!" I giggled. "I don't know. I just got it. There are no song titles and I haven't listened yet. They might just be all *I'm so glad you're my friend*."

"Ooh, secretive. Like a mystery. Love it!" She rubbed her hands together wickedly; then her face dropped. "Uh-oh."

"What?" I swung my head around in the direction she was looking, and there she was, all perky and flushed, climbing the bleachers while delicately balancing two large ziplock bags in her hands.

"Hey!" Max said, way too enthusiastically. "You came early."

Minnie climbed up to our row and worked her way past me, nestling her way right in between me and Max.

Georgia noticed this and shot me a look.

"Carla came early for her shift," Minnie said to Max. "So I got to leave." She turned toward me and acted like she was just noticing me—like she hadn't practically plowed me over. "Hi Willow!" She beamed, her hand tightening on Max's arm.

Max erupted into a huge smile. "Is that baklava?"

Minnie held up the two bags. "I made some extra to bring."

"Minnie is the best baker," Max said, dipping his hand into the bag and breaking off a piece of the flaky pastry. "Here, try some." He extended a morsel to me.

I took it. "Thanks," I said and tried a bite. It was light and sweet, dissolving on my tongue into a burst of sugar. *Minnie is the best baker*, Max said, and I wondered what *best* I was. I didn't really have any spectacular talents. I was just the sideline girl. I always thought I was his best *friend*, but now, watching Max lick his fingers and smile adoringly at Minnie, I feared I was losing even that.

A woman in a crimson and gold jacket and dark bobbed hair tapped the microphone and introduced our team. Booming music thundered through the speaker system and the cheerleading squad ran onto the mat. The crimson skirts swayed to and fro as the team simultaneously did a round-off, handspring, double handspring tumbling pass in perfect unison.

The crowd applauded and cheered. The team parted into two evenly divided sections as pairs of cheerleaders took turns doing flips and tucks together to the pulsating beat of the music. Finally, as the two lines of girls formed a V shape, Mia emerged from the back. There was a pause in the music, a buildup, and from the bleachers I saw a look of panic slide across her face. I stood up and her eyes rose to meet mine high up in the stands. I held my hand in the air, rubbed my thumb and forefinger together. I saw her do the same with her hand, discreetly tucked by her thigh. The music began to pump again. Mia took a breath with a renewed look of confidence, and then she tumbled forward, doing a round-off, a handspring, and the fancy Arabian move she told me about; then she plowed into a front handspring-punch round-off double flip. She landed with a perfect thud and the audience went wild. Several rows below us, I saw a man and woman jump up out of their seat, whistling and yelling Mia's name. I recognized them as her parents from the photos at Mia's house.

"That was awesome!" Minnie yelled. "That means we'll advance to the regionals, I'm sure!"

"She nailed that pass!" a girl in front of us said.

"She was really nervous about that," said a familiar voice behind me. I turned and saw Quinton one row above us. He smiled at me, and out of the corner of my eye, I saw Max notice. The cheerleaders ran off the mat and the competition ended.

Everyone in the stands began to climb down and exit the auditorium. As Georgia and I climbed down the bleachers, I noticed Quinton by my side. I looked over at him.

"Hey," he said to me.

"Hey," I said back, my cheeks flushing involuntarily.

"It's cool they won," Quinton said.

"Yeah," I agreed.

"Mia did great," he said as we reached the bottom of the bleachers.

I nodded. "Absolutely."

"Why did you stand up?" He waited as I hopped off the bottom stair. "You know, when she was getting ready to flip."

"Um," I stammered. "I couldn't see that great and I was, um, excited."

Quinton smiled and playfully pointed at me. "You're lying. Look at you. Your cheeks are all red."

My hands flew up to my face.

Quinton laughed.

To my left, Max slowed down and watched our interaction with interest. Minnie tugged on his arm, but he seemed intent on watching me and Quinton. I had a zing of satisfaction so I grinned widely toward Quinton.

"You did something with your hand," Quinton said. "And Mia did, too."

Crap. I pulled him over to a quieter spot in the corner of the hallway. I didn't want anyone to hear about our hand signal. I needed to keep the hypnosis a secret. For one, I don't think Mia wanted people to know. She had a reputation to protect, after all. Plus, I didn't want Mom to somehow find out. But suddenly Quinton—gorgeous, tousled-haired Quinton—seemed really interested in my answer. And out of the corner of my eye I saw Max lingering—watching us intently. And Quinton's teasing was so charming. My mind thought back to Georgia's crazy TV plots and how jealousy helped unlock true emotions. What if Max saw another boy actually interested in me? Fascinated by me? How would he feel about that?

So I tucked my wayward hair behind my ear. Then, in a hushed whisper, I explained that I used hypnosis to help Mia battle her fears.

Quinton's face was pure awestruck delight. "You helped Mia do that?"

"Ssh!" I said. "You can't tell anyone."

"Wow."

We walked outside together into the bright afternoon sun. Quinton touched my arm. "Can I ask you something?" His golden hair shimmered.

"Sure," I said, my heart racing. I had no idea what to expect.

Could it be possible that gorgeous Quinton . . . *liked* me? I tried not to be too obvious as I scanned around for Max.

His eyes darted around a little then he leaned in and spoke softly. "You're going to think I'm crazy. Remember in English class when I talked about my sleepwalking?"

Oh. I nodded. "Uh-huh."

"It's like getting worse instead of better, and I just hate going to sleep and worrying that I have no idea what I'll do, where I'll go."

I didn't like where this was going. "Uh, Quinton . . . ?"

"Can you imagine next year at college?" He continued. "God knows what I'll do. What if I walk around the dorm naked? I hate the idea of doing something humiliating or embarrassing and having no control to stop it." He leaned in closer. I knew what was coming, and I was dreading it. Because I couldn't say no to Quinton. But I didn't want to keep doing hypnosis on my friends. I was lucky that it worked this time. What if Max was right—if I messed up, they'd hear my voice in their brain forever. "Do you think you could help me?" Quinton said. " Like the way you helped Mia?"

I should just tell Quinton no. I should stop using hypnosis. It'll only make Mom mad if she ever finds out and it would certainly fracture any sliver of a chance I have at a relationship with my grandparents.

But out of the corner of my eye, I saw Max waiting across the parking lot at his car. Minnie was talking to him, but he was eyeing our exchange with interest. I looked into Quinton's chocolate eyes, desperate for help. And the idea of being able to help someone control his life was so appealing. And the idea of Max possibly being jealous was so inviting. And the idea that the ultimate hot guy was touching my arm and looking at me—well, it was just too close to perfection.

And all at once I was caving. "Of course I'll help you," I said, smiling.

Quinton flashed a grin and invited me to come to his house after school on Wednesday—the only day he didn't have football practice.

"Sure," I agreed, and turned to walk back toward Max with a smile of my own.

14

Monday morning, as I walked into English class, I had a small flutter of nerves about seeing Mia. She had called and texted me a thousand times to thank me but I still worried that somehow she'd found out I leaked our secret to Quinton. I had betrayed a friend for a hot guy. *When did I become that person?* I had never been the kind of person who put interest from guys before a friend. Maybe because I had never really been the kind of person who *got* interest from guys before.

But when Mia walked in, she ran over to me and wrapped her taut arms around my neck. "Thank you so much!" she gushed, smiling what looked to be a genuine smile. Not the stage-ready variety.

"You already thanked me," I said, relief coursing through my veins, because obviously Quinton had held up his end of the bargain.

"My parents were thrilled." She sat down at her desk and pulled out her notebook and four-color pen. "We went out to eat and Dad said it reminded him of when Mom was the cheerleading captain in college and how he loved watching her do flips and you just couldn't wipe the smile off her face. It's the most fun we've had in ages!"

"Well, you're welcome." I smiled.

Mrs. Stabile worked her way to the front of the room and announced that we were going to be assigned an oral report project for *A Midsummer Night's Dream*. She would distribute topic assignments individually. There was a general grumble of disapproval. But nothing could make me sad.

At the end of the day, Max met me at our usual spot by the small footbridge that led to the student parking lot. "Well," Max said, popping sunglasses on his face, "all I heard today was one thing: *Can you believe Mia did that flip?*"

I smiled. "Pretty great, huh?"

"Are you going to do it again?" he asked with a strange look on his face.

"I don't know," I answered, feeling a little guilty for lying. He was quiet as he unlocked the truck and tossed his bag haphazardly into the backseat. He turned the key in the ignition then uncharacteristically turned the stereo volume down instead of up.

"I just don't think you're considering the long-term effects of using hypnosis."

"Since when did you become an expert?" I asked.

We were all the way past Main Street and cruising down West Avenue and he still hadn't responded. He drove half a mile down the road and pulled into Poplinger Park. He stopped the truck and turned to face me. But he didn't say anything. The silence was killing me.

"Why are you acting all weird like I'm doing something wrong when I'm just trying to help someone?" I asked, trying not to sound too defensive.

"I'm not questioning your motives," he said quickly. "But come on—you're not exactly trained in this. What you did—it's totally different than what you and your mom did in Vegas." He looked out the windshield at the ducks swimming in the large pond, thinking a minute. "Remember when we were nine?" he said, still looking ahead. "And we were joking around and you tried to hypnotize me?"

I laughed. "Of course. That was hysterical."

"It wasn't hysterical! I broke my arm! We were just fooling around and I got hurt. You could hurt people, Willow, messing with their minds. And not just physically."

I looked at him. There was something in his eyes—something that I didn't understand.

"Is your mom okay with this?" he asked, like somehow he knew she wouldn't be.

My face fell. Because now I really felt like I was doing something wrong. Of course Mom would not be okay with this. And then I thought about Grandma. It wouldn't be okay with her either.

But somehow, I still knew that I wanted to go through with it. So I just stared out at the ducks, not answering Max, until the silence became unbearable and he turned up the music on the stereo, cranked the ignition, and drove me back home.

By the time Wednesday afternoon came, I was feeling much more confident about my skills. I had raided my mother's bedroom again. This time I found even more stacks of books and the jackpot—a digital camcorder, fancy and new, sitting on top of a huge textbook, *Healing with Hypnosis*. On a whim I rewound the footage and pressed play, watching the small viewing screen come alive. There was Mom, looking very serious, dressed all in black, actually talking about using hypnosis to heal and change habits, followed by a brief segment where she began going through the process of putting someone under—like she was hypnotizing the viewer. I couldn't believe my luck. I'd never seen her so fanatical. She never practiced or recorded herself in Vegas but I guessed this was new to her and she wanted to make sure everything was perfect.

After watching Mom's video, taking copious notes and practicing in front of the mirror, I was still a little bit nervous but feeling more confident by the minute. I had just walked out the door of the school when I ran into Max, digging for something in his backpack.

"Hey!" he said. "Hang on a sec, I'm just trying to find my keys." He pulled out his key chain and smiled. "Found 'em." We started to walk together. At the footbridge, I paused, and he gave me an inquisitive look.

"Um, I'm meeting Quinton here," I said. "I'm going to his house today."

"Oh." Max's forehead folded into a series of little lines like maybe the idea of me meeting Quinton in our meeting spot, me riding in Quinton's car, was pushing a few buttons.

A small ripple of satisfaction ran through me.

In the distance, Quinton walked toward us. The afternoon sun cast a golden shimmer atop his mess of thick, disheveled hair.

Max reached up and ran the palm of his hand over the short black fuzz that had been growing back over the past few weeks. "Okay, then," he said, a little bit louder than he normally spoke. "Have fun or . . . whatever." He smiled with only the lower half of his face, his eyes holding still, looking dubious and maybe just a little bit rejected.

"Hi!" Quinton greeted me enthusiastically as Max walked away. "I'm so ready to do this," he said. "Last night I didn't sleepwalk, but I had a dream that I was at college and I was living in a dorm with all the football players and I went to sleep and in the middle of the night I walked over to my roommate's dresser, opened the drawer, and *peed* into it. All over his clothes."

"Oh no." I tried not to laugh, but Quinton started laughing, so we laughed together. I wished I had mom's camcorder, so I could record this moment and anytime I felt invisible I could replay the day when the hottest guy in the universe was laughing and joking with me.

"I woke up all frantic," he said. "You know how sometimes it takes a minute to figure out if a dream really happened or not?" He opened his car door for me and I climbed inside. Quinton drove a compact sports car, trendy and well designed.

"And even though I hadn't actually done anything," Quinton continued, "it was almost as bad—just dreaming about all the possibilities of humiliation." He turned the ignition, left the stereo volume low, and used the turn signal even just to exit his lane in the parking lot. "I hate the idea of not being in control of myself."

"I totally understand," I agreed, thinking maybe we had more in common than I'd realized.

And even though he drove a sports car, he drove exactly the speed limit. The car was immaculate, but partly, I thought, because it looked brand-new. The stereo was set to ESPN on satellite radio. No music thumping, just the drone of an announcer talking about the latest sports news.

He pulled into a neighborhood with pear tree–lined streets and yards with flower gardens and flags that read WELCOME! His house was inviting, with a cobblestone walkway twisting its way to a white front door bordered on either side with potted spiraling shrubs. We walked inside and his mother greeted us with a warm smile. We sat at the large breakfast bar at the end of the kitchen island.

"Willow," she said, offering me a bottle of water. "You have such interesting eyes."

I blushed. "Thanks," I mumbled.

"Oh yeah, they're cool, right?" Quinton said.

A small wave of contentment coursed through me. Cool *is definitely an upgrade from* wicked.

"So," Quinton's mom said as she leaned against the counter to talk to us. "Quin tells me you two are working on an English project together."

Under the bar stool, Quinton kicked me in the shin.

"Um, yes," I answered. "Shakespeare. *A Midsummer Night's Dream.*"

"*A Midsummer Night's Dream,*" she said dreamily. "I saw the play back when I was in college." She smiled and shook her head. "So funny. Love can make you do crazy things." She glanced over to the picture pressed into a corkboard of her and her husband, outfitted in orange life vests, swimming in some tropical lagoon. "Love, love, love," she sang, turning back to the sink.

"Mom, please," Quinton said, trying to sound embarrassed, but really, he had a little smile on his face and I thought it was great that his parents could still be in love after all this time. My mother had never dated a man through an entire calendar year, and I expected it would be nice to have the same face greet you every day.

"Okay, we're off," Quinton said, pushing back his bar stool. I followed suit.

His mom turned halfway around and looked at him. "Honey, can't you study out here? At the table?" She gave him a meaningful look that clearly read, *no girls in the bedroom.* I blushed again, excited that she would think I was the kind of girl Quinton could be interested in.

"Mom, Willow is totally just a friend," he said quickly. "No worries. Plus it's an oral report and it's kind of . . . embarrassing to read the Shakespeare lingo out loud, okay? Just let us go to my room. Trust me—total friends."

He said *friends* again as if even entertaining the thought of me as anything romantic had never entered his mind. Never entered his realm of possibility.

I tried to disguise my crestfallen face. It wasn't that I wanted to date him necessarily. I mean, I understood the improbability of it. But *still*, maybe there was a small piece of me that hoped this hypnotism gig was letting people view me in a whole new light. But no, here I was again, just the friend.

"Well, all right," Quinton's mother conceded. "But leave the door open just a crack."

"No problem," Quinton said, and he took off, climbing the long staircase two stairs at a time.

Quinton's room was exactly as I'd imagined it: neat, masculine, preppy. His bookshelves were lined with both academic and athletic trophies and awards. On one side of his desk, a collection of college brochures and applications was organized into piles marked *dream schools*, *possible football scholarships*, *possible academic scholarships*, *apply early admission*, and *safety schools*. In the center of his desk there was a card, all pink and flowery, lying next to an unmarked envelope. I wondered if, after all his insistence of no dating during the school year and his *Willow's just a friend* talk, maybe it was because he had a girlfriend. So I crafted a distraction.

"Hey, maybe you should pull out your copy of *A Midsummer Night's Dream* in case your mom walks by."

"Good thinking." He bent down to look in his bag.

Quickly, I cracked open the card and inside I saw a handwritten note: *To the best Mom in the world. Happy Birthday.*

I tapped the card shut just as he rose up from his book bag. He placed the book on his plaid bedspread and climbed on the bed next to it. "Ready?" he asked.

I stood there for a moment, still a little awed by his sweet card. I looked at him all gorgeous and perfect. He was smart and athletic but kind and respectful. No wonder Max felt threatened. Five minutes with this guy and the whole world paled in comparison. *If only I could make Quinton want to date me, Max would go out of his mind with jealousy.* I began the hypnosis induction and within minutes, Quinton was under. I began making suggestions about controlling his sleep, controlling his actions. I watched him, breathing so deeply, the muscles in his chest expanding and contracting with every inhale and exhale.

If only he could see me as more than a friend, then Max might be able to do the same.

I caught a glimpse of *A Midsummer Night's Dream* lying on the bed next to him, and his mother's words rang in my ear: *Love can make you do crazy things.*

I thought about the magical flower in Shakespeare's play and the miraculous love spell that made Lysander immediately fall in love with Helena.

And as Quinton sat there all relaxed and susceptible and under my control, I got an idea.

15

Thursday morning I walked around the school hallways like a jittery windup toy, like when Mom drinks one too many cups of coffee and decides to suddenly clean out the junk drawer. I couldn't focus. The only thing that ran through my head was: *Did I really do it?* And, more importantly: *Will it work?*

It started with just a few words: *You will see me, Willow Grey, in a new light. You will see me as beautiful and enticing.* But then the more I looked at Quinton's gorgeous face, the way his lips formed the perfect little bow at the top, well, I *might* have gotten a little carried away.

You will be mesmerized by my charm.

You will want to date me.

You will treat me like the most special girlfriend in the world.

Then I probably went a touch overboard.

You will want to pamper me and shower me with romance.

You will think I'm sexy and alluring, but you will be chivalrous and never ever pressure me in any way.

In other words, you will treat me like a goddess of love.

Okay, I know, but come on, can you blame me? The situation just lent itself to so many possibilities.

I walked into English class and sat next to Mia and Georgia. Quinton walked in, but he was talking to some guy as he passed me so our eyes never met. I couldn't get a good read on him.

Mrs. Stabile talked about hidden symbolism in literature when Georgia nudged me in the shoulder. I leaned back and she whispered into my hair.

"Quinton is like, totally staring at you."

"Really?" I asked softly. "Like how?"

She thought for a minute. "Sort of like in the movie *Juno* when Jennifer Garner's character Vanessa holds the little baby boy in her arms and her face is plastered with that *I can't believe I've just met you and already I love you this much* look."

I glanced out of the corner of my eye and saw him, pressed forward on his desk with an eager look of curiosity and intrigue, almost like he was seeing me for the first time.

You will see me in a new light.

I got a flutter in my stomach. *Could it be working already? This fast?* The remaining thirty minutes of class dragged like a snail in sand until finally the bell rang. I took my time gathering my books in hopes of meeting up with Quinton at the door.

Mia came over. "Guess who called my house last night?"

"Who?" I asked.

"Coach Graham. She called to say the University of Georgia's head cheerleading coach is coming to our next competition to look at our team, and specifically *me* about a possible scholarship!" She squealed and looked like she was ready to bust into a back hand-spring right there if only the desks weren't in the way.

Quinton ambled over to our little circle. Mia, Georgia, and I all turned in his direction.

"Hey," he said to all of us, but he was looking right at me.

Georgia dug her elbow into my side and looked like she was going to implode. I inconspicuously shoved her away and walked alongside Quinton.

When Georgia and Mia had fallen a little distance behind us, Quinton touched my arm and said, "Thank you so much for coming over yesterday. I slept so well last night. No sleepwalking, and no weird dreams."

"Oh, good," I said. "I'm so glad."

"You know, it's weird," he said. "I *feel* different this morning. Like something has . . . changed."

Small tingles pulsed inside me. "Well, maybe it's because you finally got a good night's sleep." We stopped at the end of the hall.

"Maybe," he said. "You know, in this light, your eyes—wow—they don't just look like keyholes, they look like . . . portals . . . to your soul." He shook his head, embarrassed. "Sorry. I don't know what just made me say that."

"Well, don't say something nice and then apologize for it." I said, beaming. No one had ever said anything like that to me before. The warning bell rang for our next class.

"I've gotta run," he said. "But I was thinking that maybe Friday I could take you out." His cheeks flushed scarlet. "Like as a thank-you for the hypnosis."

I didn't remind him that he'd already thanked me. I just said,

"That sounds really nice," and turned and ran to class before he could change his mind.

I didn't tell Max about my upcoming date. Even though he was the inspiration for the love spell, for some strange reason, I kept quiet. Maybe I just wanted to really see if Quinton's interest was going to manifest beyond a thank-you date. Because even though I was in love with Max, a big part of me was really excited to be going out with Quinton.

Either way, during the car ride home Friday afternoon, I was uncharacteristically quiet. I listened to Max complain about a physics quiz that made no sense and I nodded enthusiastically when he told me they'd found a new bass player for their band.

"Mom's going to let us practice in the garage. A real garage band—isn't that funny?"

"I'd like to hear you guys play," I said.

"Really?" Max asked. He smiled at me then looked back at the road. "Well, let us work out the kinks first. Maybe next week."

"You got it." I slid out of the car, told him to have a great weekend and that I'd text him tomorrow. Then I ran into the house, eager to primp before my first date with Quinton.

Quinton arrived at 7 p.m. sharp, looking gorgeous in a striped polo and khaki shorts. As he walked into the foyer, I noticed that his hair had a little bit of gel in it, so while it still had that disheveled look, it was a more structured mess. And my insides flipped to think that he actually prepped for me.

From the corner of the family room, Oompa eyed Quinton with suspicion. His ears pointed and his little squished nose twitched around. Slowly he crept in Quinton's direction, circling around his legs, and for a moment I thought he was going to lift his leg and pee on the carpet surrounding Quinton, marking his territory, saying, *Willow belongs to me, buddy.* But instead, Oompa sprang up in one bouncing swoop and attached himself to Quinton's leg and began humping just like at the park, showing his alpha-dog status.

Here we go again.

Mom ran from the kitchen, mortified. She started swatting at Oompa. "Get down! What is wrong with you?" she scolded.

But Oompa hung on.

I laughed, partly due to nerves and partly because it was funny, but Quinton finally got a desperate look on his face. "Sing, Willow, *please.*"

I no longer thought this was about Oompa being homesick, but I indulged them with Cher. "*What am I supposed to do? Sit around and wait for you? Well I can't do that. And there's no turning back.*" How appropriate, I thought. Maybe I should call up Max and sing it to him. Let him know another guy was interested.

Oompa jumped down and retreated toward my bedroom. Mom stood by Quinton, looking baffled. "That dog is so bizarre," she said.

Quinton and I said good-bye and walked out toward his car. He opened the door for me, and once inside, I saw a large wicker picnic basket nestled on the floorboard of the backseat. "Are you taking me on a picnic?" I asked as he backed the car out of the driveway.

"Not just a picnic: I'm taking you to Screen on the Green." He waited for a reaction but I didn't know what Screen on the Green was. When he realized my ignorance, rather than making me feel stupid, he explained. "In downtown Atlanta, every summer they have a huge movie screen in Piedmont Park that plays movies on Saturday nights. So, here in Worthington, we decided to do our own version. We drape a huge white sheet across the Recreation Department building in Poplinger Park and the whole town votes on what movies to show. Tonight they're playing *The Notebook*."

"That is so neat," I said and wondered if I had mentioned in passing how much Mom and I loved romance movies.

"I've never seen *The Notebook*," he said. "Have you?"

I nodded.

"Oh." He fizzled.

"No, no, I LOVE *The Notebook*! I can't wait to see it on a giant sheet screen and point out all my favorite parts to you."

He brightened a bit and drove into the entrance of the park. He slowed the car down at the basketball court, the site of our very first encounter weeks before. Our minds must both have simultaneously played out the scene of Oompa bolting out of the bushes and attacking his leg, because Quinton and I both burst out laughing.

He looked over at me and smiled his crooked smile. "I had to get stitches on my back, you know."

"Oh my God, are you serious?" I gasped.

"No." He laughed. "But you're gullible."

I playfully swatted him. "That was mean." *But it wasn't. It was the perfect way to ease first-date jitters.*

He drove around a bit then found an open parking spot. He reached back and got the picnic basket off the floor. Then he popped the trunk and took out a thick red blanket. Together we walked toward the wide-open green lawn, where families and dates were collecting on blankets with similar baskets and having picnic dinners before the movie began.

Quinton spread out the blanket next to an oak tree so we could use the thick trunk as a backrest. He opened the picnic basket and pulled out clear plastic plates and plastic forks. Inside a small cooler was an assortment of drinks, and he leaned the tub in my direction, letting me choose. He peeled open aluminum foil packages and examined the contents in a way that made me suspect his mom had put together the dinner, but I didn't care. Because the sun was setting and the huge white sheet was now illuminated with the soft incandescent glow of the movie projector, and the Sprite I was drinking was just as fizzy and bubbly as my mood.

From a huge set of oversize speakers, the first bursts of audio filled the warm night air. Around us, fellow picnickers grew quiet, just chewing and snacking on their food as the movie began to play. Quinton and I leaned back against the grainy bark of the tree, propped our ham-and-cheese sandwiches in our laps, and shared a bag of barbecue chips. He smiled at me and I smiled back. I leaned closer to him and said, "Look, watch, this is important."

And as Noah and Allie found love on the screen, Quinton draped his arm around my shoulders, pulling me close into him. And even though it was September, the air was still thick with the humidity of summer, and for a fraction of a second I thought how our body heat stifled the air around us. But then an unexpected gentle breeze blew through the park like a reprieve, wrinkling the faces on the giant cloth movie screen, making everyone chuckle.

It felt fabulous. I felt fabulous. Surprised, actually, at how quickly I felt swept off my feet by Quinton. Sure, I knew he was gorgeous and smart and funny. And I hoped going out with him would make Max jealous. But I never really thought about how much I might genuinely enjoy being with him. I had a sudden feeling that everything I wanted in moving back to Worthington was about to come true. Like all I had to do was dream — and all my wishes could be granted, just like that.

16

Saturday morning, Mom was sprawled out on the carpet in tight spandex shorts and a lime-green T-shirt, following the yoga instructor on TV. My exercise consisted of stretching my facial muscles into a smile every time I thought about Quinton and our date. My phone rang and I saw it was Quinton. I worked my cheek muscles again as I answered.

"I was thinking," he said, and it felt so intimate to just skip the awkward introduction. "If you didn't know about Worthington's Screen on the Green, you probably don't know much else about our town now. It's been like, what, ten years since you lived here, right?"

"Nine," I answered.

"Why don't you let me show you around?"

"Okay, that sounds great." We agreed upon a pickup time and I headed to my bedroom to get changed. Mom sprang off the ground and followed me. She flopped on the carpet, stretching her calves as

I held up two different tops. She pointed to the daisy yellow Roxy tank top.

"Really?" I asked, wanting to make sure I looked my best. I held it up to my chest. "It doesn't make me look like a banana?"

"No! Yellow is a happy color. Wear it."

"Okay." I hung the other shirt back in the closet.

"So, tell me more about this Quinton," Mom said. "How did you meet? Is he in any of your classes?"

I sat down on the floor next to her and told her the story of our accidental meeting in the park thanks to Oompa.

Mom tipped her head back and let out a hearty laugh. "Well, that's memorable," she said, and I loved how it felt between us. Just so easy and open, like the companionship of giggling friends rather than mother and daughter. And I wished Grandma could see this connection between us—something to be proud of Mom for.

When Quinton showed up, he drove us the six miles from my house into downtown Worthington. Friendship Plaza—a parklike area in between all the downtown shops and cafés, was filled with benches and manicured flower gardens. As we walked next to the old metal slats of railroad tracks, Quinton pointed. "Every spring in the center of town, there's an event called Bark in the Park—it's kind of like our very laid-back version of the Westminster Dog Show. People bring their dogs to perform tricks and the judges hand out prizes to the cutest puppy, the smartest dog." He laughed. "You should bring that crazy dog of yours. He may not win any prizes, but I think he'll entertain everyone for sure."

I laughed and loved how easy it was to be with him. It was like he was just confident that everyone liked him. He didn't have to worry or be nervous or try to impress me. "So much has changed since I lived here," I said.

"Yeah," Quinton agreed. "It's changed a lot even since I moved here in seventh grade. When my parents first told me we were moving from Atlanta to Worthington, I was like, where? You're taking me to some hick town?" He laughed. "But it's built up a lot. There's actually a bunch of cool places to eat and hang out. It's a pretty nice place to live."

Even nicer that you're here, I thought. I followed him into Mike's Bikes, a small shop nestled between a jewelry store and a children's clothing boutique. He walked up to the gray-haired man at the counter and asked to rent bikes for the day.

"Sure thing," the counterman said, disappearing into a back room for a moment. He emerged wheeling two bikes toward us, with two helmets dangling from his hand. At the sight of the ten-speeds, my stomach turned into a flutter of nerves. When was the last time I rode a bike? Many years ago, when Mom dated this mountain-bike enthusiast and she dragged me along on some ride down a sandy desert trail. I'd wobbled behind her the whole time. *This is going to be a disaster,* I thought. *I'm going to humiliate myself, and Quinton is never going to take me out again.*

But as I watched Quinton hold the heavy glass door for me, smiling with a look of genuine happiness, I remembered something. Inside Quinton's mind, a soft, quiet voice was urging him to like me. To see me in a new light. To want to date me. And all at once, I relaxed. *If this hypnotic love spell is really working, I could ride this bike straight into a pile of mud and Quinton would probably think it was adorable. Hopefully.*

I swung my leg up and over the hard bike seat and climbed aboard with a newfound relaxation. We rode side by side through the small historical part of downtown, weaving our way through an old residential neighborhood filled with elegant pillared mansions that had been restored to house local businesses. Quinton called back to me, "Careful up ahead!" The sidewalk erupted into hills and valleys due to the two-hundred-year-old tree roots sprouting up and splitting open the cement. We bumped over them, laughing as our bikes wobbled. He stopped at a four-way stop.

"This is my favorite road," Quinton said, pointing to the right down Tree Line Drive. On either side of the road, the sidewalks were lined with full, green-leafed trees. "In the spring, these dogwoods all suddenly bloom overnight. Like one day they're little green buds and the next morning—boom, the whole street is full of white flowers. It's like waking up to a first winter's snow." His cheeks pricked with a flush of embarrassment. "Sorry, that was cheesy. What's wrong with me? Maybe it's all that Shakespeare we're reading."

"No, that was beautiful. I love flowers!"

"Yeah? What's your favorite?"

"Purple irises," I answered without hesitation.

He smiled broadly. "Somehow I knew it wouldn't be the rose. Nothing conventional about you." He grinned at me in a way that made me look away. "I'd love to live in one of these old houses." He pointed down his favorite road, then started pedaling, turning to the right.

I followed him and imagined us, years from now, living at number 423, the two-story home painted cream with black shutters, and long trails of ivy spilling from the window boxes. We would sit on the black rocking chairs, a large glass pitcher of sweet tea resting on the table between us, our two teenage boys, both miniature versions of Quinton, collecting their football gear and bounding down the front steps.

And that's when I knew something had changed. On Wednesday afternoon, planting the seeds of love in Quinton's mind had more to do with Max than anything else. But now I was beginning to wonder—*was I falling for Quinton?*

When we returned to Mike's Bikes, windblown and sweaty, the door of the neighboring Worthington Diamond Center opened. Georgia walked out. "Willow? Is that you?"

I pulled off the neon pink helmet. "Hi!"

Georgia's eyes bulged out of the sockets as she looked from Quinton to me. "Quick," she said, grabbing my elbow, "come inside and help me with something."

"Go on," Quinton said. "I'll return the bikes and be over in a minute."

Georgia and I disappeared inside the jewelry store. "Oh. My. God. Are you on a *date* with Quinton Dillinger?!"

I nodded, bursting with pride.

"What did you do? Where did you go? Did he kiss you? Hold your hand? Ask for another date?"

"Today we went bike riding. Last night we went to Screen on the Green."

"LAST NIGHT?! You went out LAST NIGHT and you didn't call me?!"

"I was going to tell you today." My cheeks ached from all the smiling. "He didn't try to kiss me but he did put his arm around me last night, and today . . . well, not much physical contact is possible when you're on a bike."

Georgia nodded, thinking as she sat down in front of a clear-glassed counter, a long gold chain twisted into a knotted mess in front of her.

"What's that?" I asked.

"Oh, when my mom bought this store there was a ton of old inventory lying in a box in the back room. Mom put me to work untangling them. Fun, huh?"

"ANY WORK IS HONORABLE WORK, GEORGIA," her mother's familiar voice boomed from some unseen location.

Georgia rolled her eyes. "How does she always do that?"

"Here, let me see." I sat down next to her and examined the knots. I took a pen from the desk behind her and used the tip to separate the center of the huge tangle and began to work the twisting chain apart.

"He's thinking long term," Georgia said as I worked the necklace. "Screen on the Green, bike ride through town—these are thoughtful, planned-out events. He's wooing you!"

I felt a tingle as I remembered the flash of my future life with Quinton. But what about Max?

A bell above the glass door dinged as Quinton walked through. "What are you doing?"

"She just fixed a necklace for me!" Georgia squealed as I delicately pulled the last knot apart and dangled the straight gold chain on my finger.

"Beautiful *and* talented." Quinton patted me on the shoulder, and I blushed. Georgia's eyes went wide.

"It really is a beautiful necklace," I said, handing it over to Georgia. "I love the charm." Attached to the delicate gold chain was a small locket with the word *remember* engraved in cursive. I opened it. There was an open slot just waiting for a picture to go inside.

Quinton and I walked toward the door, but Georgia scurried after us. "Wait! Let me take your picture!" She whipped her cell phone out and Quinton draped his arm around me. She snapped two shots. "Perfect!" she said. "It's important to document special events." She leaned in and whispered to me, "I'll pull this picture out five years from now at your engagement party."

"Ssh!" I giggled, shaking my head, and caught up with Quinton at the door.

When I got home, I was dying to tell Mom about my date. "Mom?" I called as I opened her bedroom door. She acted all flustered as I walked in, like she was hiding something under her covers. She was dressed in conservative black pants and a black top, her hair pulled back into a sleek, simple ponytail. "Are you . . . going somewhere?" I asked.

"Oh, um, I just got home."

Home from where? There was a time when I always knew where she was and she always knew where I was. How had that slowly changed without either of us really noticing it?

She pulled her hair out of the ponytail and it cascaded down into perfect sheets of glossiness— there was no crinkle mark left from the rubber band, like there always was in my hair. She slid out of her clothes and put on her yoga pants and lime-green top from the morning. "So," she said. "You're all glowing and flushed. You've got that look. The look of *love.*" She sat on her bed and patted for me to sit next to her.

"He's *perfect*, Mom," I said dreamily. I told her all about our day. "He's smart and funny and so thoughtful." The more I went on and on about Quinton, the more Mom's face transformed from excited to nervous. Her eyebrows slanted slightly into a little V, giving her the look of a principal disciplining a wayward student.

"What?" I asked her, fearful that she had somehow figured out my secret. Like to the world someone as ideal as Quinton would never fall for someone as average as me. Did she know I'd used hypnosis?

"I know how you're feeling, and I know it's new and exciting and every touch makes you feel like you're going to explode. . . ."

"Oh my God, Mom, please."

"No, Willow, look, we need to have this talk."

"I swear to God, we don't."

"Guys this age have one thing on their mind."

I had to force myself not to smile, because in this case, since I had controlled Quinton's mind, I had specifically stated that he *would not* be a typical teenage horndog. He would be kind and considerate of my timing and pacing. After all, I was embarrassingly inexperienced in the physical department. I could only imagine that someone as gorgeous as Quinton was not.

"I'd love to preach abstinence, but I'm not so naive."

"Mooooooooom," I whined.

"You *cannot* get pregnant," she said adamantly. "I'm not saying I regret getting pregnant at sixteen, because you were the best thing that ever happened to me. You know that. But it wasn't easy. And you're so smart, Willow; you have so many options with your life. I don't want to see you restrict your life because you have a baby on your hip. . . ."

"MOM! He hasn't even kissed me."

"Oh," she said, looking startled. Then her face eased into a smile. Her eyes got glassy. "Of course he hasn't. God, you're such a good girl, Willow." She reached over and wrestled me into a hug. "You're smart and you're cautious and you're all the things I'm not."

I pulled out of her viselike grip. "You're smart, Mom."

She ignored me and yanked me close again. "Still," she said into my ear. "Maybe we should get you a prescription for the Pill. Just in case."

"Mom!" I pushed her away. "Not. Even. A. Kiss."

"Not even a kiss," she repeated, laughing like a crazy person. She hugged me again, harder, tighter, smothering me. "I love you so much."

"Geez." I tossed her aside, onto the bed.

She flopped on her back and giggled in a fit of laughter and relief, and I tried to suppress all the guilty feelings I had about lying to her.

Monday morning, when I walked into the kitchen to grab a Pop-Tart before school, I saw a shiny new wicker basket propped on the counter. Inside were not fresh homemade muffins or even bakery-fresh bagels—rather, the white-painted basket was stuffed with boxes of Trojan condoms, a list of three different gynecologists in town, and four pages, printed off the Internet, on how to say no to peer pressure when dating. I was irritated. *Why does she have to be so blatant in everything she does? I mean, it's hard enough that her clothes are so flashy, why does she have to bring attention to me, too?*

Just then I heard a knock at the door. *Hmm, that's weird. I didn't hear Max's truck.* I opened the door and saw Quinton.

"Morning," he said.

"Wow, I wasn't expecting you!"

"Thought you could use a ride."

There was a rustling from the family room; then Oompa came barreling across the carpet and jumped onto Quinton's leg.

"Whoa," Quinton said. "Could you please get this dog a girl-friend or a boyfriend or even just a *Playboy*?"

From outside, I heard the familiar rumble of Max's truck speed-ing up the driveway. *Uh-oh.*

"Oompa, down!" I clapped my hands loudly. But Oompa kept going.

Quinton reached down and tried to pry him off, but Oompa just started licking his hands. Quinton made a face and wiped them on his jeans. I breathed an inward sigh of relief that, thanks to the pow-ers of hypnosis, even *this* couldn't make Quinton stop liking me. It was very freeing, really.

"Um, hey." Max walked up beside Quinton in the doorway, eye-ing Oompa with suspicion. He moved through the threshold into the family room, just feet away from the kitchen counter. *Crap. My new boyfriend. A humping dog. A basket stuffed with sex parapherna-lia. Max is going to think he walked in on some weird orgy.*

I tried to back casually toward the kitchen counter to block his view without drawing too much attention to myself, but suddenly Oompa barked, making Quinton flail backwards and knock into me. I swung my arms backward for balance—right into the white wicker basket, which fell sideways. A square blue box toppled out and skid-ded across the counter. *TODAY'S SPONGE—The Vaginal Contra-ceptive Sponge—the reversible, over-the-counter, barrier method of birth control!*

Oh sweet Jesus.

I heard a muffled laugh from Max.

"Um, help!" Quinton called, still trying to disengage from my dog.

"Oompa!" Mom's shrill cry startled all of us. She clapped her hands sharply and Oompa hopped down obediently, snorting a little. He walked over and rubbed his square head against Max's leg, looking more like a purring cat than a dog.

"Hey," Quinton said, pointing at Max. "How come he doesn't get the leg hump?" He shook his head. "I need to change my cologne."

"Um, Oompa is just a little senile," I stammered and hastily tossed a dish towel onto the basket, but the shift in weight made the entire thing tumble on its side again. Two boxes of Trojans skidded across the counter and fell onto the tiled kitchen floor. The stack of white papers fluttered through the air and landed at Max's feet.

Oh. My. God.

I dropped to my knees and quickly gathered the sheets into a messy stack.

Max squatted down beside me and picked up the two Trojan boxes. He turned to me. "For you," he whispered, arching his eyebrows. "Or no, wait, I guess I should give them to Quinton."

"Shut up, Max," I said and shoved the boxes inside the silverware drawer. I shot a look at Mom. *Hello? Humiliating enough?*

She shrugged, silently motioning to the two guys standing in our house. *How was I supposed to know they'd show up?* her face said.

"Um, guys?" Quinton stood motionless, his cheeks matching the color of the red roses plastered across the *You and Your Virginity* pamphlet. Which had landed right at his feet. "Sorry to interrupt." He looked at me. "Did you . . ." Quinton glanced quickly over at Max and then back at me. "Did you already have a ride? Because I can just meet you at school—"

"No, no," I said, standing up. "I want to ride with you." I glanced at Max, feeling simultaneously guilty and annoyed. "Sorry," I said. "I'll see you at school."

The smug look fell off of Max's face. "Oh, okay," he said, sounding both shocked and maybe a little hurt. He glanced at Quinton then fixed me with a long, intense stare. "See you at school." He passed Quinton on his way out, patting him on the back.

Once inside the car, Quinton started to laugh. "Dude," he said to me. "First the dog, then the basket . . . I'm beginning to think you're like one of those naughty librarian types."

"Huh?" I asked, sort of afraid of what he was going to say.

"You know—prim on the outside but secretly you're like . . ." Suddenly, a blank look crossed his face. He reached over and turned down Sports Center. "I respect you, Willow," he said, his voice sounding very far away. "I want to be considerate of your timing and pacing. I don't want to be some typical horndog."

I sat very still.

He shook his head. "God," he groaned. "Sometimes I don't know why I say the things I do." He leaned over and turned the radio back up.

"No," I said quickly. "It's cute. I'm glad you say those things." I reached over and took his hand. He held it tightly, and grinned.

"God, Willow," he said. "You really are special."

We rode the rest of the way in silence.

When we got to school, Quinton held my hand as we walked across the parking lot. It felt amazing to be physically attached not just to a boyfriend, but to Quinton. People noticed, whispering and commenting the minute we passed. He continued to escort me down the long hallway toward my locker. When I told him that it was okay, he needed to get to his locker before the homeroom bell rang, he shook his head no and said he wanted to stay with me and watch me open my locker.

I thought that was odd, but when I dialed my three-digit combination and pulled the door open, inside there was a beautiful bouquet of towering purple irises. I gasped. No one had ever sent me flowers before. I reached over and hugged him. "Thank you!"

"Did you know that the iris is the flower of the Greek goddess Iris, who is the messenger of love?" He gave me a sheepish look. "I had to look up what an iris was because I didn't know."

I bit my lower lip to stop it from trembling because that was the sweetest thing I'd ever heard.

He leaned down but then stopped. "I want to kiss you. Is it okay if I kiss you?" he whispered.

I nodded yes and he bent over and gently kissed my lips. When I fluttered my eyes open, he was smiling.

I looked back at the deep violet petals and felt a surge of emotion. I felt so special. He had listened to me. I tried to ignore the fact that he was only doing it because I'd hypnotized him to. *Maybe he's really falling for me, after all?*

The bell rang. Quinton squeezed my hand. "See you later."

"Thanks again," I said. I shut the metal door, leaving the vibrantly colored flowers behind, but I took the feelings along with me, nestled deep in my heart. And as I turned to walk in the opposite direction, I saw Max, standing alone by the water fountain, watching me. I tried to wave, but he quickly walked away.

"He gave you flowers! That's so romantic!" Mia gushed in English class. She sighed. "Guess the last time Jake gave me flowers."

"Your birthday." Georgia craned her neck from her desk into our conversation.

"No," Mia said, a little sadly.

"Valentine's Day," Georgia tried again.

"No." Mia shook her head, the sadness morphing into something like anger.

Georgia scrunched her face up. "Christmas?" She raised her voice hesitantly, aware that nine months was an awfully long time ago.

"Jake has never given me flowers."

Georgia gasped like this was truly horrific news. And I was surprised that Mia was letting down her facade to us—showing us the imperfections in her perfect relationship. I had yet to see her do that elsewhere. It made me feel important.

"Well," I said, "maybe he doesn't know you like them?"

Mia shook her head again. "Last fall we walked by the Flower Pot and I made a huge deal about how much I loved the smell of fresh flowers. Then, a few months later, when he didn't pick up on the hint and we were heading into February, I casually told him how sure, I loved roses like the rest of the world, but I really preferred white roses—not red or pink. February 14 arrived and the fool gave me chocolate-covered cherries. And I hate cherries."

"Oh," I said, not sure what to say. "I hate cherries too."

"And for my birthday? He gave me a duffel bag. A duffel bag! And I had hinted for like weeks that I really wanted these pretty earrings I saw in a jewelry store window. He just doesn't listen to me," Mia said. "You're lucky."

"A duffel bag for your birthday." Georgia cringed. "Sometimes I truly believe that guys just need a manual."

"That'd be a best seller," Mia said.

Georgia shot her finger into the air. "I'm going to write one!"

"You're not even dating anyone," I whispered.

"I spend an average of four hours a day watching TV and movies.

That's twenty-eight hours a week, fifteen hundred hours of carefully crafted and plotted romance a year. And that's not even including my reading habits." She pulled out a sheet of paper and began scribbling ideas.

Mrs. Stabile hushed the class and began her lecture. Mia passed a note over to me. *Come over this afternoon?*

I nodded. *Sure,* I mouthed, thrilled that we were becoming true friends.

Behind me, Georgia continued to write. I glanced over my shoulder and caught the top line, bold and in caps: *IF GUYS ARE MEMBERS OF THE ANIMAL KINGDOM, SURELY THEY CAN BE TRAINED.*

When the bell rang at the end of class, we all walked into the hallway. By the lockers, Jake and a few other football players, Hayden and Davis, were talking. Mia flew over to them. As I walked away, I saw her thousand-watt stage smile plastered on. So different from how she'd just been with us.

That afternoon, when Mia and I walked into her house, Mia's mom was decked out in an apple-red T-shirt with big white letters UGA stamped across the chest. Underneath in cursive, it read CHEER-LEADING. She had on a pair of white cotton shorts and her blond hair was pulled back in a high ponytail.

"Hi, hi, hi!" she sang. "Did Mia tell you the wonderful news? That the University of Georgia coach is coming to scout her this weekend?" She was practically bursting with excitement, but when I glanced over at Mia, her smile looked frozen and forced.

"She did," I said. "I'm so excited for her."

Mrs. Palmer smiled at me; then Mia and I walked back into Mia's room. She flopped on her bed, stretching out her petite body into a huge X but still barely spanning the distance across her queen-size mattress. "I need your help again," she said, staring up at the ceiling.

"Okay," I said, flopping down next to her. She scooted over and we lay there, side by side.

"I need another session. You've got to help me make it through this next competition."

I turned and faced her anxiously. "Won't it be easier this time? You've already done the tumbling pass, so you should be more confident—less afraid, right?"

She exhaled loudly then turned to face me too. "Mom went to UGA."

"So I figured, from the getup," I said.

Mia sighed. "The glory days. She was, like, the best cheerleader to ever walk the campus. So when she found out the coach was coming to scout me—she freaked. She's sooo happy. And I'm glad, of course, because lately she's, well, she hasn't been happy."

I raised my eyebrows, unconvinced. Her mom seemed like the poster child for happy.

"No, it's true," Mia said. "Lately she's all mopey. Sensitive. Not in front of guests, of course, but when it's just us. Dad's been working late and he's been distracted, and she thinks it's about her. I tried to tell her, Dad's a doctor—he has patients and an office to run and it has nothing to do with her, but she doesn't listen."

The image of the perfect beach photo floated in my mind and I wondered if Mia's mom was sad when they took that picture. If the whole family had mastered the art of the thousand-watt stage smile.

"Anyway, since she found out that the UGA coach was coming, she's been bouncing around all perky and excited, and that puts all kinds of pressure on me to do well. Then, last night, she decided that I need to do her move."

"What do you mean, 'her move'?"

"When Mom was at UGA in the early nineties, she created her 'signature move.'" Mia pulled herself up and walked across her room to her laptop resting on the desk. I got up and followed her over. She opened the computer and typed into a search engine. "Mom's move is called 'walk in heels, stretch, double down.'"

"Sounds . . . interesting." I leaned over to look at the computer screen.

"There's no video on the Web of her, of course, but here's a clip from *Cheerleader Nation*—that show on Lifetime about the squad trying to win the national championship." She clicked on a link and a video started. Three girls elevated a fourth up into the air. The girl held her leg up; then the three base girls tossed her high into the air. "See how much height they have to achieve so she can do a double down?" She saw my confusion and explained. "I'll have to spin twice in the air, so they have to toss me really high and *ugh*, it's just . . . scary. Plus, I have to do it perfectly because *IT'S MOM'S MOVE!* I can't screw it up." Her face went pale.

I put my hand on her shoulder. "It's okay. Calm down." I reached over and hit the replay button to watch the move again. Mia turned away from the screen.

"Can't you just do the other move? The one that you've practiced?"

She turned back and looked at me with the first sign of tears in her eyes. "But Mom's so happy. I heard her singing in the shower. She hasn't done that in months."

I wanted to tell Mia that it made no sense that a double flip could completely change someone's outlook on life, but she seemed so desperate. So scared. So in need of my help. So I touched her arm gently and said, "Come on. If we're quiet, we can do the hypnosis right now."

When I got home from Mia's, I pulled my cell phone out of my backpack. I had three messages from Georgia:

Chapter 1—Hey, my dog walks on a leash; surely I can train my boyfriend to go where I want to hang out.

Chapter 2—If I can teach my dog not to sniff my crotch, surely I can train my guy to quit reaching for my pants.

Quick question: If people use shock collars to train dogs, do you think it's feasible to suggest using a Taser? It could be quite effective. Bad birthday present? TASER! Not gonna happen again!

I had four missed calls from Max, with one final message. *Call me.*

So I quickly typed a response to Georgia: *U R insane.* Then I put in a call to Max. He answered on the first ring. I tried to be all casual. "Hey, what's up," I said, but in my mind I was replaying the box of condoms falling onto the floor and my kiss with Quinton in the hallway. I could feel the heat of embarrassment in my face. I was glad he couldn't see me.

"Hey," Max said, and I heard a guitar pulsing in the background. Max said something to someone and the tinny vibrations stopped.

"Are you practicing with your band? 'Cause I can call back later."

"No, no, they're just leaving. 'Bye, man," he said and I heard what sounded like some hand slapping. "So . . ." He returned to me but then said nothing else.

"So," I said, and for the first time ever it felt a little awkward between us.

"So, you and Quinton—you're, like, together?"

An involuntary grin spread across my face. Was my plan working? Was Max jealous? "Yup, I guess we are."

"How did that happen?"

I tried not to be offended, not to jump to that conclusion that everyone was baffled that Quinton could like me, because Max was my best friend and I had to believe he wouldn't think that. I sat down on the floor of my bedroom and stared at my toes. "I don't know. We're in English class and we've been grouped together a few times."

He was quiet.

"What?" I asked.

I heard him tap his drumsticks on something, making a fast clickety-clack beat. "I'm just not convinced that he's the right guy for you. I mean, he's nice and everything, but his whole life is football and school, and you can't stand sports."

"It's not that I can't *stand* sports, it's just something I've never really been involved with or appreciated before."

"Yeah, but he's all, like, a pretty boy. Like an Abercrombie and Fitch guy."

"What does *that* mean?" *That I'm not pretty enough to be with him?*

He tapped his drumsticks again. "I don't know what I mean. I just think you guys seem mismatched." He paused. "What about your broken heart? The one you told me about the night you stayed here? I guess you're . . . over him."

I took a deep breath. No, of course I wasn't over him. But what did it mean if your heart fluttered for two different guys? I heard something outside my window and walked over and peered outside. But Max wasn't there, just some squirrel rustling in the shrubs. "How come you didn't just come over to talk?" I asked, pressing my hand against the slick surface of the window.

"Because for all I know, Quinton is over there, anxiously sorting through your basket of goodies. I can't just show up anymore. This changes everything."

"Oh." My finger drew a circle against the pane. "Well, you said Minnie didn't change anything, so Quinton doesn't have to change anything either."

He was quiet and I realized the circle I was drawing had morphed into a heart. He didn't respond, so I said, "Quinton and I do have a lot in common, actually. But thanks . . . for caring. And nothing has to change between us."

"Except the rides to school."

"Well, yeah, I guess that'll change. But that's all."

"That's all," he repeated; then we both were quiet again. "Well, I told Trent I'd call him."

"Okay," I said, glad that at least he wasn't running to Minnie. "Good night."

" 'Bye."

I put the phone down, staring vacantly at the smeary smudges of hearts on the window. One heart connecting to another and another. Sure, maybe Quinton and I were mismatched, but somehow we still had a spark between us that lit us up like fireflies. Maybe the hypnosis was the kindling that ignited the fire, but the connection between us was real, wasn't it? I imagined it worked the way it helped Mia. She was innately a great athlete—the hypnosis didn't create that; it just maximized her potential by erasing her fear.

So in my mind, the hypnosis had brought Quinton to me, but after that, how we felt about each other was real. The funny thing was, that initially my intention was to spark some jealousy in Max. And it seemed like it had. But unexpectedly, dating Quinton seemed to be everything I never realized I wanted. He listened to me and paid attention to me. He wanted me to be happy. Sure, part of my heart would always be wrapped around Max—after all, he was my first love. But with Quinton, this was what grown-up love felt like, I was sure. It wasn't just fantasies that one day we would end up together—this was real.

Maybe I didn't need Max after all.

Saturday, Quinton picked me up to go to Mia's competition. "Thanks so much," he said, "for coming to my football game last night."

"I wouldn't miss it," I said, buckling my seat belt.

"Some girls think football is boring." He reached over and took my hand. "I'm just so happy you came."

Maybe the actual game was boring, I admitted to myself, but the experience wasn't. Being at Quinton's game—as his girlfriend—I felt like the prom queen. Every time Quinton looked my way, I felt myself flush. Every time he made a good pass or a tackle, people smiled at me like I was somehow responsible.

We drove into the crowded student lot now and parked. "Did I tell you that I haven't sleepwalked in a week? You're like a miracle worker."

"Really? That's amazing!" I crossed my fingers that the hypnosis worked as well for Mia, because she was really stressed about today's competition.

"I was thinking about having a party at my house tonight," Quinton said. "Something small. Sound good?"

"Sure."

"You can invite Georgia if you want."

I squeezed his hand. "Thanks."

The auditorium was packed, even more crowded this day than at the last competition. Quinton held my hand and led me up the bleachers to our group of friends. He used his hand to clear any crumbs or dirt from the bench before I sat down, and I loved how everyone noticed this—noticed Quinton taking care of me. We sat, and Quinton draped his arm around me.

Across the gym, Max and Minnie walked in and headed our way. They quickly climbed the bleachers as the cheerleading coach made her announcements. I waved to Max and he smiled at me. He looked over at Quinton; then steered Minnie into a bleacher several rows below us and sat down. I tried to flag him over and signal that there was plenty of room by us, but when he looked up at me one more time, he barely saw me; he was too busy eyeing up Quinton and his arm on my shoulder. I thought about jealousy and wondered if that was what I was seeing on Max's face.

The music thundered through the gymnasium and the squad

ran onto the mat and began performing the same routine as at the last competition. But as the bass pounded and thumped toward the finale, the squad lined up into a new formation. Three girls hoisted Mia up into the air. As she kicked her leg up and held it for a split second, the rest of the gym faded away and it was just me and Mia, signaling at each other. Then the girls tossed her high up into the air, and the crowd came roaring back. Mia spiraled twice and landed perfectly into their arms to a burst of frenzied applause. I saw her mom spring out of her seat, jumping just as high as the cheerleaders she clapped for.

After the competition, Quinton told a bunch of people about the party at his house later that night. As I followed the crowd down the steps, listening to Georgia talk about the latest plot twist on *True Blood*, something caught my eye. I blinked and squinted, sure I was imagining things. But as we walked closer, I saw it was true. Grandma was standing by the door. Our eyes locked and she gave me a closed-lipped, tentative smile.

I pushed past the crowd of people, trying to make my way over to her, to ask her what she was doing. Was she there to see . . . me? But by the time I weaved my way to the door, she was gone. Vanished.

And I wondered if I just imagined it all.

19

That night everyone went to Quinton's house for a post-competition celebration. Quinton's parents were out of town for the weekend so we had the entire house to ourselves. Everyone congregated in the finished basement. It was the perfect party space—a huge plasma TV hung from the wall; a pool table and a Ping-Pong table were across from a huge wet bar.

One by one, random girls I recognized from the lunchroom or the hallways came up to me, peppering me with questions.

"Oh my God, how did you get Quinton to break his no-dating-during-football-season policy?"

"Oh my God, you are so lucky. Quinton is so hot."

"Oh my God, you guys make the cutest couple!"

Georgia came over. "Thanks so much for inviting me," she said. "It's, like awesome, being here. Sadie Wilson spilled her beer all over me and I said, *No big deal*, and she said I was cool. Cool! And you—not only are you, like, in the *in crowd*, you're like part of Quinton's family already."

"What?" I asked her. She led me over to the living room area, and there, on the coffee table next to the huge leather couch, was the picture she'd taken of me and Quinton last weekend. It was blown up to five by seven and framed in a bronze picture frame.

"That took a lot of work," Georgia said. "I sent the picture to his phone, so he had to download it, crop it, enlarge it, print it, and frame it." She smiled. "He's totally into you."

"Wow." I reached over and picked up the frame, noting how he had even removed the red-eye from my pupils. "That *was* a lot of effort." Inside, I was glowing. This thing with Quinton—it definitely seemed real. He had my picture on display, something I harassed my mom for never thinking to do! A little voice inside me said that we had only been dating for a week and, well, it seemed kind of . . . soon. But I shook it off. That's how real love was, I supposed—when the puzzle pieces click, why look back?

Suddenly, from above, a static-filled noise leaked out of the built-in speakers nestled into the ceiling as someone turned on the stereo.

"Everyone," Quinton said loudly, standing in the corner of the room by a huge stereo system. He secured his iPod on a docking station and turned the volume up. "I've created this playlist for my new girlfriend, Willow."

"Awwwwwww," all the girls gushed. Across the room, Mia was talking to Sadie, with the thousand-watt smile plastered on. But when she heard Quinton's announcement, for just a second, her happy face changed into something more wistful.

Overhead, Eric Clapton sang "Wonderful Tonight."

Quinton smiled at me and a flutter of butterflies flew in my stomach. I smiled back as he went over to talk to Jake.

Across the room I saw a familiar pair of flip-flops coming down the stairs. Max. When his face came into view, he scanned the room until he found me. I waved him over. Georgia went over to the bar to get a drink.

"Well," Max said with a provoking look in his eyes, "I guess I was wrong. You and Quinton do have something in common—a love of cheesy music."

"Eric Clapton is classic," I said defensively.

"Most of the time," Max countered. "Except this. *Go to a party and everyone turns to see this beautiful lady,*" Max sang with a mushy look on his face.

"Quit." I laughed, pushing his pretend microphone down from his face. "Well, I'm sure you've made a special playlist for Minnie. Hell, you've probably written her a song."

Max's smile dropped and an unreadable expression crossed his face. His denim-blue eyes held mine, and it seemed like the entire chaos of the party just evaporated behind us. "Willow," he said softly, not teasing anymore. "I want to ask you something."

He looked over at Quinton then back to me. His face was serious—nervous almost. Oh, my God, what if Max *was* jealous? My heart raced. That was what I originally wanted, right? I looked at Max—wonderful Max who made me feel calm and comforted and understood. But then I looked across the room at Quinton. Gorgeous Quinton who made me feel beautiful and special and wanted.

"Willow," Max reached over and touched my arm.

Suddenly Mia bounded over, all electric and buzzing. She took my hands and started jumping like she was on a trampoline. "I did it! I did it! I just got a text from my mom that my coach called and said the UGA coach was 'very impressed.'" She air quoted while springing like she had coils in the soles of her sandals. "They're talking scholarship!"

"That's amazing!" I said.

"Yo, kangaroo, you're making me dizzy," Georgia said, returning from the bar with an overflowing cup.

Max gave a small *oh well* sigh and his words—whatever they were—remained unsaid. "Congratulations, Mia," he said, then walked toward Trent and Conner over by the TV.

"I can't believe Quinton's playing all love songs for you tonight," Mia said. "That is so romantic." She gazed across the room to where Jake was playing beer pong. He tossed his Ping-Pong ball through the air, crashing it smack into Davis, another football player standing on the opposite side of the table.

"Score!" Jake screamed.

Mia sighed. "Jake would never do that."

"Um, are we noticing Max at four o'clock?" Georgia whispered.

"What?" I swung my head and saw Max looking our way. Quickly he turned back toward Trent and Conner.

"He can't stop watching you," Georgia whispered. "I think we have a Ron and Hermione situation going on here."

"Huh?" Mia asked.

"Harry Potter," Georgia explained. "Ron and Hermione. Friends who can't stand seeing each other with anyone else."

"So?" Mia furrowed her brow, confused.

"Jealousy," Georgia explained. "Seeing Willow with Quinton is making Max realize what he's lost."

I looked over at Max's back. *Could it be true?* I thought about our phone conversation. "You know," I whispered, and Mia and Georgia huddled closer. "He told me he wasn't convinced Quinton was right for me."

"Ha-ha!" Georgia pointed at me.

"That's crazy—Quinton is perfect for you," Mia said. "He listens to you, does romantic things for you . . ."

"Max is jealous," Georgia said confidently.

"Why should he be jealous? He has perky Minnie with her little skirts and her flaky baklava." All three of us looked over at Max, and perhaps he felt our laser beam stares, because he turned to face us. He had his hands on his hips, one thumb hooked through a belt loop.

"Look at him!" Georgia whispered fiercely. "Look at his body language! He's in a classic cowboy stance. All he needs is a ten-gallon hat and a lasso! He's trying to demonstrate his manliness to you!"

"Hush." I laughed. "He is not." *Is he?*

Max quickly looked away.

"Uh-huh." Georgia nodded. "Totally jealous."

"Who cares about Max," Mia said. "You have Quinton and he's so into you!" We all looked away from Max toward Quinton, who was talking to Hayden. He caught my eye and smiled. Overhead B.o.B. sang "Nothin' on You," and Quinton lip-synched, "*They got nothing on you, baby. Nothing on you.*"

"Aww." Mia sighed. "To have a guy like you that much . . ."

"Yeah, it's amazing," I said and it was. Quinton was thoughtful and romantic and kind. I smiled and tried to squash the little tiny voice that wondered what Max had been about to say to me.

Sunday morning Mom asked me how Quinton's party was. I told her about it and asked what she did while I was gone.

"Oh, you know, not much," she answered.

"Is it boring here for you?" I asked, because it was the longest I'd ever seen my mom without a date or a party to attend. She hadn't even brought any friends to the house, which was so unusual. All along I had suspected Mom's insistence on a more quiet and conventional life had everything to do with getting back in Grandma and Grandpa's good graces, but when that didn't pan out, I assumed she'd revert back to her nightlife. But no, she hadn't gone out all weekend, and here she was curled up on a Sunday morning with a textbook instead of a romantic comedy.

"Boring?" Mom asked. "Not exactly. I mean, life is different." She laughed. "But not in a bad way."

I nodded. "Well, that's good. Do you want to go to the mall today?" I asked, picking up her empty coffee mug off the floor and putting it in the sink.

"Oh, actually, hon, I have something I need to do today. Sorry." She winced a little. "I know we haven't had much fun lately, but rain check?"

"Sure," I said. "No big deal." But it *was* a big deal. Because she didn't tell me what she would rather be doing instead of hanging out with me. And it gave me the strangest feeling—like Mom was hiding something from me. Then I thought about all the hypnosis I'd done and I got a heavy brick feeling in my gut, because, for the first time ever, there was a fissure in our solid foundation.

I looked back at her with her nose buried in some book and then I turned and walked into my bedroom. I pulled out my cell phone and stared at it. I wanted to call Quinton, but my mind kept wandering to Grandma at the cheerleading competition. When we had our routine Sunday chat, neither of us brought up what happened at our reconciliation gone wrong. It's like we both wanted to pretend that everything was okay—that we could still fix things. Had I imagined Grandma showing up at the competition? Before I could chicken out, I dialed the numbers.

She answered on the third ring sounding a little breathless, like maybe she'd just run in from tending to her roses.

"Grandma?" I asked tentatively.

"Willow?" I heard the sound of fabric crinkling like she was pulling off her gardening gloves. "Sorry dear, let me get settled. Okay. Oh, it's so good to hear your voice."

"It's good to hear yours too," I said, and then it was quiet, like we both were tentative. "Um, was that you at my school yesterday?" My heart was speeding double time. Suddenly it occurred to me that maybe I was completely bonkers—that my mind was creating what I wanted to see.

"Yes," she said, and I felt my shoulders relax. I hadn't realized how tense they had become.

"Willow, do you think you could sneak away for the afternoon? Maybe join me here for some lunch?"

"Yes," I answered quickly, not even considering how I'd get there if Mom was using the car. I knew I'd find a way. We said we'd see each other in an hour and hung up the phone.

When I walked out of my bedroom, Mom had left a small note on the table. *Be back later.* I glanced out the window and saw that the car was gone. I was debating my options when my phone rang.

"Did you have fun at the party last night?" Quinton asked as soon as I picked up.

"I did."

"I can't stop thinking about you."

I flushed with warmth. "I can't stop thinking about *you*."

"Is it too much if I want to see you again today?"

"Actually, could you do me a favor?" I asked if he could drive me over to Grandma's. I was worried that he would think I was inviting him to meet my grandmother and I didn't want to have to explain my crazy family situation but he made no assumptions.

"No problem," he said. "Then just call me back when you need a pickup."

My heart swelled, because truly, I couldn't have invented a better boyfriend. Even if I'd sort of invented this one.

He showed up twenty minutes later. When he walked in and saw that we were alone he pulled me close and kissed me passionately. It was soft and soulful—much more passionate than at school. My entire body felt warm and tingly and perfect . . . until Oompa ambushed us.

Quinton just laughed good-naturedly. "Seriously, I need to change my cologne."

I plucked the dog off his leg and we went out to his car. "Look in the glove box," he said as he pulled out of the driveway.

I opened it up and inside I found a small gold-wrapped box. "What's this?" I asked.

"Open it," he said.

I directed him to turn onto Magnolia Lane, then peeled the gold foil off and saw a white and black sticker on the box: THE WORTHINGTON DIAMOND CENTER. Inside the velvet-lined box was the delicate gold chain with the locket that I'd admired at Georgia's mom's store. The tiny engraving, *remember*, glittered up at me. "Oh wow," I exclaimed. "This is so thoughtful. You didn't have to do this." I looped the necklace around my neck and clasped it.

"I saw how much you liked it," he said as we pulled up the long winding driveway to my grandparents' house.

"Thank you," I said, "for this, for the ride, for just being so wonderful."

He stopped the car by the walkway to the front door.

I leaned over and gave him a kiss. "I don't deserve you," I said.

He smiled. "Call me when you're done."

"Okay." I walked away from the car. On instinct, I looked back over my shoulder and saw Quinton looking at me. I raised a hand and waved. He waved back. Then I walked toward the huge double doors and rang the bell.

Grandma answered, dressed in her Bermuda shorts, a button-down shirt, and a large sun hat propped on her head. "Willow, I'm so pleased you've come." She opened the door and I followed her all the way into the kitchen, where a small circular table was set for lunch for two. A vase was filled with orange gerbera daisies she obviously had plucked straight from her garden. The formal china was in the china cabinet. Instead the place settings were light beige and casual, and I loved that all the stiffness of our living room get-together weeks ago had been rethought. This felt right—the way a grandmother and granddaughter should have lunch. Grandma took her hat off and opened the fridge.

I sat down and Grandma brought over a platter of croissants and a bowl filled with fresh chicken salad. "I didn't know if you liked grapes in your chicken salad. Well . . ." Grandma hesitated slightly. "It's been years since we've actually had a meal together."

"I like grapes." I said, excited to have a home-cooked meal.

"Good." She placed the platter on the table between us "That's what I want, Willow," she continued. "I want to know the details. All the little things you can't learn from just a phone call."

A lump formed in the back of my throat. I tried to swallow back the tears, not letting her see how much it meant to me.

She smiled, and when she shut the refrigerator door I saw an old sheet of yellow construction paper, curling and frayed at the edges, taped up to the stainless steel. It was a picture I had drawn years ago of me and Grandma out in the pasture, petting Grandma's horse. On the bottom, in the scratchy penmanship of a six-year-old, I had written, *I love you*. Beneath it Grandma had written in blue ballpoint pen, *I love you too*.

"What I want to tell you," Grandma said, "is that, while of course I wish last Friday went better, sometimes your mother can be . . ." She paused, closed her eyes for a minute. She reopened them. "Regardless of my *problems* with your mother, they shouldn't . . ." She took a deep breath, like she was searching for the right word. ". . . interfere with *our* relationship. You live just miles from me now. Miles." She smiled and reached across to squeeze my hand. "We can do all the things we talked about—have lunches, go shopping. I can teach you to garden!"

I nodded and picked at the chicken salad. I should have felt happy, but deep down I was disappointed. Because even if Grandma and I did all those things—lunches and shopping and gardening—it still made me sad that Mom wouldn't be a part of it. Then I heard Mom's voice in my head, saying: *Sure, she'll spend time with you as long as you're doing things she deems acceptable.* But what about the things *I* wanted to do? Did Grandma want to know the real me, or did she only want to mold me into her perfect granddaughter? Suddenly, I was beginning to realize how Mom must have felt.

"How's Grandpa doing?" I asked, changing the subject.

Grandma smiled. "Better, it seems. He's walking with his cane now."

"Oh, that's great," I said and wished he wasn't sleeping. I wanted to see him regaining his strength so I could erase the last image I saw of him, weak and suffering, from my mind.

When we'd finished lunch and I was stacking the plates in the dishwasher, I caught her smiling at me.

"What?" I asked, self-conscious.

"Nothing." She waved a hand. But I saw her looking at the dishes neatly arranged in the bottom bin with satisfaction on her face.

For a fraction of a second I had a wild impulse to rearrange all the dishes and make an unorganized mess. Why? I questioned. To test Grandma? To see if she'd still accept me? Still want to spend time with me?

Grandma looked over at me with a genuine smile. "Shall we sit outside on the porch?" she asked.

I clicked the dishwasher door closed and pushed away my insecurities. "Sure."

We walked out onto the back veranda and sat on the wicker swing. "What's that?" I asked, pointing to a metal tin.

"Tulip bulbs." She stopped the swing. "Come on, let's go plant them."

"Okay," I said.

For the rest of the afternoon, she taught me how to garden. It was quiet, just the sound of us scooping dirt and patting the soil. The rhythm of our work, so in sync and methodical, was peaceful. Calming. I looked over at Grandma. She took her sun hat off and wiped her hair away from her eyes with the back of her hands.

Sure, it was an activity that she picked—her hobby, her passion. And I knew the way she dictated the activity—not even asking if I was interested—would have irritated Mom. But the truth was everything about it—the silent companionship, the cool dirt beneath my knees, the satisfaction of nestling each tulip bulb into its own little cave—it was perfect. And I loved it.

20

Monday morning, Quinton drove me to school again. Since Max and I didn't have any classes together, I didn't see him all day. It was weird. I never realized his absence so much before. I mean, of course I loved how Quinton was at my locker between every class, but I found myself accidentally looking for Max, too. So after school, I decided to send Max a text.

Except he called me first.

"So, I have a question for you," Max said.

"Okay, shoot." I turned the TV to mute.

"I know your natural preference is for cheesy, dentist office love songs, but I've been working really hard to provide you with a solid musical education. But now that you're riding with Quinton, I'm concerned you're falling behind on your studies."

I laughed. "Quinton listens to ESPN."

"As I suspected," he said. "So listen, I want to take you to see this new up-and-coming band Friday night down at the Tabernacle in

Atlanta. I think they're going to be the next big thing. It'll be fun . . . if Quinton doesn't mind."

"Why would Quinton mind?"

"Because you'll miss his football game."

"Oh," I said. "Well, I went to his last one. Plus, I feel like I never get to see my best friend anymore!"

"I know," he agreed. "I hope you can go. It'll be fun."

"Is Minnie going?" I asked, suddenly wondering if this was a friends activity or possibly more than friends. I thought back to the way he looked at me at Quinton's party.

"Nah, she doesn't like concerts. She hates the crowds and the noise."

Hmm, I thought as we hung up. *No Minnie. Just me and Max . . .*

I suddenly felt a twinge of disloyalty toward Quinton. So I dialed his number.

"Hello, gorgeous," he said brightly, and I started to laugh. Then I realized he was being serious.

I casually mentioned going out with Max Friday night. "You know Max and I have been friends since we were really little," I explained.

"I know," Quinton said. "And of course it's okay. I totally trust in you and the strength of our relationship." His voice sounded weird and robotic as he said it, and it gave me a funny feeling.

"Cool," I said. I was happy that he was so amiable, but "strength of our relationship"? We had been dating for two weeks!

"I want you to be happy and fulfilled," he continued, "and I under-stand that I might not be able to fill every need that you have."

"Um, okay," I said, and for a moment I panicked that he could hear my thoughts about Max from a few minutes ago—that he knew I was excited about going to the concert alone with him.

Quinton continued. "I was doing a little research on successful courtship because I want to shower you with special moments and I was surprised to read that one of the nicest things you can do for your mate is give them space. Creative space, fun space, emotional space . . ." He sounded like he was reading off a cue card or something. What was he talking about?

"Ooookaaay," I said tentatively. He sounded more like Dr. Phil than Quinton.

"So, go with Max this Friday. Take the space you need! I want to shower you with special moments," he repeated. "Even if one of those moments is not with me."

"Um, all right," I said. "Thanks."

It was quiet for a minute. My head was all fuzzy. Why was Quinton acting so weird? Could he sense that my heart was torn? I decided to change the subject. "So how was football practice today?"

"Man, Coach busted our balls today. He made us run bleachers . . ." He went on, sounding like the normal Quinton again.

His words kept playing over in my head. *I want to shower you with special moments.* My stomach lurched—because suddenly I was pretty certain this had nothing to do with Max. I realized I had planted very similar words inside his head just two and a half weeks ago.

All week Quinton was affectionate and attentive, driving me to school each day, holding my hand as we walked down the halls and sending me notes in English class that broke the boredom and made me laugh. So any worry I had encountered on Monday afternoon floated away like the bunch of pink balloons Quinton tied to my locker Friday afternoon.

"You are so thoughtful!" I gushed as we watched the helium lift the last balloon out of sight.

"As a kid I always loved letting balloons fly up past the clouds," Quinton said as he opened his car door for me.

As we exited the student parking lot, he turned right instead of left toward my home, but I didn't think too much of it. Maybe he had to stop off at the weight room to get something for his football game that night. But then he drove right past the gym.

"Quinton?" I asked, but he just smiled, turned on his blinker, and pulled onto Interstate 75 heading south. "Where are we going?"

"It's a secret," he said. He drove down the interstate, passing the exit for the mall and passing the next three exits as well. We eased into the afternoon traffic as we drove closer toward Atlanta and I felt a mix of excitement and agitation. I had never had a surprise birthday party or spontaneous road trip before, but at the same time, I had to get home for my plans with Max.

I kind of felt kidnapped.

We drove into downtown traffic and Quinton pulled off at an exit and eased into the entrance to the Atlanta Botanical Garden.

"I've never been here before," I said. "Actually, I've never been to any botanical garden before."

"Me neither," Quinton said as he paid for our tickets. "But when you told me how much you liked irises, I thought, what would be better than a visit here?" He squared his shoulders with pride.

"That's so nice of you," I said and tried to inject some enthusiasm into my voice. *I mean, yeah, I like irises, they're pretty, but it's not like they're my favorite thing in the whole world.* But I looked over at him strutting down the walkway and reminded myself that he didn't know that. He was just being attentive and creative. He was being a good boyfriend. The boyfriend I'd hypnotized him to be.

We walked on the Canopy Walk and let the leaves from the tree-tops dangle on our shoulders. We sat in front of the waterfalls in the Cascades Garden and let the rushing water fill our ears. We held hands and talked easily. As we walked among the lush, green shrubbery, I glanced at my watch. "We should probably head back," I said. "You need to be at the football field in less than an hour, and Max is supposed to pick me up at six."

But Quinton was barely listening. He had his nose buried in a map of the gardens. "I think the Japanese Garden is up here to the left."

I looked at my watch again. "Quinton, I really think we need to go. What if we hit traffic? Won't your coach be mad if you're late?"

"Rush hour's not too bad on a Friday," he said. "It says the Japanese Garden has irises in the spring—I'm not sure they'd still be blooming in late September."

Oh, for God's sake—I just saw a bunch of irises in my locker last week! But he was walking faster, on a mission. He looked possessed.

"Fine," I said, feeling bad. He was just being thoughtful. I sprinted to catch up with him. "We'll go to the Japanese Garden. But we should only stay for a few minutes."

Ahead we saw the entrance and speed-walked past the strolling visitors. The exhibit was small but beautiful, with a glistening pond surrounded by meticulously sculpted trees.

"Damn," Quinton said. "I don't see any irises."

"It's okay," I said and turned to leave, but he just stood there next to an old Japanese lantern, swinging his head to and fro as if a collection of purple blooms were hiding from us under a tree or bush. "Come on, we need to go," I persisted. The peaceful Japanese Garden did nothing to calm my accelerating heart as I saw a text appear from Max. Everywhere I looked, I saw the rigid bamboo fence framing the garden, holding us captive, and I felt a little breathless, trapped. "Come on. We need to go," I repeated.

"Oh, I just feel bad about the irises."

"It's not a big deal. It was fun anyway."

"It is a big deal," he said as I pulled him through the garden and toward the parking lot. "I want to do special things for you. To treat you like a goddess."

Oh no. Those words sound awfully familiar. "Look, Quinton, you are an awesome boyfriend. But you don't have to go so . . . overboard. I like you no matter what. Plus, we can't just abandon our lives to look at some irises. We both have things we need to get back for." I was getting desperate.

As he opened the car door, a funny look washed over his face. "Oh, crap," he said, shaking his head. "You're right. I forgot. I'm sorry."

"It's okay." I reached over and buckled my seat belt.

"No," he said, staring at the dashboard. "It's not. I don't forget stuff. Ever. That's not me. Mom says I'm a human calendar. I don't know what's wrong with me lately."

A wave of guilt swept over me. Could it be an effect of the hypnosis? "Just go." I pointed to the steering wheel and he cranked the car. We flew out of the parking lot and drove approximately ten yards—into the biggest traffic jam I'd ever seen.

"Damn," Quinton mumbled.

I looked at my watch. Max would be showing up at my house in thirty minutes. I quickly texted him: *Running late. Can you give me an extra twenty minutes?*

Sure, Max texted back.

But forty-five minutes later we had advanced about fifteen miles north into the suburbs but still a good twenty miles from Worthington. Quinton's phone rang nonstop. First it was Jake, then Davis, then Hayden wondering where he was. Then, as we were still inching along the highway, his coach called, irate and unforgiving.

"I'm sitting out tonight," he told me after he clicked off his phone.

"Oh no, I'm so sorry."

"It's fine," he said tightly.

But I knew it wasn't. Football meant everything to Quinton, and that's when I started to get a sinking feeling in my gut that maybe my little love spell was more powerful than I realized.

When I got home, I called Max but he didn't answer. I texted him frantically but he didn't respond. "Crap, crap, crap," I said and threw my phone on the floor.

Mom walked out of her bedroom with a robe on and her hair wet, fresh out of a shower. "Where've you been?" she asked, curious, not accusatory. "Max was here." She looked at the clock above the TV. "About an hour ago. He waited for you. Said you had plans."

I sighed. "We were supposed to go to a concert. Was he mad?"

Mom twisted her mouth. "He wasn't happy."

"Shoot," I mumbled and sat on the couch.

"Were you with Quinton? Because his mom called here looking for him. She said he was late for a game."

I didn't answer, just leaned my head back and closed my eyes. I could feel Mom's brain spinning. "No, Mom, not even a kiss, today, okay? We were just looking at some stupid flowers."

Mom sat down next to me and I opened my eyes. "Remember when you were worried that Max was going to forget about you because he had Minnie?" she asked.

I put my hand over my eyes to hide my guilt. "I know. I screwed up."

Mom put her arm around me. "Everyone screws up. Just apologize. And mean it. He's your friend, and true friends are forgiving."

I nodded and felt a small prick of tears, worried that maybe my guilt ran deeper. What if there were consequences to mind control that I hadn't thought about? What if it wasn't all good?

21

Saturday, Quinton was climbing bleachers and running laps in full pads in the brutal afternoon sun as punishment for his Friday escapades. I spent the day trying to get in touch with Max to apologize but he wouldn't pick up my calls or answer my texts. The only good thing that happened was when Grandma called and invited me to lunch on Sunday at the Village Porch in town. The next day, when I pulled Mom's car into the packed parking lot, I saw the Sunday church crowd all dressed up in skirts and blouses, and I glanced down at my vintage wash jeans and American Eagle raglan T-shirt and wondered if Grandma would frown in disapproval the way she always criticized Mom's clothing choices.

But she didn't. When she saw me walk in, she stood up and waved me over to her small square table, her silver charm bracelet clinking with the shake of her arm. She was beaming.

I crossed the crowded restaurant to sit with her.

"I ordered you a ginger ale," she said with a smile. "I noticed that's what you drank at my house last week." She slid an envelope across the table.

"What's this?" I asked, taking it in my hands.

"Open it," she said.

I slid my finger under the sealed flap and opened the envelope pulling out two shiny tickets. "*The Nutcracker*?" I asked, a little breathless. "You remembered." The last time we visited, so many years ago, Grandma and I had decided we were going to see *The Nutcracker* at the Fox Theatre in Atlanta. She said she'd pay for the airfare for me to fly back and for the show tickets. I just needed to show up. But that was the year Grandma and Mom had their huge blowup and the holidays slid by, both of us knowing dreams of *The Nutcracker* were just that—dreams.

"Of course I remember," Grandma said.

I slid the tickets into the envelope safely and handed them back to Grandma. She tucked them inside her clutch.

Grandma folded her hands in her lap. She leaned in a little toward me. "So," she said. "I've heard a little gossip around town."

My hands started to sweat. I thought about Grandma at Mia's competition and panicked at the thought of my hypnosis. I hadn't exactly kept that a secret. But no, Grandma was smiling, showing her perfectly aligned teeth, as creamy white as her pearls.

"I heard"—she cocked her head slightly and pointed her manicured finger at me—"that you are dating a young man. A Mister Quinton Dillinger the Third, to be exact."

"Oh," I said, startled, laughing a little with relief. "Yes, I am."

"I was at Jordan Paul Salon on Thursday and Margaret Williams told me Quinton's mother mentioned it at the tennis club. She said Quinton was just smitten and that you—you were wonderful. She said you came over to help him with his Shakespeare report and that you were so smart." She folded her hands again and straightened her posture. "I knew you'd have a gift for literature. Just like I always did."

The waitress came over and placed our plates of quiche and toast on the white tablecloth. When she left, Grandma reached over and patted my hand. "I'm so proud of you," she said; then she picked up her fork and pierced the fluffy quiche.

As I buttered my toast, I couldn't help but think I didn't do anything.

A refined couple about my grandparents' age walked over. They were dressed up in their Sunday church clothes. Grandma got up, kissed each of their cheeks, and chatted about some charity event at the church. "Lorraine," Grandma said, "I would like to introduce my granddaughter. This is Willow."

I stood up and shook their hands.

"She's dating the oldest Dillinger boy, Quinton," Grandma said, beaming.

"Oh?" Lorraine raised an inquisitive eyebrow. "Judge Dillinger's grandson?"

"Indeed," Grandma said, and Lorraine and her husband nodded their approval. They chatted for another minute about silent auction items while I sat there and smiled uncomfortably. Eventually they hugged and the couple left. Grandma sat back down, smiling at me. "Quinton's grandfather and your granddaddy worked very closely together for many, many years. The Dillingers are a fine family, Willow. Fine. I'm so proud of you," she repeated.

And as I sat there and ate another bite of my quiche, I knew I should just move on and enjoy this time with my grandmother. It was all the things I'd dreamed about—an actual lunch date, tickets to the ballet. But I couldn't stop rehashing all the times Mom said she could never earn Grandma's pride. What had I done, exactly, to earn her approval? "Why are you proud of me?" I asked tentatively.

"Because, darling . . ." Grandma set her fork and knife neatly on her plate. "You're dating the right kind of boy. A good boy. Nowadays, with the stories you hear on the news with teenagers getting into all kinds of trouble with naked pictures on their cell phones and promiscuity, I'm just proud that you had the good sense to select someone like Quinton."

I released the grip on my napkin and breathed. I was about to tell her the story of the irises and the necklace, but then Grandma's face fell.

"Your mother," she said, reaching up to clench her strand of pearls. "Sometimes I think she brought home her boyfriends just to get a rise out of me—I swear I think she did. Some of the boys she dated . . . ugh." She visibly flinched.

"Well, one of those *boyfriends* was my father," I said very softly, very slowly, trying so hard not to get angry. *Grandma said she wanted a relationship with me*, I reminded myself. *She wanted to know the details.* I didn't want to screw that up. I waited for her to apologize, for her to say of course she didn't mean my father. But she didn't. She slid two twenties out of her wallet and placed them on the black folder next to the check, then stood up.

"Willow," she said, "really, it doesn't matter about the mistakes your mother has made, because somehow you've managed to turn out just perfect, with a good head on your shoulders and a strong sense of responsibility. I know what a good student you are. Principal Bigham's wife is a member of the League, you know. I know you're good friends with Dr. Palmer's daughter, Mia. I know that you're making good choices and are a good person and *that* is why I'm so proud of you."

Was I making good choices? I felt my throat go dry.

I wanted to stand up, look Grandma in the eye, and say that everyone makes mistakes, not just Mom but me, too. And just because Mom did things differently from Grandma didn't mean the things she did were wrong. But the words stuck in my throat. Because I didn't want any more fights. I didn't want any more judgment. And I definitely didn't want to hear that certain things were unforgivable, because what would Grandma say if she knew the *real* reason Quinton was dating me?

Grandma had bought tickets to *The Nutcracker* because she wanted a relationship with me, and maybe it wasn't as perfect as a family photo on the beach, but still, it was something, and I couldn't risk losing it.

It should have been enough. All the nice things that Grandma said should have been enough to allow me to overlook her jab at Mom. But still, the entire ride home from the restaurant I re-scripted our conversation to a version where I was gutsier. Not so afraid of losing something I barely had a hold of. In my playbook, I told Grandma that she should give Mom some credit because she raised me as a single parent and if Grandma was so proud of how I turned out, then she should be proud of Mom for how she parented me. The quiche and toast and two glasses of ginger ale sat thickly in my stomach, and I couldn't help feeling guilty, because only in my head was I brave enough to say these things.

When I got home, Mom was sitting at the kitchen table with her checkbook open and an envelope and letter in front of her. "How was lunch?" she asked.

"Good." I smiled, not wanting to say too much for fear I'd explode and spill everything. "What's that?" I pointed at the letter.

Mom made a disgruntled face. "It's a letter from the neighborhood association. Did you know they send you a monthly bill? Homeowner's Association dues just to live here? That's ridiculous. Like I'm not paying a mortgage already."

I sat down and picked up the letter.

"They say it covers road maintenance, upkeep of the clubhouse and activity room. I haven't used the clubhouse or activity room." She gave me a look like, *So why should I have to pay?*

I glanced over the letter. "Didn't they mention the dues when you bought the house?"

She exhaled in defeat. "I don't know, maybe? I've never bought a house before. I had to sign a bazillion things." She shook her head. "I guess it's just another thing I've screwed up."

I thought about a lifetime of Grandma's criticism. I leaned over and put my arm around her. "You didn't screw anything up, Mom. Look, I have some money stashed away from birthdays that you could use."

"Oh my God, no, I'm not taking your money, Willow." She leaned into my arm, and for a second it felt like I was the mom and she was the kid. "Thanks, but I'll manage."

"You always do," I said and felt tears prick at my eyes.

Mom pulled back and saw my glistening eyes. "What's wrong with you? Are you PMSing?"

We both laughed and I flung the letter at her playfully. "Go pay those dues, then." I went into my bedroom and called Quinton. I wasn't intending to, but before I knew it, I was talking to him about my lunch with Grandma, explaining to him that I felt so torn between wanting a relationship with her and loyalty to my mother. When I was done rambling, Quinton spoke in a soft, comforting voice.

"It must be so tough for you," he said. "To be caught in the middle like that. Sometimes I'm just completely mesmerized by you—by how strong you are. How resilient. I really respect how you won't take sides but see the best in each of them. You are wonderful. Beautiful. No matter what is happening in your life, I want you to know I'll always be there to support you."

I sighed a little, because even though everything Quinton was saying was nice, it felt so canned. I didn't feel like hearing about how great I was. I wanted someone to hash out the situation with me. His constant affirmations were smothering me rather than comforting me.

But I didn't want to seem ungrateful, so I thanked him for being so supportive, and hung up. I sat on my bed and stared at my phone. I really wanted to call Max. Max would understand. He had endured years of his grandparents' disapproval of his father. I remembered the hurt in Max's voice as he described their arguments to me. Max would know what to say.

I scrolled down my list of contacts, but when I found his name, I hesitated. I knew he wouldn't answer. So I put my phone down and reached into my backpack for *A Midsummer Night's Dream*, hoping to distract my spinning mind.

Monday morning when Quinton picked me up he seemed really pleased. He wore a small smile of contentment the entire time he drove us to school, and I wondered if there was going to be another vase of flowers in my locker. *Or maybe he's just satisfied with his comforting skills from our phone conversation.* But when we walked into school, people kept looking at me with these bizarre expressions. I checked to make sure I had indeed put clothes on this morning; then I whipped out a compact to see if I had anything on my face, but all was clean.

"What's going on?" I asked Quinton, but he didn't answer, just kept on smiling that little smile he'd had all morning.

We passed a group of freshmen and one of the girls looked at me and said, "I *liked* you!"

"Huh?" I questioned, but she was already halfway down the hall. We reached my locker and there was no huge floral arrangement, no helium balloons. Quinton kissed me good-bye and I grabbed my books, utterly confused. As I walked toward my first class, Georgia came up to me.

"You saw, right?" she said cryptically.

"No. What's going on?" I had a swell of both anxiety and irritation.

"Quinton created a fan page for you on Facebook."

"WHAT?" I shrieked.

"A fan page—like you're a fan of Zac Efron or a fan of the Jonas Brothers. Your page is Be a Fan of My Awesome Girlfriend, Willow Grey."

All the blood in my body rushed into my face. I pulled out my cell phone and logged onto Facebook. Georgia grabbed my sleeve and pulled me into the bathroom to shield me from having a public meltdown. Immediately my screen filled with an image of my face, zoomed in close and red-eye reduced. *Willow Grey is my girlfriend,* the description of the group read. *And she is a goddess of love.* A brick landed in my stomach. *She is beautiful and special and sexy and alluring.* Oh my God. Those were *my words.* The words I had planted in his head! There were several more pictures—pictures I never even realized he had taken of me with his phone.

"Look, you have 247 fans already!" Georgia said.

"He called me a goddess of love!" I shrieked. "On the Internet! Where everyone in the world can see! Oh my God, this is humiliating. How could he not think this would be humiliating?"

"Maybe he thought you'd like the attention?" Georgia suggested.

I thought about all those times I stood behind the curtains and wished I could be front and center like Mom. When I hypnotized Quinton, I thought being pampered and showered with overt gestures of love would make me feel special. And at first, they did. But everything was escalating so fast, now it just felt out of control.

"I really like Quinton. He's so nice, and come on, he's so hot, but I just think there's a basic problem in our relationship." I wanted to tell her the problem was that my love spell was spinning out of control, but I couldn't. So instead I said, "He lays it on really thick, and publically, too. Like the announcement and the love songs at the party? And the constant handholding and all the gifts? And now this. I know some people might really like that, the public displays of affection, but for me, well, sometimes it's a little suffocating."

Georgia's eyes widened. "Are you saying you're going to break up with Quinton?"

"I don't know," I said truthfully. "I don't know what to do."

In third-period English class, Georgia and I discussed the Facebook situation again. Mia walked over and sat down. She pulled out her notebook then leaned over toward our conversation. "I heard about the fan page," she said.

"Ugh," I grumbled.

"What?" Mia asked.

"Yeah, she's pretty pissed about it," Georgia said.

"Pissed?" Mia look confused. "Really? Why? He's just trying to be romantic."

I was tempted to tell Mia that this romance was one big fabrication that was spinning so outside the realms of my intention that it scared me. But I didn't, because Quinton walked into the classroom.

He smiled a cocky grin in my direction that told me he was clueless as to my reaction. He came over to my desk. "Hey, gorgeous," he said in that same lilting voice he used every time he was quoting my love spell back at me.

"Quinton," I grunted through gritted teeth, "please do not post things about me—about us—online."

"You don't like the fan page?" he asked, clearly mystified.

The whole class was listening. I wished he'd lower his voice.

"No," I whispered. "It's totally humiliating. Totally embarrassing. I feel . . . violated."

"I. Am. So. Sorry," he gasped. His eyes were wide with concern. "I had no idea you'd feel humiliated. Embarrassed. Violated." He spouted my words back to me. He pushed his shaggy hair out of his eyes. "I only did it to show the world how great you are. Because you are. Great." He leaned his hands on my desk and angled himself toward me. "Please forgive me."

The entire English class was holding their breath. Even Mrs. Stabile seemed curious, her pen suspended in midair, waiting, like everyone was waiting, for my answer.

I gave a small, quick smile. "Of course I'll forgive you." Because what other choice did I have? Everyone breathed a collective sigh.

Quinton smiled his gorgeous smile and retreated to his desk in the back of the room. As the class returned to normal, I held onto the sliver of hope that maybe this was all that was needed—a little upheaval. Maybe Quinton needed to hear me say what was too much to put a mental stop sign in front of the subconscious commands that drove his actions. And maybe it would bring us back to the way it was in the beginning, when things felt fizzy and full of potential.

On the drive home, Quinton apologized again and I told him it was fine, he didn't need to rehash it. As long as he deleted the fan page we would never have to talk about it again. He was quiet, remorseful, for the remainder of the drive. And I thought maybe the subject was closed. But when we pulled up my driveway, a small smile crept across his face and I caught a glimpse of what looked like a purple velvet carpet on our front porch. I walked up the steps and saw purple petals artfully scattered across the porch spelling out SORRY.

"I had to call every florist in town," Quinton said, "to get enough irises."

I stared at the petal message. "When did you do this?" I reached up to pull the delicate chain away from my neck. The locket suddenly felt heavy, weighing down on my neck.

"I skipped calculus and physics."

"You skipped calculus and physics?" He never skipped class. "What are you doing? You're in the running for an academic scholarship. You're already in hot water with football. You can't throw away your academics, too, just to go pluck flower petals!"

"But they're for you." Just then, as if on cue, Quinton's phone rang. He looked at the caller ID and saw it was Coach Hammond. He answered it and I could hear the yelling from the other end of the phone. "Yes, sir," Quinton said. "I'll be right there." He clicked off his phone. He looked down at his watch. He shook his head and a look of concern crossed his face. "I've gotta go," he said suddenly. "I'm late for practice."

"Are you in trouble?"

"Maybe," he said seriously. Then his face changed abruptly back to smitten. "But if I am, it's totally worth it just to spend these few minutes with you. To repair whatever little problem we had today. Because I never want you to be mad at me. You're so special to me. I can't stop thinking about you." He came over, took my face in his hands, and kissed me. It was perfect—just the right amount of passion and pressure. His hands were soft and strong. But here's the problem: It didn't feel amazing. Not this time. It didn't even feel that good. It felt suffocating, like that damn necklace was pulling me down and his lips were blocking my air. Really, I just wanted him to leave.

Quinton finally pulled away and looked at me with deep, penetrating eyes. "It's like someone carved out a section of my brain and planted you in there." He laughed a little.

I forced a laugh, too, and waved my hand through the air, like, *What a preposterous idea!* Then that familiar lead brick landed smack in the pit of my gut once again.

23

By Wednesday afternoon, Max still hadn't called me back. I saw him once on Tuesday afternoon. He was walking by himself down the hallway. I tried to smile at him and he didn't frown or turn away; he just sort of looked sad and walked right past me.

I sat on the couch after school, trying to work on my English report, but couldn't stop thinking about Quinton and the web I'd spun. I pushed my notebook aside and grabbed the laptop. I stared at the Google homepage, not sure exactly what even to search for. *When hypnosis goes wrong . . . How to undo hypnosis . . .* Finally, a link popped up that looked promising: *How to remove a posthypnotic suggestion.* I clicked on it. I skimmed through the text, getting fearful when it said that hypnotic suggestions could be lifelong if not undone. A flutter of panic swept through me, but then I read something else: *Simply re-induct and de-suggest.* In other words, if I could get Quinton back under hypnosis, I could influence his mind back to normal.

I put the laptop on the coffee table and picked up the phone.

He answered right away with a lift in his voice. "Hey special girlfriend."

"Hi," I said, staring at the instructions on the computer. "I was just thinking, it's been over a month since I did the hypnosis for your sleepwalking and I think maybe it's time for another session. A tune-up! Really make sure you kick the habit."

"Not necessary," he chirped. "You did such a great job the first time around I haven't had a problem since. I'm cured for life!"

Damn!

"And thanks," he continued, "because I absolutely hated the idea of walking around doing absurd things I never would do otherwise."

Guilt, guilt, guilt. "Okay." I tried not to sound so deflated. "Well, I better get back to my homework."

"Hey, I can come over and we can work together."

"No! Um, no, thanks." I softened my voice. I yanked the gold chain away from my neck. "Actually, um, Mia is coming over later," I lied. "But I'll see you tomorrow."

"Okay. Have fun with Mia. Miss you, my goddess." He hung up.

I reached behind my neck and unclasped the gold chain and put it on the end table beside me. The words on the laptop screamed, *Simply re-induct and de-suggest!* Simple—not so much. I was about to start a new search when my cell phone buzzed that I had a text from Mia. *Hey, can I come over?* My stomach felt queasy, like maybe this mind control had gotten so out of control that all I had to do was mention something and it influenced the behavior of someone I'd hypnotized.

I texted Mia back. *Sure.*

Fifteen minutes later, Mia pulled up the driveway and came inside. "Are you working on your oral report?" she asked, seeing the computer in my lap. "I'm sorry, I didn't mean to interrupt."

"No, it's a welcome interruption. Sit down." I placed the laptop on the coffee table and clicked off my Google search about hypnosis gone wrong.

Mia sat down. "So the UGA coach contacted Coach Graham."

"Did you get a scholarship?" I asked excitedly.

"Not yet." Mia slumped onto the couch next to me. "She requested some video clips of me. I guess to show the athletic director and some other people."

"Well, it'll happen, I'm sure of it."

"Coach Graham suggested that I really knock it out of the park next week at districts."

"What do you mean?"

"She wants me to have a 'Mia move'—my own signature move." Mia inhaled sharply. "We decided I should do a triple flip backward in a tucked position." She twirled her index finger in three loops in the air. Her eyes widened. "It's the most difficult move in artistic tumbling. Here, let me show you." She reached for my laptop and clicked through a few links and pulled up a video clip of a girl flipping through the air at a national cheerleading competition.

I thought about my hypnotic suggestions to Quinton—my simple intention to make him like me had spiraled into a borderline obsession. What if my hypnosis to erase Mia's fears had turned her into a reckless daredevil? I shook my head. "No, sorry, I don't think we should do any more hypnosis. Look at that Mia. That looks really dangerous. I bet that girl practiced for a really long time. You can't just expect hypnosis to replace good training."

"But I *know* I can do it!" she insisted, tucking her feet under her legs on the couch. "I'm just afraid, that's all. I've been doing tumbling and gymnastics and cheerleading since I was four, and I know the mechanics of the move—I just need help with the . . . psychology of it. *Please.*" Her light green eyes pleaded. "Everyone is expecting something big from me. My coach, the college recruiters, the squad, my parents. Especially my parents. You don't understand how disappointed my mom will be if I don't get into her alma mater. And my dad? These last three competitions have been the most I've seen him in a year. I don't want to go back to when he's working all the time." She looked so desperate, hanging on to that pointy apex of the pyramid with only her tiny, muscular arms. I never realized perfection came at such a price.

I looked back and forth from the computer to Mia. "Okay," I relented. "But this is it. No more. I don't want you to come over next week and beg me to help you do seven flips off the roof of your house or something."

She bounced up off the couch and clamped her arms around me, surprising me with her strength. "You're the best! The best!"

"Well, come on," I said. "Let's just go do it now."

"Yay!" She got up and skipped toward my room. I followed her, but this time I wasn't filled with the pleasure of being needed. Instead that heavy brick settled in my stomach with the fear that maybe I wasn't being helpful at all.

But Mia was all smiles, planted on the beige carpet and leaning up against my bed. So I walked through the motions, putting her under quickly, influencing her mind not to be scared. Thirty minutes later, when we were through, we walked back into the family room and Mom was sitting on the couch, legs crossed, a very serious look on her face.

"Oh, um, hi Mom," I stammered. "When did you get home?"

"A few minutes ago," she said, eerily sitting there not doing anything. The TV was not turned on. She wasn't snacking or holding her phone or even thumbing through a textbook. She was just sitting. And staring, listening to the *tick tick tick* of the second hand on the clock across the room. "Hi Mia," she said.

"Hi Mrs. Grey!"

"Vicki," Mom corrected.

"Right, Vicki. Good to see you, but I've got to get home, and Willow needs to get back to her English report." Mia gave me a huge grin. "Thanks," she said, and I saw Mom scrutinize our exchange.

I closed the door behind her quickly, before she said anything that would reveal our secret to Mom. I breezed through the family room, picking up my laptop in a flash, and scurried into my bedroom. Two minutes later, Mom peeked her head in. She still wasn't smiling.

"What's going on?" she asked. "What were you two doing?" It wasn't a casual question. She was using a tone of voice I had only ever heard her use directed at old boyfriends.

"Nothing," I said, my heart pumping faster. "Mia and I were just hanging out, talking about Quinton and her boyfriend, Jake. She thinks Jake's not romantic enough, not like Quinton, who's so mushy." I clamped my mouth shut. Too many unnecessary details. I remembered reading that people who lie or are guilty of something often over-explain with too many details.

Mom narrowed her eyes at me, like maybe she'd read that too.

"And why is Quinton so romantic?" she asked, and for a fraction of a second I thought maybe she was thinking about sex again. But then she squinted at me, leaned forward. "Did you *hypnotize* him to be that way?"

Oh crap.

"Are you using hypnosis to get a boyfriend? To get him to treat you the way you want to be treated? Because I overheard a few things from your room and I swore I heard the word *hypnosis* . . ."

My whole body felt hot, panicked. Caught. I forced shock. I bristled up. "What? Do you think that's the only way I could get a guy to actually like me? By *forcing* it? Like I'm so undesirable that no guy would ever . . . just . . . like . . . me?" Without planning to, I suddenly was heaving with tears, gulping in air. "Just because I'm not as pretty as you . . ."

"Sshh! No, I'm so sorry." Mom came over and tried to hug me, but I pushed her away. "Please," Mom said, and she took my hand. "Of course you can get a boyfriend. I'm sorry to even suggest otherwise. I"—she bit her lip a little—"I don't know . . . I feel this void with you lately. Like you're hiding something from me," she said, sounding a little desperate.

"What about you?" I turned it around. "Don't blame the void on me. You're all . . . serious and sneaky, like you're the one hiding something. It's different between us because you never have fun anymore."

"I'm trying to be your mother and not just your friend, okay? I want to set a good example, Willow. I don't want to be the irresponsible parent that can't pay the bills and keeps you out late at night because we're 'having fun.'" She sat down on my desk chair and lowered her voice. "When Grandma called us in Vegas four months ago and told me that Grandpa had a stroke, she said she was afraid Grandpa was going to die and never see me make a decent life for myself. And for you." She blinked her eyes, then smiled weakly. "So that's what I'm trying to do, okay?"

"Okay," I said softly.

"And I'm sorry." She reached out and took my hand. "For accusing you of hypnotizing people." She laughed a little. "I guess it's just the more I learn about using hypnosis for long-term medical reasons, the more I get scared. It's pretty intricate and amazing—the ability to influence someone's mind and bend their will. I guess I'm just afraid I'm going to screw someone up!" She laughed and my heart plunged. "I didn't mean to put that on you. It has nothing to do with you. It was all me and my fears."

I gulped. *Screw someone up?*

"It's okay," I said, forgiving her for her accusation when in fact she was correct all along. She knew me so well.

"Want to go out and get some dinner?" Mom asked, sounding more like herself.

"Sure," I said. "Sounds great." But there was no way I could eat with the ten-ton brick of apprehension filling up my belly.

24

When Mom and I got home from dinner, I took Oompa for a walk to try and clear my head. I walked down the street and turned into the pillared entrance of Poplinger Park. Overhead spotlights lit up the tennis courts to the right, and smaller solar lights hid underneath bushes and plants, lighting up the walking trails. I took the leash off Oompa, picked him up in my arms, and sat down to swing.

"I have really made a mess of things," I said into his spiky fur. He snorted his agreement. My phone buzzed in my pocket. I reached for it, and when I saw it was Max, I frantically pressed the talk button, accidentally dropping Oompa off my lap. He landed with a thud on my pinkie toe. "Owww!" I hollered then, and, although it really wasn't that painful, I just exploded into tears, all the anxiety leaking out of me in blubbering sobs.

"Geez," Max said on the phone. "I admit I gave you the freeze-out, but I was just upset that you bagged on me for the concert. But I'm over it, so stop crying. I'm sorry."

But I couldn't stop crying, which was weird because I typically wasn't the emotional one. Usually it was me rolling my eyes as Mom wept at a Gerber commercial. And Max knew that I was normally pretty levelheaded. I think it freaked him out.

"Where are you?" he asked.

I squeaked out, "The park."

"I'll be right there."

Ten minutes later I had managed to wipe the snot from my nose and smudges of makeup from under my eyes. Max's truck rumbled into the parking lot adjacent to the swings. His headlights shone brightly on me and Oompa, and I hid my face behind my hands. A minute later he was over on the swing next to me, and I was glad to be enveloped in the evening darkness. Oompa jumped off my lap and onto Max's. Max scratched his ear, kicked into the dirt, and started to swing. He didn't say anything, but having him there, my best friend, was the comfort I needed.

I took a breath, looked over at him. "I just had a fight with my mom," I said, not knowing how else to explain the tears. "I mean, of course I'm upset by your freeze-out." I smiled. "But"—I looked down—"that wasn't really why I was crying."

"Are you okay? Is everything with your Mom okay?"

I nodded. I looked back over at him, and the spotlights cast light and shadows on his face and shone little puddles of light onto his hair. "I'm sorry about the concert. I didn't mean to blow you off. It was just—"

"You don't need to explain," he said. "It's okay. I'm sure Quinton wasn't too thrilled with the idea of us going out."

I turned in my swing to face him more, the chains twisting above me. "No, that wasn't it."

"Really? 'Cause Minnie wasn't too happy about us going."

"She wasn't?" The chains began to unwind, spinning me in the opposite direction. I laughed a little, not meaning to sound so happy at Minnie's jealousy.

"I wound up taking her instead of you," he said flatly.

"Oh well, I guess that made her happy."

He looked down at Oompa, whispered something in his ear. Then he straightened back up. "It was fine. I mean, she went and sat through it but she just wanted to be there so you weren't. She didn't have fun. *We* didn't have fun—not the way you and I would have." He stopped swinging and just looked at me. My heart thumped. "Minnie and I are pretty different," he said. "I like action. I like karate and playing my drums. I like music and concerts and doing stuff in the outdoors, and Minnie—she never wants to try anything new. She wants to lounge around and bask in the sun. I just sit there all antsy like, *come on!*"

"But she's so sweet," I said, because I didn't know what else to say.

"Yeah, she is sweet and she's a great person but I don't know, it's not . . ." He paused, not moving his eyes from mine. "It's not like when I'm with you."

My palms felt slick against the chain ropes of the swing. Something was happening between us. For a moment it was silent, only the background chorus of the crickets chirping and the tree frogs croaking filling the air. Max used the toe of his foot to inch his swing closer to mine; then he reached over and grabbed my chain and inched me closer. He started to lean in my direction, and my heart was convulsing now, because I was almost positive that Max was going to kiss me.

Then Oompa sprung up off of Max's lap and his back claws pierced Max's thigh.

Oompa rocketed through the air and ran toward the walking trail nestled in the trees. My heart stopped its frantic beat and plummeted to a screeching halt, because Oompa had run right up to Quinton, who was walking toward us with a huge smile plastered on his face.

"I knew you'd be here!" Quinton called. "I went to your house and your mom said you'd taken a walk, and I just *knew* you'd come to the site of our first encounter and our special date."

Max wiggled off the swing.

Quinton walked closer, and he had a wild look in his eyes, like he didn't even see Max—all his attention was focused solely on me. He got down on one knee like he was ready to propose. "Facebook devotion is too public for you, okay, I accept that. So here . . ." He reached into his pocket, and for a very scary second I thought he was going to pull out a ring. But he didn't. Instead, he brought out a pile of colorful construction paper cut into rectangles and stapled together to form a booklet. "It's a coupon book of love," Quinton announced proudly. "If you're in the mood for a massage . . ." He flipped through the pages and flashed a picture of a stick figure man rubbing a stick figure lady's shoulders. "Here's your coupon! In the mood for a candlelight picnic?" He flipped through and found the appropriate coupon. "Here you go!"

Max looked at Quinton and then back at me. A look I couldn't identify passed over his face. He got off the swing and began walking toward his truck.

I jumped up. "Please don't go, Max."

"I . . . I shouldn't have come," Max said, turning around to face me. "You've got Quinton. He should be the one comforting you."

"Wait," I said. "Max . . . I . . . you . . ." I wanted to say the missing word. *Max, I want you.* Or *Max, I love you. I've always loved you.* But Quinton came up behind me. He flipped through his coupon book for more evidence of his devotion.

"If you're trying to tell me that you need a little alone time," Quinton said as I continued to walk away from him toward Max. "I've made a coupon for that too!"

Max got in his truck, started the engine.

"Max!" I yelled.

He rolled down the window. "He's your boyfriend, Willow. So either go to him or . . . change that." He rolled his window up and drove away.

What? What was he saying? If I broke up with Quinton . . . ?

Quinton walked around to face me. "You're so sexy in this light," he said. "Sexy and alluring."

I put my hands on his shoulders and squared him to look me in the eye. "I swear to God, I'm not, Quinton." I said. "I'm not sexy. I'm not alluring. You are *not* mesmerized by me." I tried desperately to undo the mind control.

"Of course you are." He beamed. "And I am! You're my goddess of love!" He leaned over to kiss me, but I stopped him.

"Look," I said. "I think we need to cool things down a little. Maybe take a break."

"Take a break?" Quinton shook his head. "No, I could never stop loving you! It's like you're etched into my brain!" He wrapped his arms around me and squeezed the very last ounce of hope out of me. I knew I wouldn't be able to reason with him. What if I'd screwed him up forever—just like Mom had said?

The next morning, Quinton showed up to pick me up for school, all chipper and mushy like he never heard a word of my attempted break-up. After leaving the park, Max hadn't answered his phone or any of my texts. I had tossed and turned all night. So this morning, I had zero energy to even care that Quinton hadn't heard me. I climbed into his car and let him go on believing everything was hunky-dory, because what other choice did I have? It was like talking to a brick wall. But I knew somehow I would have to get inside Quinton's head and fix this mess I'd made. And I needed help.

I cornered Georgia in English class and whispered, "I have a problem. A top secret, major problem. Do you think you can help?"

Georgia blossomed at the idea of drama in real life, not just on her TV screen. "I would *love* to," she said. "Your house or mine?"

I thought about Georgia's hovering mom. At least my mom wouldn't be home until after work. "Mine," I said.

"I'll be there." She clasped her hands in excitement.

I told Quinton he didn't need to drive me home and I met Georgia in the parking lot. We were buckling our seat belts in Georgia's lemon-yellow VW Bug when Georgia said, "Okay, spill. I'm dying to know what's going on."

So I took a deep breath and told her everything. She was frozen with shock and intrigue. For once she was speechless. "And here's the thing," I continued. "I think Max actually might like me. *Like me,* like me. I think he wanted to kiss me. But he won't make a move as long as he thinks Quinton and I are dating. And I can't seem to break up with Quinton because he's so enchanted from the hypnosis." I explained how the conventional method to stop a hypnotic suggestion required me to get him back under hypnosis—something I couldn't do since he no longer was sleepwalking.

Georgia was wide-eyed and fascinated. She parked in my driveway and turned the car off. "Well," she finally said, "let's go find a way to re-hypnotize the guy." Then she got out and confidently strode toward my front door.

An hour later, all thirteen of Mom's textbooks were stacked on my bed. "I think the handshake method is your best bet," Georgia said, referring to the rapid-induction method, which stated that you could re-hypnotize someone with a quick jerky handshake. It only worked on people who had been successfully hypnotized before.

"How's that going to work?" I argued. "We've kind of moved past handshakes."

Georgia reached for one of the textbooks again. The she abruptly put the book down. "Wait," she said. "Do you have a video of your mom's show?"

"Our show," I automatically said. "Yes. Why?"

"Because, *hello*, have him watch it. Maybe listening to your mom hypnotize the volunteers will hypnotize *him*."

"That's actually not a bad idea," I said. "I'd have to really set the mood, make sure there's no distractions. Maybe find Mom's CD of ocean waves and play it softly in the background. Oh no, wait, my stereo is broken."

"You could dim the lights," Georgia suggested. "Have soft candlelight."

I went into the living room and rifled through our DVDs until I found it. "It could work," I said, suddenly reenergized.

"And if it doesn't work," Georgia said, "resort to the handshake.

Pop in a horror movie and hold hands. At a scary moment suddenly jump and jerk his hand."

"Yeah." I nodded. A plan and a backup plan. I was feeling good.

Georgia smiled and together we went in search of candles. I felt certain that if I could get Quinton back under my control, I could fix this giant mess I had created.

Friday morning when Quinton picked me up I casually suggested, "Hey, want to come over Saturday night and just hang out? Watch a video or something?"

"Sounds great," he said.

The trickier part was convincing Mom to leave the house. But as luck would have it, Friday afternoon, when Mom came home from work, she told me a few of the ladies from work were going out to celebrate the receptionist, Brenda's, fiftieth birthday.

"Why don't you come?" she asked. "We can have some fun."

I felt bad. I had just the other day spouted that Mom and I weren't having any fun and clearly she had listened. She was trying. But I had a much more important agenda. Once I fixed Quinton, I'd have plenty of time for Mom.

"Sorry." I shrugged. "I already promised Quinton I'd hang out. Plus, it's not like I know your work friends."

She smiled weakly. "Okay, no problem." But as she spoke, she put on her big stage smile—something I'd never seen her use for me before.

Saturday night, five vanilla-scented candles burned on the end table next to the couch. I couldn't play the melodic sounds of crashing waves because of my broken stereo, so instead, I plugged in the box fan and let its soft hum serve as our spellbinding background noise. The lights were turned down low.

When Quinton walked in, he surveyed the scene, and a crooked grin spread across his face. *Oh God.* He probably thought he was getting lucky.

Trust me, I thought. *Fixing your mind will be way better than sex, I promise you.*

"So," I said, "I was thinking maybe I'd play the video of Mom's and my hypnosis show from Vegas. I mean, it's a . . . part of my past I'd really like to let you see." Geez, I sounded just as cheesy as he did.

"Okay, sure," Quinton said, plopping on the couch and adjusting the pillows. Clearly he thought this was all code for *Let's get it on.*

I slid the DVD into the player and pressed play. Oompa appeared from my bedroom. He eyed Quinton stretched out on the couch. Oompa waddled over and sniffed around at Quinton's leg. Then, for the first time, he didn't jump and attach himself. He just snorted one loud snort then lay down next to my feet. It was like Oompa knew Quinton was no longer a threat—that my affections had waned. I reached down and scratched his ears. I sat close to Quinton but didn't touch him. I didn't want anything to distract him from the hypnosis.

On-screen, Mom appeared. She pulled fifteen volunteers from the audience. Slowly she began the hypnotic induction, using her low, sexy voice. I watched Quinton's face. It was softly illuminated by the orange flickering glow of the burning candles. The shadows below his cheekbones angled his features, making him look older, more mature. Sexier.

Oh, I thought miserably. *If only you had liked me without the mind control.*

Mom's sultry voice droned, flat and mesmerizing. *Surely this will work*, I thought encouragingly. Quinton seemed drowsy.

Then suddenly, Quinton laughed. "Do you see what's happening here?" he said, pointing down at Oompa.

On the floor at my feet, Oompa's head had flopped to the side. His pointy ears rested back against his head and his tongue hung out.

Oh, for God's sake.

Quinton laughed harder, clearly not the least bit hypnotized.

I clapped my hands together in one sharp smack. "Oompa!" His head snapped up. He looked at me, blinked his eyes two times, then lumbered across the living room in a zigzag fashion and headed back to my bedroom.

"That is one crazy dog," Quinton said.

I scrambled over to the DVD player and ejected the disc. *Time for plan B.* "Uh, have you ever seen *The Blair Witch Project*? It's such a great movie." Total lie. I hate scary movies. I had to borrow it from Georgia.

Quinton nodded. "Yeah, it's awesome."

"Want to watch it?"

"Sure."

I slid the new disc into the player. I returned to the couch and took Quinton's hand. He smiled down at me. The first preview started. I wrestled my way out of our interlocking grip and grabbed the remote. "Come on, come on," I said as I fast-forwarded through the coming attractions. "Okay, there." I put the remote down and snuggled into him. I took his hand in mine and replayed in my mind the text I had read. The handshake needed to be quick and abrupt, with a jerky flick of the wrist. *Okay. I can do this. I have to do this.*

Suddenly the creepy music began to play—the telltale sign of impending horror. I held his hand tightly. The music got louder. On-screen, a girl screamed.

Quick as I could, I yelled. "AAAAAAHHHHHH!" I yanked his hand and wrenched his wrist as hard as possible.

"Shit!" Quinton gasped, pulling his hand away from my grip. His elbow flailed out in the sudden movement, colliding with one of the five burning candles on the end table.

"Oh no," I screamed as one of the candles toppled off the table and fell onto the ground. The circulating fan blew the flames just enough for them to ignite the edges of the glossy *People* magazine stashed next to the couch

"Shiiiiiiit," Quinton yelled. Definitely. Not. Hypnotized.

I stood up, panicked, as *People* continued to burn. *What to do?* I ran toward the kitchen to get water. I grabbed the first container I saw—Mom's coffee mug—and filled it up from the tap. I darted back into the living room to find Quinton, shirtless, patting out the flames with his Worthington High Football T-shirt. I set the coffee mug down on the coffee table and slumped in exhaustion.

Quinton stood up, holding the charred T-shirt in his hand. If I wasn't so dejected, I might have noticed his rock-solid chest and abs. As he turned, I saw a tiny little scar on the small of his back. Evidence of our very first encounter, when things were just silly and embarrassing. Before all the madness took over.

Above us, the fire alarm began to sound. *Shriek. Shriek. Shriek.*

"What a night," Quinton groaned.

He only knew the half of it.

Quinton got a chair to climb up and disengage the alarm. With each pulsating blast of the siren, I felt the clock ticking, warning me, that if I didn't fix Quinton's head soon, things would only get worse.

25

Sunday morning I stared up at the loose wires dangling down from the dismantled fire alarm. I wished it were as easy to break whatever connections were misfiring in Quinton's brain. Wires I could deal with, but Quinton's brain was turning out to be an incomprehensible challenge. I called Georgia and replayed the night's disaster.

"We'll figure something out," she said.

Twenty minutes later, she arrived at my doorstep holding a small plastic bag. She handed it to me. Inside was a wad of tangled necklaces. "You work on those and I'll search for ideas. Where's your computer?"

I brought the laptop from my bedroom and set it up on the kitchen table. "I've searched for everything," I said, but Georgia sat down and started typing with determination.

I sat down across from her and pulled out the first tangled bundle of chains. Georgia clicked away on the computer, occasionally huffing in frustration or cocking her head in fascination while I used the sharp point of a safety pin to create a small window of separation between the two tangled chains.

"I think maybe we need to investigate other options," she said.

I looked up. "What do you mean?"

"Well, obviously getting Quinton back under hypnosis no longer seems like it's going to happen."

I sighed. "But what else can we do? It said if unbroken, a hypnotic suggestion can be lifelong. LIFELONG!" I was beyond trying to camouflage my panic.

"Right, but listen, I have an idea. In *Midsummer's Night Dream*, the fairy puts a love spell on Lysander to make him fall in love with Helena, right?"

"Right," I said, uncertain where she was going.

"Well, essentially you used hypnosis to put a love spell on Quinton."

Hmmm. "Okay, so?"

"So rather than focusing on undoing the hypnosis, maybe we need to explore how to undo the love spell."

Interesting. "A love spell? Is there really such a thing?"

Georgia nodded and smiled. "Oh, there is. And look, I think I might have found our answer."

"What?" I scooted to her side of the table and peered at the screen. " 'Head Cleaners'?" The page was an eerie shade of plum purple, with sparkling yellow stars twinkling all over the site. In the upper right corner was a candle with the flame's pixels twitching. "What kind of website is this?" I asked suspiciously.

She clicked on a link. "Look, it says she's the number one–rated spell caster for authenticity and honesty and glorious results. *Glorious results*, Willow!"

I leaned in over her shoulder while she read out loud.

"It claims she can formulate a cleansing drink to reverse any spell gone wrong."

"I don't know," I said, leery. "This seems so . . . weird."

"Well"—Georgia threw her hands up in the air—"what other options do we have?"

I looked up at the dangling wires of the fire alarm and recalled the suspicious look in my mother's eyes. The clock was ticking. Quinton was spiraling. It wouldn't take much longer before Mom figured out what I had done. And if she did . . . "Okay." I turned to Georgia. "How does this Head Cleaner thing work? How do you get the cleansing drink or whatever you called it?"

"Well . . ." Georgia puckered her mouth. "It's forty bucks to get a custom-built potion."

I thought about the maxed-out credit card. "I can't use my mom's credit card for this," I said. "She'll figure it out. But I have cash saved that my grandparents send me for my birthday every year . . ."

Georgia thought for a moment. "I have an emergency credit card my mom gave me that I've never used. I could just be on the lookout for when the new statement comes in the mail and grab it before my mom sees it."

"I could give you the cash right now," I offered.

"Deal." She dug into her wallet and plugged the numbers into the computer.

Instantly an online chat box appeared and a prompt asked: *Tell me exactly what kind of cleansing potion you require.*

So I typed in a thorough description of the problem. A little hourglass appeared on the screen, telling me whoever was on the other side was hopefully thinking long and hard about my predicament. Finally the response appeared.

To restore balance and harmony you must concoct the following recipe. Heat it over an open flame and recite the following passage. Then let the person with the altered mind drink this potion, and within twenty-four hours, Karma Cleansing Potion will reestablish proper order.

"O-kay." Georgia clapped her hands together. "Let's see, we need oil and water and salt. . . ." She started rummaging through the cabinets.

I stared at the words. It seemed crazy. A wacky anti-love potion, seriously? But at least it was a plan, and I had run out of any other options. So I read it and joined Georgia in the preparation. "Do you think we should wait and do this tomorrow? Mom's yoga class ends in, like, twenty minutes."

Georgia looked at the clock. "It's up to you. Do you want Quinton's love spell to linger any longer?"

I clenched my jaw and grabbed the laptop. "What else do we need? A sprig of cherry blossoms for new beginnings," I read. "Cherry blossoms?"

"Hmmm," Georgia thought, sitting on top of the counter as she pulled things off a shelf. "Well, all the cherry trees bloom in the spring. Maybe just pull some leaves from a cherry tree?"

I shrugged. "I guess that'll work." I walked outside to the end of our driveway and reached up to pull some drying leaves off the branches from our cherry tree. When I went back inside the house, Georgia was holding a large chili pot in the air.

"Do you think this constitutes a 'suitably large vessel'?" she asked.

"Looks good to me."

She measured out the water, oil, vinegar, and salt and added a pinch of thyme.

I crinkled the yellow and orange leaves into the pot; then we placed it on the stove. I turned the gas flame on and waited until the mixture came to a boil. I held my hand over the pot and read off the computer in a deep, solemn voice. "*Fire warm, fire bright, fire glows in the night.*"

Georgia giggled.

I hushed her and continued. "*Fire shines like the sun. Now the transformation has BEGUN!*"

The front door swung open with a whoosh and Georgia and I screamed. "AAAAHHHHHHHH!!!!!"

"AAAAHHHHHHH!" Mom shrieked in return, clutching her hand to her chest. She stared at us. "What are you doing?"

"Science experiment," Georgia answered quickly. "Look." She turned to me, all serious. "The leaves *did* disintegrate under a certain amount of heat."

"Right, right!" I reached over to the computer and clicked it shut inconspicuously. "So, um, here, let's pour the um, *scientific evidence* into this Nalgene bottle to um, bring to school tomorrow."

"Right," Georgia said, carefully pouring the potion from the chili pot into a Nalgene bottle "Just be careful," she said slowly, "not to mix this up with *Quinton's Gatorade bottle at lunch* because who knows what would happen if he *drank it.*"

"Hmm," Mom said. "I don't ever remember doing science labs at home," she mused, grabbing a Ding Dong from the basket. "But maybe that's because I missed most of my chemistry labs. I was too busy making out with Tommy DeVito behind the art building!" She chuckled then slipped off into her room.

Georgia handed me the plastic bottle. "Guard this with your life."

We nodded in unison both of us hoping for a good outcome.

The next day I wrestled Quinton's blue Gatorade from his backpack while he was busy unloading his football uniform from the trunk of the car. I poured out half of the blue liquid and added our cleansing potion. I shook it vigorously then returned it to his backpack.

At lunch, when he sat down at our table, he had a cup of ice water on his tray along with his pizza. My stomach got all twisted with anxiety. The potion needed to be consumed within twenty-four hours or it supposedly lost its magic. If he waited until football practice, it might be too late. I glanced down at his backpack. Quinton took a bite of his pizza. Mia asked me something, but I didn't hear her, I was too distracted, willing Quinton to get his Gatorade.

Then suddenly he reached down, pulled out the blue bottle, and placed it next to his tray. I sighed relief.

"Are you okay?" Mia asked me. "You're acting kind of . . . strange."

"Oh, I'm fine. Good," I said as I dropped my banana. "Ooops."

Quinton squinted at me. "You're kind of jumpy." He reached for his cup of water.

In desperation, I shot my arm out and knocked the whole cup out of his hand. "Oh, shoot," I said. "Sorry, sorry," I said as ice landed in his lap. I grabbed some napkins and just sort of tossed them into his lap. "No sense in getting X-rated, ha-ha-ha," I blabbered.

Mia screwed up her face. "Did you drink too much caffeine or something?"

"Yeah, maybe," I lied. I sat back down and tapped my toe nervously.

When Quinton had dried himself off, he took another bite of pizza but didn't reach for the Gatorade. So I crafted a quick distraction.

"Look!" I pointed. "Sadie cut her hair into a pixie!" Everyone at the table turned and I swiftly sprinkled some salt onto Quinton's pizza.

"That's not Sadie," Jake said. "It's Mr. Robertson."

"Oh gosh, really? My mistake." I innocently took a bite of my turkey sandwich.

Quinton took a bite of his pizza. His mouth puckered and he reached for his Gatorade. He chugged half of the bottle in one giant gulp.

Oh, thank God.

He ran his tongue over his teeth, then reached into his mouth and pulled out what looked like a bit of leaf. "What the . . . ?" He stared at it.

Cherry blossoms, I thought, *please do your magic.*

All day, Georgia and I sat on pins and needles wondering if and when we would notice a change.

But late that night, Georgia called and said she'd just heard a song dedication on Star 94, the local Atlanta station. *This song is for my beautiful love goddess, Willow Grey,* the DJ announced, then spun some sappy love song.

The next morning when Quinton picked me up he handed me

an envelope. Inside was a white sheet of paper with individual letters from magazines and newspapers cut out and taped onto the paper to spell out: *I will always treat you like the most special girlfriend in the world. Love, Quinton.* When I looked up at him, he had that look in his eyes again—that wild, possessed look. It was starting to really scare me.

I showed the note to Georgia in English class and we both agreed with a huge wave of disappointment that the cleansing spell had obviously not worked. We needed to find another option. And fast.

Georgia reassured me not to fear. The re-hypnosis had gone down in flames. The cleansing potion was a washout. But she had a new plan. I crossed my fingers and thought, *Third time's the charm.*

26

"Voodoo?" I asked, frowning. "Are you serious?"

"I think it could work," Georgia said, and opened the browser on my computer to the website.

Voodoo is the most powerful means a person has to control their situation and make their life better, the description read. Well, I had to admit I liked how that sounded.

We needed to order two dolls—one that would represent me and one that would represent Quinton. Georgia used her secret credit card and placed the order. In the meantime, I needed to collect a sample of Quinton's DNA. The website suggested a sample of hair, snipped directly from the head, as it seemed to work better than samples obtained from a hairbrush.

So the next morning, I stashed a pair of scissors in my purse. On the ride to school I kept my hand pressed inside my bag, ready to grab the scissors and snip, but I decided not to do it while he drove. Last time I startled him, we'd had a fire. We couldn't risk an accident.

"You're quiet this morning," Quinton said, stroking my knee.

"Just tired, I guess." My hands were sweating. *Where should I cut so he won't feel it? So it's inconspicuous? Just behind the ear?*

"Jake told me that Mia told him she saw the nominations for Homecoming Court, and guess what, baby? We're both on the list." He smiled at me.

"Oh wow," I said. I wondered if after Quinton's love spell vanished and we broke up, my sudden popularity would dwindle as well. Probably. But, truthfully, I didn't care anymore. Because I didn't want popularity and attention if it came at the price of permanently altering someone's life.

We got out of the car and walked toward Quinton's locker. I lingered by his side. He looked down at me and smiled a dopey grin. I reached up and ran my fingers through his disheveled hair. My heart rate accelerated. With my other hand I gripped the scissors from my purse. Slowly I sneaked them behind his ear. I sectioned some hair between my two fingers and snipped. *Got it!* I almost yelped with glee!

Quinton ruffled the back of his ear like he had an itch, and I eased the hair clipping into my pocket. *Score!*

"Miss Grey!" A cold, reprimanding voice silenced the hallway.

I spun around. It was Mr. Robertson, the calculus teacher.

"Scissors are not allowed outside the classroom."

"Um, ah, I just had a loose string here hanging from my sleeve. I was going to, you know, snip it off."

"Oh!" he gasped. "Those are not even school-approved safety

scissors. Those look like kitchen shears! They are strictly forbidden on school grounds!"

"What?" I caught my breath.

"You need to come with me," he said, pointing down the hallway.

"Mr. Robertson, come on," Quinton said, but his charms were useless.

"Right now!" Mr. Robertson barked.

I scampered over and followed him down the long hallway. My heart raced. My throat closed up. *Was I going to the principal's office?*

Mr. Robertson went inside to talk to Principal Bigham, leaving me to sit on the hard-cushioned bench outside. My eyes burned. My life was a mess. A complete mess! And just when things couldn't get any worse, who should turn the corner and walk right toward me but Max.

I wanted to dive under the bench and hide, but it was too late. A huge smile broke across his face. He walked toward me. "Well, if it isn't Willow Grey," he joked. "Sent to the principal's office, eh?"

"It's not funny," I said.

"I think it's pretty funny. What did you do?"

I started doing that awful thing were you can feel your nostrils flaring back and forth, your eyes are blinking, and your throat is convulsing, all because there's a big pool of tears just waiting for the dam to break.

"Hey," Max said. "I'm just kidding."

"Well, so maybe I'm *not* adventurous anymore, okay?" I sort of screamed at him. "Maybe I'm not like that brave, hilarious girl you grew up with. Maybe sitting here outside the principal's office scares the crap out of me. Maybe I've just been trying really hard to make everyone think I'm fun and dynamic and cool—the life of the party—but really, deep down, I'm just boring. Dull."

"What are you talking about?" Max asked. He sat down next to me. The warmth of his body enveloped me.

"Maybe it's all been one big lie," I said softly.

"Why would you lie to me?" Max asked. And he had that look on his face that he had at the park—serious, honest, maybe even a little bit of longing. Or was that just me looking for it?

"Or is it Quinton you're lying to?"

I swallowed.

"Because you don't ever have to lie to me. I'll always be here for you, no matter what."

As a friend? Or as more? I needed to know. I had to ask. At the park it had seemed like he was telling me to break up with Quinton. Was I misunderstanding him?

"Max," I said. "I'm—"

The glass door swung open. "Willow Grey," a voice boomed. It was Principal Bigham. And I had no choice but to leave.

I got off with a warning. And they confiscated the scissors. But I still had Quinton's hair in my pocket and a newfound inspiration to fix this mess. Not only did I need to undo the love spell to free Quinton from mind control, but yet again I'd gotten the impression that I could have a chance with Max if I wasn't dating Quinton.

"The voodoo has to work!" I said to Georgia as we sat at my kitchen table and tore open the box that had been FedExed overnight from New Orleans.

"Weird," Georgia said as she extracted the two voodoo dolls. They were made from two sticks tied into a cross with thick stringy wire—Spanish moss, the paper said—then wrapped in fabric. Two stuffed heads were attached and marked with two buttons as eyes. Georgia looked over at me. "Do you have the strands of Quinton's hair?"

I nodded and pulled out the ziplock bag of hair.

Georgia sighed. "He really does have nice hair."

"Focus!"

She snapped back to the instruction sheet. " 'The doll is an energy-focusing tool. It represents the spirit of the specific person you identify.' "

I looked at the diagrams. "It says to affix the DNA sample according to the illustrations, but to be careful not to interact with the doll in any way until you're ready to begin the voodoo." I used crazy glue to stick Quinton's hair to the top of one doll's head. Then I pulled some strands out of my head, and we glued those on the other doll.

"Okay," I said. "We need to spread this red string from his chest to mine. Then we use the corresponding red-tipped pin to stick the string into each doll's heart. This represents the current relationship." We laid the string accordingly and used the pins to adhere each end. "Now I'm supposed to use very sharp scissors to cut the string right in the middle to sever the love." *Shoot.* Our scissors were sitting in Principal Bigham's office.

I went into the kitchen and found a sharp knife. "I don't know," I said. "Maybe we should go to your house and get some scissors. I mean, I think we should follow the instructions exactly."

"How will I explain to my mom why we drove all the way there to get scissors? Plus we need to do this before Quinton's hair strands have been separated from their DNA source for too long. The instructions say that recent connection to the person is vital."

"Okay," I said and held the knife above the string. "Should I saw at it? Like a piece of steak?"

"Here, give it to me." Georgia took the knife and placed it under the string with the blade facing up. In one quick swoop, she sliced the knife through the string. But the rapid movement plucked the pins out of the voodoo dolls and flung them across the room.

"Oh no!" I cried, and raced to pick up the pins. "What do I do? Stick them back in?"

"I don't know," Georgia said, still holding the knife. "Does the red pin, like signify the heart? Are you feeling any pain? Tightness in your chest?"

"I don't know," I said, grabbing at my chest. "My heart has been racing ever since we started this."

"So no change?"

I shook my head.

"Maybe it means now you're *heartless*? Like the Grinch."

"WHAT?"

"No, no, just kidding!" she cried, but I was on the floor, scrambling to pick up the red pins. I raced over and shoved them back into the voodoo dolls.

"Whew," Georgia said. "That was close."

I sat back down and tried to catch my breath.

Georgia looked at the instructions. "Now it says to use a yellow string and yellow pins to connect your hearts to signify that you are still connected, but as friends."

I placed the end of the yellow string over the Quinton doll's chest and jabbed the yellow pin into the fabric.

"Careful!" Georgia shrieked. "Don't break his ribs or give him a heart attack!"

"Okay," I said. Just as I was gently repositioning the yellow pin, Oompa jumped up into my lap, jolting my hand and causing me to make a small tear with the pin. A long strand of Spanish moss poked out.

"Oh my God, you've punctured his intestines!" Georgia said.

"Oh no!" I pushed Oompa down and used the yellow pin to frantically stuff the protruding string back in. "Do you think we should use some scotch tape?"

"I don't know! Let's just get this yellow string attached. Fast!"

I looked down and saw I had frayed the ends of the yellow string. I frantically reached for the knife, sawed a nice sharp edge, and re-stuck the pin into the fabric one more time. By the time the voodoo doll sequence was complete, we were both frazzled and sweating like we had just performed open-heart surgery.

"It's fine," I said, panting. "Everything's going to be fine."

I gently placed the dolls inside an empty camcorder box I'd found shoved in the corner of Mom's closet and eased the dolls under my bed just as Mom walked in the door. She eyed us with a look that made my insides go squishy.

"What are you guys up to?" she asked.

"Oh, nothing," Georgia said, then gave me a wide-eyed *this is going to work* look. She gathered her things and left.

It has to work, I thought. *The clock is ticking. Quinton is spiraling. Mom's getting suspicious. And if Quinton's love spell stays, I may forever lose my chance with Max.*

The next morning when Quinton picked me up, I noticed a rip straight through the fabric at his chest. My mouth gaped open.

Could it be? I reached over and touched the rip. "What happened?" I asked.

He looked down. "Oh man, I didn't even see that."

"How are you feeling this morning?" I prodded. "Does your chest feel funny? Is your heart racing? Upset stomach? Feel like . . . your insides are coming out?"

"No," he said, laughing. "You're weird." He reached over to hold my hand for a minute, then started the car and drove us to school.

All day Georgia and I threw long, anticipatory stares toward each other, waiting anxiously for Quinton to change. For him to suddenly want to cool off our relationship and just be friends. I tried not to deflate when he held my hand as we walked down the hallway. I even ignored it when he offered to hand-feed me potato chips from his lunch. *Surely the voodoo powers would infiltrate his heart any minute now!*

"The instructions said it could take up to forty-eight hours," Georgia reminded me.

But the next day he insisted on putting his arm around my shoulder as we walked from the student lot into school. When I told him it was kind of awkward to walk and half-hug at the same time, he said it was just a show of his growing affection. Still, I held out hope that a change of heart was just around the corner.

But I was wrong. Instead, when we literally turned the corner, I saw my locker covered top to bottom in gold foil wrapping paper with a huge red bow stuck to the center.

"What?" I asked, taking in the Christmas extravaganza in early October.

"Open it!" Quinton said eagerly.

"Open it!" chanted a chorus of excited girls who had congregated by my locker.

I tore the gold foil off in one big swoop, and underneath there was an enormous locker-size photo of me and Quinton. Our faces in the picture I recognized from the picture Georgia had snapped after our bike ride, but somehow he had Photoshopped a beach scene behind us and changed our clothes to a white halter wedding gown and a black tuxedo. He had created a locker-size imaginary wedding day.

"Oh my God!" Mia chirped behind me. "You are so romantic! You totally understand a woman's heart!"

Jake rolled his eyes.

Quinton turned back to me. "Open the locker."

It was the last thing I wanted to do, but with everyone watching, I had no choice but to spin the combination. When I pulled the metal door open, an enormous ten-pound white teddy bear dressed in a tuxedo, holding a fake red rose toppled out onto me and began singing "You Are My Sunshine" in a tinny electronic melody.

"Oh man," Jake said, smacking Quinton on the shoulder. "You are totally whipped!"

"Nothing wrong with a little affection, Jake," Mia said curtly. But Jake kept on teasing Quinton. Mia's face fell, but she tried to play it off.

The warning bell rang and the huddle of people surrounding me scattered. As the crowd dispersed, I saw Max, standing on the other side of the hallway, frozen, taking in the scene. I tried to step in front of the enormous wedding picture, but I could tell that Max saw it. He looked from me to the life-size wedding dress, then back to me. His face was blank. Then he turned around and walked away.

I wanted to yell, *Wait! Please come back!* But he was gone.

I picked up the gigantic teddy bear and shoved it back into my locker. "*You make me HAPPY when skies are gray*," the electronic voice boomed from behind the metal door. As I leaned against the locker door to make sure it shut all the way, a thought occurred to me. "Quinton?" I asked. "How did you get this bear inside my locker? How did you get the irises inside my locker last month? I never told you my combination."

"Oh, I just came by early one morning and started trying different numerical combinations. I think I tried about six hundred different ones until I hit the jackpot."

I stared at him, unbelieving. "Wasn't that a little . . . tedious?"

"Nah." He wrapped his arm around me. "Nothing is too tedious for my love goddess. All I want to do is spend my life pampering you!"

The bell rang.

"Well, thanks," I said, and raced off to class with my stomach in knots. In English I whispered to Georgia, "The hypnosis is taking over his brain! He said the only thing he wants to do is pamper me!"

"What are you talking about?" Mia came up behind us.

"Um . . . just the locker thing from this morning," I said.

"Oh." Mia sighed dreamily. I loved that she was just herself with me now. All honesty—no stage smile or presentation of how she thought the queen bee should be.

"Do you really think it's romantic?" I asked quietly. "You don't think it's a little . . . over-the-top?"

"No," Mia answered vehemently. "I think it's fantastic."

Maybe it would feel fantastic if it were genuine. If the relationship were real. I wondered, briefly, how I would feel if it were Max who was showering me with attention.

At the end of class, Quinton walked me to the end of the hallway. Just as we parted and I felt a swirl of fresh air and freedom from his constant presence, I turned the corner and lost my breath.

Because pressed up against the lockers, in a full-on open-mouthed passionate kiss, were Max and Minnie.

27

I was standing in our kitchen, staring at the still-dismantled fire alarm. "My life's a disaster. The world's most perfect guy is obsessed with pampering me, but all I want to do is run the other way. And the boy I do love is clearly still in love with someone else!"

Georgia paced around the kitchen, twirling a finger in one of her corkscrew curls. "Max could be playing you at your own game." She looked over at me. "He knows your class schedule. He knew you'd be walking down that hallway."

I thought about that while I picked up the large black Hefty bag on the floor. "What's this?"

"Oh. Mom said you were so good at untangling all those neck-laces, maybe you could help with our Christmas lights."

I nodded. "Sure." I pulled a giant mess of green cords and little multicolored bulbs from the bag. It's funny how my heart slowed down a little and my shoulders relaxed as I worked my way into the center of the knot. *If only I could untangle my own life.*

Georgia dug into her backpack. "Do you care if I rehearse while we brainstorm? Auditions for the play are in two weeks."

"No, go ahead," I said.

She flipped through a pile of white papers in her hand. She stood up straight, lifted her chin, and began in a theatrical voice. "Every day I question . . ." Georgia squinted her eyes. "Wait a minute." She dropped her pages.

I looked up from the Christmas lights.

Georgia ran over to the laptop. Her fingers flew across the keyboard as she nodded her head and said, "Uh-huh. Yeah. Bingo."

"What?" I asked.

"I'm trying out for the part of Sister Helen Prejean in *Dead Man Walking*, right?"

"Right."

"Well, Sister Helen is a spiritual advisor to Matthew—the murderer."

"Yeah, so?"

"Sooooo, a spiritual advisor's job is to offer guidance for life's problems. Well, I think we both agree we have a major problem here. Maybe you need a *spiritual advisor*!"

"Are you seriously comparing me to a murderer?"

"Look." Georgia turned the laptop to face me. "Silver Rain can sense your energy field and guide you to healing and transformative options to fix deep-seated problems."

"Who?" I asked as I pulled the long green wire through an opening in the knot, coming one step closer to straightening out the jungle of lights.

"Silver Rain," Georgia said, tapping the computer screen. "She's a high priestess."

This was getting ridiculous. The cleansing potion, the voodoo dolls—none of that worked—why should I expect Silver Rain to have any great solutions? I wanted to be able to fix my mess myself— to have the satisfaction of untangling the final knot and pulling the strands straight again. I didn't want to hand my bag of snarled knots over to someone else to unscramble. But my mind was blank. My heart was distressed. I sighed. "How much?" I asked.

Georgia shrugged. "Each session is tailored to the individual problem."

"That sounds like a lot." I made a skeptical face.

"Well, do you have any other suggestions? We're getting desperate here. Max is never going to stop making out with Minnie if he thinks you and Quinton are designing your future engagement rings! For all we know Quinton is Photoshopping your faces together to create your imaginary offspring! Do you want THAT on your locker?!"

Oompa jumped up off the ground into my lap, a little scared of Georgia's bug-eyed hysterics.

"Okay, okay," I relented. "Let's call Silver Rain."

We put the phone on speaker and laid it on the table between us. Together Georgia and I explained our predicament to the breathy-voiced woman on the other end.

"What you need," Silver Rain pronounced, "is a banishment spell."

"Yes! A banishment spell!" Georgia agreed enthusiastically. Oompa barked enthusiastically. "What's a banishment spell?"

"For sixty-five dollars, I can send you a kit with the appropriate ingredients for a banishment spell. For an additional thirty-five, I'll throw in two hematites—grounding and balancing stones—and a tool to use directly on the problematic person. The direct contact between the stones and the person in question is the most surefire method to expel the negative energy."

"Yeah, yeah, we want that!" Georgia said, and the next thing I knew, she was reciting her emergency-only credit card numbers once again.

Later that night my cell phone rang and I saw it was Grandma. I watched as her name flashed across the screen, but for some reason I couldn't make myself answer it. Instead, I held onto the bundle of entwined Christmas lights, still working on the mess. When I saw the voicemail icon light up, I put down the twinkle lights and listened to the message. Her chipper voice asked if I would like to go to the mother-daughter luncheon at the Junior League next weekend.

"We'll make it a grandmother-granddaughter event, ha-ha!" she announced.

I wished I could call her back and suggest all three of us go. *Three generations of Grey women together*, I could propose. Or that she take Mom—her daughter. But my fingers wouldn't dial her back. I'd thought we were going to be the perfect family, but I was wrong. Her criticism of Mom rang too fresh in my ears. Mom's desperate need for acceptance was still too evident in her sad eyes. And my mess from hypnosis swarmed all around me, making it impossible to focus on anything else. My biggest fear was if Grandma found out, she would judge me the way she'd judged Mom—preventing our family from ever being whole again.

I pulled the green cord one more time through an opening and, magically, the long strand of bulbs untangled. I stretched one end all the way to my wall and plugged the cord into the socket. Instantly the tiny bulbs lit up in a twinkling array of primary colors. I pulled my blinds down and turned off the overhead light, letting the Crayola colors sparkle in my hands and cast my room with colored light. Untangled and illuminated— just how I'd thought my life would be once we started over. Once we reconnected with my grandparents. Once I had a boyfriend. Once I had the spotlight.

But my life was exactly the opposite.

Two agonizing days later a large box arrived. Georgia and I placed it on the kitchen table and used a sharp knife to slice through the thick packaging tape. Inside were four small vials of oil, two flat brown stones, and a large tongs-shaped contraption.

"Interesting," Georgia said as she picked up the tongs and pressed the handles, clamping the ends in and out.

I picked up the instruction manual tucked inside and began to read.

"Peppermint oil," Georgia said, sniffing one of the vials.

"Wait a minute," I said, pointing at the print. "We can't do this."

"Why not?" Georgia continued to press the tongs in and out with fascination.

Oompa came over and sniffed the end of the tongs. He whimpered loudly, then turned and waddled off toward my room.

"Because," I said, "it says using this hematite stone dipped in the banishment potion and applied with the application tool will *literally push the problematic person out of your life.*"

"That's good!" Georgia insisted, still playing with the tongs.

'Listen!" I looked back at the paper. " 'Sometimes the person will find him- or herself accepting a job out of state or moving out of the country. In rare circumstances' "—I raised my voice—" 'the person winds up in *jail*, but this only happens in cases where the person is dangerous.'" I tossed the paper down. "This is *crazy*, Georgia! Silver Rain and banishment spells. What are we doing?! I can't risk Quinton going to *jail*—I've messed up his life enough already!"

Georgia put the tongs down. "Well, how are we going to reverse the love spell, then?"

I thought about asking my mom for help. She had done hypnotism for nine years. She would know what to do. I felt a sting of tears. But she would be so upset with me. "Maybe we can just wait it out," I suggested. "Maybe if I just pull myself away from him a little each day..."

There was a knock at the door. Georgia and I eyed each other with delirium. We ran around wild-eyed, flinging the vials and stones and tongs back into the box. The person knocked again.

"Coming!" I called as Georgia threw a *People* magazine on top of the return address marked *Spiritual Assistance from Silver Rain*.

I opened the door and saw Quinton standing there.

"Hi!" he said.

"Oh, hi," I said, startled. "What are you doing here?"

Oompa came running from the bedroom at the sound of Quinton's voice. But when he saw the large box of banishment tools still sitting on the table, he sniffed, growled at the box, and turned away, running off back to my room.

Quinton pointed to the large red canoe strapped to the top of his car. "I've done some research," he said. "There's a lake up in the north Georgia mountains where one cove is filled with ducks."

I stared at him like he was a lunatic. *Why is he talking about ducks?*

"I've rented this canoe, and I'm going to drive us up to that lake so we can paddle through hundreds of ducks and re-create the love scene between Allie and Noah from *The Notebook*. Remember? Our first date, the first movie we ever watched together?"

"Quinton," I said in a slow, calm voice like, I was talking someone off a ledge, "why are you here with a canoe, talking about ducks and the north Georgia mountains when it's 4 p.m. and you're supposed to be at football practice?"

He just kept on smiling. "Because this is more important. You are more important." His eyes were glassy and dazed.

"NO. NO, I'M NOT!" I stated emphatically. "You're going to mess up your chances for the football scholarship. I can't be responsible for that!"

"You know, I've been thinking," Quinton said calmly. "We haven't discussed after graduation. I need to know where you plan on going to school so I can tailor my applications."

"No, no, no!" I grabbed his shirt. "Look at me! Your future does *not* revolve around me!"

"Your eyes," he mused. "They're so mesmerizing."

"Oh, for Pete's sake." I let go of his shirt, thwarted. "I can't go up to the mountains today," I said. "I've got things to do."

He smiled. "No problem. Rain check?"

I forced a smile. "Okay." I turned and walked back inside. "Open that box," I said to Georgia. "Desperate times require desperate measures."

All night I fidgeted on the couch, waiting for Mom to go to sleep. I crossed and uncrossed my legs.

"Oh look," Mom said, flipping through the channels. "*The Notebook* is on."

"No! Turn it off!" I said a little too sharply.

Mom looked over at me. "Is everything okay? You're acting strange."

"I just, um, I'm tired of this movie. I just saw it last month with Quinton in the park, remember?"

"Right," she said slowly, still looking at me inquisitively. "Is everything all right between you and Quinton? I haven't heard you talk about him lately."

I slumped back into the couch.

"What's wrong?" she asked.

"Oh, I don't know. I think maybe he likes me a little more than I like him."

Mom nodded understandingly. "Feeling smothered?"

I nodded. "Like I can't breathe. Like this stupid locket he gave me is fifty pounds and dragging me down."

Mom reached behind my neck and unclasped the necklace. She placed it on the end table next to her mug.

It felt so great to talk to her, like old times. I just wished I could have been honest with her.

Mom put her arm around me. "I think it's time for you to cut ties," she suggested. "Move on to greener pastures."

I sighed. *If only it were that easy.*

Mom squeezed my arm in sympathy, then got up and went to her bedroom. I waited quietly by her door until her breathing turned slow and rhythmic; then I whipped out my phone and texted Georgia. *It's GO time.*

28

I met her on the front porch and we snuck back inside the house, where we mixed fifteen drops each of pine oil, peppermint oil, rosemary oil, and olive oil from the small brown vials into a cup. We dropped the two flat stones into the mixture, careful not to splash ourselves with the banishment potion, as the instructions said the oils were very potent. Then I used the clear plastic gloves provided to lift each stone from the mixture and adhere them to the pronged ends of the long tool. I removed the gloves and scrubbed my hands.

Georgia pulled out two pairs of black yoga pants and two black hoodies. I climbed into them then slipped on the black cap she handed me. I felt like a cat burglar.

"Isn't wool a little warm for October?" I whispered.

"We need to camouflage."

I nodded and tucked the ends of my blonde hair up under the cap.

We loaded everything into Georgia's dad's truck and drove through the dark night toward Quinton's house.

"We can't park in front of his house," I hissed.

"But the ladder?" Georgia whined. "What are we going to do, carry it a mile?"

I bit my lip and looked around. "Just go a little bit down the road."

She drove three houses down and parked.

We got out. I stuffed the pronged banishment tool into the kangaroo pocket of my hoodie. We quietly shut the truck doors and tiptoed around to the back and extracted the large metal ladder from the flatbed.

"You take the front. I'll take the back," I instructed.

We heaved the ladder off the flatbed, gripping each end between our hands. It really wasn't too heavy, just cumbersome. We darted between Quinton's house and the neighboring brick colonial, whacking off the tips of a boxwood shrub with the swaying ladder.

"Sorry," Georgia called quietly.

We turned toward the back of the house and I pointed up to the window at the far left of the second story. We set the ladder down into the grass.

"Okay." Georgia lifted one end of the silver ladder and I grabbed the other side and we hoisted the opposite end up into the air until it crashed against the brick house with a whack.

"Ssshhh!" Georgia and I yelled at the ladder.

Something bolted from the shrub beside us.

"Ahhh!" I screamed as a squirrel scurried over my foot and climbed the young, spindly tree next to the house.

We swung our heads back and forth in search of Quinton's

family, neighbors, or local policemen, whom we were certain heard the racket. When no one appeared with handcuffs, I pulled the black wool cap further down on my forehead and Georgia copied me. She held the bottom of the ladder as I climbed the rungs slowly, sweating as the top ends scraped loudly against the brick with each movement I made.

Georgia began to climb up the ladder behind me, until we were both near the top, ready to enter the house.

I stood there on the top rung and wondered how it had gotten to this point. A week ago I was crying because I was sent to the principal's office and now here I was breaking and entering—a felony. Or at the very least, a misdemeanor. I couldn't believe the turn my life was taking. The whole situation seemed like my hair: The more I tried to fix it, the more of a mess it became. But what could I do? Hair was just hair, but this was Quinton's mind. And my life. I had to repair the damage I'd done.

To my relief, I saw that the window was open. Keeping one hand on the ladder, I used my other hand to jimmy the screen up. It required more force than I expected, and I heaved with one big push. The screen screeched up and a huge puff of yellow pollen dust shot out from the window ledge and hit me in the face. I immediately coughed and spluttered.

"Ssshh!" Georgia said, and I clamped my fist over my mouth, but my chest kept convulsing.

Inside, Quinton tossed in his bed.

I ducked down, hitting Georgia in the head with my butt. "Sorry," I gasped between coughs. Finally, I caught my breath and my hacking died down. I looked down at Georgia. "Ready?"

I swung my leg over the windowsill and crawled inside Quinton's bedroom. It was dark inside, just the neon glow from his digital alarm clock lighting the space. Suddenly a burst of fear shot through me. *I can't do this! What if I get caught? How would I explain myself?* I squinted over at his desk and noticed that his stacks of college applications, once so neatly organized, had fallen to the floor. Instead, covering the desk was a sheet of heavy-duty art paper, a palette of watercolor paints, and a paintbrush. I leaned closer and saw that the paper was covered in black lines and numbers—like a paint-by-number set. As I focused my eyes, I realized with horror that the image was me. I put my hand to my mouth. He had sent a photo of me to some company that had created a paint-by-number canvas in my image.

This had to stop. I turned back to Georgia with renewed courage. I pulled the banishment tool from the pocket of my hoodie, and crept quietly over toward his bed.

He looked so peaceful sleeping on his side with his knees pulled up and his hand draped over the top of his plaid bedspread. His perfectly bowed lips were parted just a sliver and his golden brown hair, shimmering in the light of the full moon, was rumpled and cascading over his forehead. He really was beautiful. I glanced around his room—so neat and tidy, all his trophies dusted and arranged according to size. *He is such a great guy,* I thought. He was the perfect boyfriend—for a short time. Before everything went so horribly wrong. And maybe he would have been in real life, too—if I hadn't hypnotized him to be something he wasn't. *It's not fair what I've done to him. I need to fix it. To undo my mistakes.*

I pressed on the tool, opening the ends of the tongs with the flat stones, and held it up to his head. I opened them more so the space was wide enough to place each stone on his temples like the diagram demonstrated.

Georgia started to giggle. "Sorry!" she whispered. "It just looks funny. Like you're giving him electric shock therapy."

"Hand me the metal stick," I whispered.

Georgia reached into her pocket and produced the long, thin metal probe.

I held the tongs with my left hand, making sure to keep the stones on his temples, and used my right hand to bang the metal stick against the handle of the tongs. The entire tool began to vibrate, making a soft humming noise like a tuning fork.

Quinton bolted up in bed like he'd been struck by lightning.

CRAAAAAAAP!

Georgia and I hit the floor like we were bowling pins knocked down. We wormed our way under Quinton's bed as he jumped out of his covers, searching around his room all disoriented.

"Who's there?" he asked manically.

"Oooh, he sleeps with no shirt on," Georgia whispered. "Look at those pecs!"

"Hush!" I elbowed her.

Quinton walked over to the open window and stuck his head out.

Damn, we're going to get caught! How am I going to explain this?

As he turned around, Georgia and I both saw the banishment tool lying in the middle of the carpet. He was walking right toward it. He was going to trip right over it! Georgia reached up and pulled off her wool cap. She angled back her arm as best she could in the confined space under his bed and whipped the cap across the floor.

It flew out from under the bed, skidded across the carpet, and landed on the opposite side of the room.

"Who's there?" Quinton asked again, walking briskly to the other side of the room.

Without hesitation, Georgia and I slid out from under the bed, crawled hastily on hands and knees across the carpet, picked up the banishment tool, and flung ourselves out the window. Georgia scurried down the ladder. But when I heaved my legs across the windowsill, I missed the swaying top rung, and my leg crashed into the side of the house. I held onto the top edge of the ladder as it started to lean, then slide, then fall, scraping me along the scratchy brick and mortar of the house until I plunged into the spiky leaves of the shrubs. The ladder slammed down into the grass beside me in a racket. Suddenly, the sprinkler system turned on, sending a misty waterfall down on me, as I hovered in the shrubs.

"Oh my God, are you okay?" Georgia was by my side.

Above us, Quinton stuck his head out the window. "Who's there?" he called down.

We stayed hidden in the bushes until he disappeared back inside his room.

Quickly we got up and hoisted the ladder up off the ground. My hip ached, but we had no time to dawdle. So I hobbled as fast as I could, awkwardly clutching my side with one hand and the ladder with the other.

We made it back to the truck, breathless from exertion and relief.

"Holy crap," Georgia said when we were far enough away to feel like successful fugitives. We both burst into a fit of exhaustion- and anxiety-induced giggles.

Georgia drove quickly across town. In the distance, the first slivers of sunlight were peeking over the horizon.

The next morning Quinton picked me up for school. As I climbed into the car, I noticed it right away: Quinton's sideburns. They were singed from the banishment tool! I started to panic. *He has to know. He knows we were there last night. He thinks I tried to hurt him.*

I was stiff. Rigid. Like if I moved even an inch, Quinton was going to snap his head toward me and say, *I know everything!* I wished he would talk to me. Instead, he had his attention focused on his driving and the damn ESPN announcer on the radio. I could feel the tension in the air. I wasn't caught by the police, but I was caught by Quinton. And that might have been worse.

He pulled into the student parking lot and parked. He sat in the driver's seat for a minute and I braced myself. He turned to face me. "I dreamed of you last night," he said.

"What?" I asked, thinking I heard wrong.

"I dreamed that you were an angel floating around my head and sprinkling me with light beams of love." He smiled and unbuckled his seat belt. Then he walked into school in a delusional stupor.

As we walked, I texted Georgia. *OMG, his sideburns are singed! He has burn marks on his temples!*

She texted back. *Does he look like Frankenstein?*

GEORGIA!

More importantly, she texted, *was he at all suspicious about last night? Did he mention anything?*

I glanced over at him, happily walking toward his locker with a dopey grin on his face. *He said he had a weird dream, that's all.*

Still lovey-dovey? she asked.

Still lovey-dovey, I texted back.

Don't lose hope.

In English class we began our oral report presentations. First up was Kayleigh Mathews—a quiet girl whose topic was the character Hermia's idea of love.

When Kayleigh finished, Mrs. Stabile announced that Quinton was up next for his report. He walked to the front of the room looking relaxed and assured. He sat down on the chair at the front of the room but then angled it so it was facing directly toward me. He cleared his throat.

"Let me sing you a love song," he said without reciting his topic, and I tensed a little. "About what's in my heart." He touched his chest with two fingers. "Irises refuse to bloom whenever we're apart."

My stomach knotted. *What was he talking about?*

There was a general murmur of confusion.

"I've held others before, but it was never like this," Quinton's eyes bored into me. "My thoughts revolve around you in heavenly bliss."

Mrs. Stabile shuffled through papers on her desk. "Quinton," she interrupted. "I'm a little confused. Your assignment was to do a character analysis of Puck." Quinton looked at her blankly, and she sighed. "You know, the quick-witted sprite who sets the play's events in motion with his magic?"

Quinton just smiled at me, holding his index cards in his hand.

"I'm sorry if you accidentally thought you had a different topic," Mrs. Stabile said. "Do you think maybe you could just talk off the cuff a bit about Puck's capricious spirit and humor? Maybe touch on how he is good-hearted but capable of cruel tricks like using the magic flower and love spell to create wild confusion?"

"I'd rather just finish my love poem for Willow," he said. "It came to me last night in the middle of a bizarre dream—like an electric jolt of inspiration."

The muffin I ate for breakfast felt heavy in my stomach.

"I have to feel your tender touch. . . ."

"Mr. Dillinger," Mrs. Stabile said sharply, "I'm willing to give you some leeway here, but no, you may not recite a love poem to Ms. Grey in my classroom. Now speak a little about Puck's character or I'll have no choice but to give you a zero."

But Quinton kept on spouting lines of mushy devotion. Mrs. Stabile shook her head and used her red pen to scratch notes in her book. But what she didn't realize was that Quinton really should have gotten some credit after all.

Because, sadly, the description of Puck and his cruel tricks sounded an awful lot like me.

"It didn't work," Georgia said into the phone that was resting on the table between us. "We've given it two days and nothing has changed."

Silver Rain breathed heavily on the other end. "Did you follow the instructions precisely?"

"Precisely!" I cried.

"And you're absolutely sure you made direct contact?"

"Oh, we're sure," I answered. "There are burn marks to prove it."

"Hmm," Silver Rain mused. "If banishment didn't work, I think the answer is a Cut the Mojo love charm."

"Huh?" Georgia and I both said at the same time.

"You need to create a talisman—that's a charm made out of dough. . . ."

"How much?" I cut her off. "Because I'm going to be broke by the time this is all through."

Silver Rain sighed. "Well, since the banishment didn't work, I'll give you the recipe and instructions for free. You just need to provide the materials."

Georgia grabbed a pen and paper and together we took notes as Silver Rain assured us that this would work. She was positive.

I called Quinton and told him I'd be unable to attend his football game Friday night, but Georgia and I had a pressing matter to take care of. I thought maybe he'd be aggravated, but of course he wasn't.

"I'll pick you up Saturday to go to Mia's competition," he said cheerily.

"Okay. Good luck," I said, and we hung up.

Georgia and I mixed the dough recipe using salt, flour, and water. We shaped the dough into a small, charm-size heart then used a knife to carve an X through the center. I held my hands over the dough and recited Silver Rain's words: "*You were once my burning desire. You once lit my heart on fire. I loved you then you see, but the flame is gone: Let me be. But together we stay, friends all the way.*" I carved my initials into the back of the charm and placed it on a sheet of aluminum foil. I slid it into the hot oven.

Twenty minutes later Mom walked in. "Yum, what are you baking?"

"Cookies," I answered, and smiled at Georgia: It had been her idea to slip out to the grocery store to buy some slice-and-bake chocolate chip cookies.

Saturday, when Quinton picked me up, I had the Cut the Mojo charm safely wrapped in tissue and nestled in the pocket of my jeans. Georgia was going to swipe a chain from her mother's jewelry store long enough to let the charm hang right above his heart. We drove forty-five minutes to the high school where the regional cheerleading competition was held.

When we arrived at the gymnasium, Quinton spotted Jake and Hayden high in the bleachers and climbed up toward them. I saw Hayden sitting next to mousy Sarah. They were laughing and flirting with each other. Well, I thought, at least there was that. With all the mayhem I had created with Quinton, at least I could tell myself I had helped Hayden and Sarah. And I had helped Mia. I hoped God graded on a bell curve where some of the good could cancel out a lot of the bad.

I scanned the bleachers looking for Georgia but my eyes fell on Max. He looked over and saw me. I tentatively waved. He smiled and gave a quick wave back. Then he turned and sat next to Minnie. It made me sad to think that we had crossed the line from friends with potential to barely friends at all.

Across the gym, Georgia spotted me and began to wave. I flagged her over. She climbed the bleachers and squeezed in next to me. Sarah smiled at Georgia.

"Heard you did great at drama tryouts," Sarah said.

Georgia smiled. "Thanks."

After a few minutes of chatting, Georgia gave me a knowing look and said, "I need to go to the bathroom before it starts. Want to come?"

"Sure," I said. We got up and walked back down the long set of bleachers, deciding to find a bathroom that would be empty and quiet. As we wormed our way through the shuffling crowd, a woman caught my eye, sitting on the opposite side of the room. She was wearing a powder blue top and her silver hair was coiffed into a glossy bob. *Could it be?* My heart thumped. *Why would Grandma drive all this way?* I squinted and thought of her unanswered invitation to the Junior League luncheon and the two more voice messages she'd left since then. It was unlike me to ignore her calls—we both knew that. But as the mess with Quinton escalated out of control, I found myself pushing Grandma away. It seemed inevitable that this fiasco would soon erupt, and if Grandma found out I had used hypnosis just like Mom—actually, in a worse way than Mom ever had—I didn't even want to imagine what she would think about me.

Georgia tugged on my sleeve, and the next thing I knew, I was swept through the open doors away from the crowds and down a long hallway. We ducked into a girl's bathroom, and crammed into a stall together. Georgia pulled a thick silver chain out of her pocket and we threaded it through the round opening we had punctured in the dough love charm.

I held it in my hand with a determined look on my face. "It has to work."

"It *will* work," Georgia said.

We nodded one sharp nod of solidarity, then headed back into the gymnasium. As we squeezed through the ever-thickening audience, I scanned the opposite bleachers for powder blue, but it was just a sea of colors, all blending together into a hazy rainbow. We climbed toward the top, and I sat next to Quinton. Georgia took her seat just behind us, next to Sarah and Hayden.

"I have something for you." I smiled demurely at Quinton.

"Oh yeah?"

"I made it." I pulled out the tissue-wrapped love charm and handed it to him.

He pulled open the ends of the white tissue wrap. "You made this charm for me? That's so nice."

"Here, let me help you put it on," I said, unhooking the silver clasp. As I reached the ends of the necklace toward his neck, Quinton's forehead wrinkled up.

"Wait," he said, pulling the charm closer to his eyes. "Why is there an X through the heart?"

"Um . . ." I suddenly felt hot and a little dizzy. What if it was too obvious? "It's um, because . . ."

Georgia leaned in between us. "X marks the spot," she said quickly. "Like, *there he is—that's my man. That's the heart that belongs to me.*"

"Right, right." I nodded furiously. "X marks the spot!"

"It almost looks like it's cutting the heart in half," Quinton observed. Quite rightly.

"Because half of your heart belongs to Willow now, right?" Georgia said, grabbing the chain. "Here, let me help you get it on. It'll be easier for me back here."

"Wait, I want to look at it some more," Quinton said.

Just then a fit woman with a swingy ponytail positioned high on her head took center stage, tapping the microphone and welcoming our high school squad and supportive fans. The crowd erupted into applause, and all around us students stood up and clapped. Quinton stood up and I reluctantly folded the necklace back into my hand. I turned around and gave Georgia a desperate look. When the crowd returned to their seats, Georgia reached over and took the necklace from me.

"Here," Georgia said. "Let me help you clasp this."

The cheerleading squad took their positions on the mat below. Music pulsated from the ceiling and thumped through the wooden bleachers beneath us.

Georgia placed the necklace around Quinton's neck, but he swatted at her hand. "Hold on," he said. "I can't get a good look at it."

Georgia shot me a look that screamed, *Distract him so I can get this thing around his neck!*

"Oh, Quinton," I said, leaning toward him. "I just wanted to make you something that um . . . physically represented my feelings." On the mats below, the cheerleaders did running round-offs followed by back tucks. I grabbed Quinton by the collar of his shirt and pulled him into a passionate kiss.

Georgia strung the silver chain around him and clasped the hook. The love charm plopped against his T-shirt with a plink.

As I pulled away I saw Mia, standing on the mat, looking up in my direction with panic etched across her face. She was waiting for my signal to rub her fingers together. I tried to stand but Quinton pulled me toward him, going in for a second round of kisses. I tried to give him a quick, closed-lip smooch, but then he was angling me to sit on his lap. I yanked away, tried to stand again, tried to turn to catch Mia's eye, but it was too late.

She was springing up into the air, doing her triple flip backward in a tucked position. As she spun around for the third time in the air, people jumped up off their seats, applauding with fury.

But then the crowd gasped collectively. Mia hadn't released fast enough, and she crashed down onto the mat, still partially tucked. There was a deafening thud.

The crowd went silent.

The team froze.

The music stopped.

The stadium was bone-chillingly quiet as Coach Graham ran over toward Mia. Mia's mother and father flung themselves off the bleachers and onto the mat. Mia's mother bent down to embrace her but Dr. Palmer put his hand up to stop her. He said something inaudible but he gestured to the awkward position Mia was sprawled on the mat.

Mia's mom burst into tears, causing the mascara to run down her face.

Her dad turned to Coach Graham and it was easy to see from his lips that he said emphatically, *Call 911.*

30

The drive to Worthington Medical Center was torture. I kept telling Quinton to go faster, follow the other students' cars that kept cruising past us.

"I know you're worried," he said. "But it's not worth risking a speeding ticket or an accident just to arrive there five minutes faster."

I slumped back into the passenger seat as I saw Max's black Ford pickup speed past us in the left lane. I sighed with worry.

Quinton reached over and grazed his hand along my cheek. "It'll be okay," he said in an artificial voice.

Quinton's craziness was my fault, too. My tally was climbing— the number of people whose lives I'd damaged was growing. *Please,* I silently prayed. *Please do not let Mia be seriously hurt. Do not let her be immobile or paralyzed because of me. Please.*

The guilt pummeled down on me until I couldn't take it any-more. I pulled out my cell phone and dialed my mom. To confess? I wanted to, desperately. Like maybe if I admitted my awful mistakes it could somehow make them disappear. But when she answered with her perky, "Hey kiddo," I just started to cry. Quinton grazed his hand on my face again which made me weep louder.

"What's wrong?" Mom asked.

Everything. Instead, I told her that Mia had fallen and was being rushed to the hospital.

"I'm getting in the car right now," Mom said. "I'll meet you in the lobby."

I felt myself relax a little, just knowing she'd be there. By the time we found a parking spot in the jam-packed visitors' lot and ran into the waiting room, most of the senior class was milling around, eating candy from the vending machine and talking in hushed tones. Mom weaved her way across the crowd and took me in her arms.

Georgia came over to us. She was uncharacteristically quiet, just smiling a small, tight smile of concern for a friend. To the right of us, Coach Graham was consoling the squad members. "She's going to be all right," she said, although there had been no word from the doctor yet.

"I told Mia the triple flip was too risky," one of the cheerleaders said, tears welling in her eyes.

"I know," Coach Graham agreed. "She kept pushing the limit. I warned her that she could injure herself but"—she shook her head slightly—"it was like she had something to prove."

I thought back to our hypnosis sessions, all the times she said these difficult moves were expected of her. *Could that have been all in her head? Could all of that pressure to overachieve come from some insecure part of her own mind?*

"It was like—" one of the cheerleaders began. "I don't know, it was sort of like she was hypnotized when she would get ready to do those dangerous stunts."

My heart froze in my chest.

"What do you mean?" Coach Graham asked.

"It was like she had no fear," Sadie agreed. "She'd be nervous a few days before, but then as soon as it came time to do the stunt, she'd be strangely detached—like her mind was somewhere else." Sadie lowered her voice to an insinuating tone. "And she'd always want to know if Willow was in the stands."

Boom, boom, boom. My heart went into overdrive.

"Willow?" Coach Graham. "The new girl?"

"Yeah," Sadie said. "The one from Vegas. The one who had a hypnosis show."

I felt Mom stare down at me. *I had told people about our show.*

Georgia began to squirm. "Um, I could use a drink," she said. "Want to come?" She reached for my arm.

"We all saw Willow do hypnosis at a party," a different cheerleader said.

There was a general mumbling of agreement. I began to panic. My hands started to feel sweaty.

"Do you think Willow was hypnotizing Mia to do more dangerous stunts?" Coach Graham asked Sadie. Her voice thundered across the hospital lobby. "Where's Willow?"

Suddenly, a thousand sets of eyes turned toward me. Students, parents, teachers—they all looked at me with both confusion and accusation written across their faces. Then I saw Max's denim-blue eyes looking at me with an unfamiliar expression—one I thought was a mixture of incredulity and disappointment. *Boom, boom, boom.* My heart banged uncontrollably. The stares were smothering me. I couldn't breathe.

Quinton placed a consoling hand on my arm, but I brushed it aside. Then I saw my mom. I couldn't stand the pained expression on her face. I needed to escape. I scanned around frantically for an exit. This was it—all the chaos of my life for the past few months was boiling over. I tore through the packed waiting room, squeezing between the crowds, ignoring the calls of my name, and raced through the electronic sliding glass doors out of the hospital. I bent over, hands on my knees, and tried to catch my breath. My chest squeezed in tiny bursts of air. My head was spinning. My heart was pounding.

The sliding doors of the hospital opened and Quinton emerged, shielding his eyes from the sun and scanning around for me. I dropped to my knees and hid behind a white ambulance. I took another deep breath, trying to calm my drumming heart. Suddenly I saw a pair of black heels stop beside me. I looked up and saw my mother.

"Please tell me it's not true about Mia. *Please* tell me you're not that stupid." She sounded desperate.

I burst into a fresh swell of tears. "I'm so sorry."

"What were you thinking?" she gasped.

"I don't know!" I sobbed. "I'm so sorry." I leaned back against the ambulance, the weight of all my mistakes crashing onto me.

"Do you have any idea how much damage you may have caused? That girl is lying in a hospital bed!"

I covered my face with my hands, sobbing and shamed.

"I told you to leave hypnosis behind!" Mom cried. "I'm trying so hard to earn back Grandma's respect and," she blinked her eyes. "It's not an easy thing to do. If she hears about this, she's going to think"—her voice caught—"I corrupted you—her perfect granddaughter."

"I'm *not* perfect," I garbled. "I'm terrible. I've been lying to everybody—trying to do things I didn't know how to do, trying to be someone I'm not."

"Why?" Mom asked with tears in her eyes.

I shook my head. "I don't even know," I admitted. "It was a new place. I thought maybe I could be a new person." I sniffed. "Someone . . . fascinating. But I'm not." I covered my eyes and started to cry again. "I'm just selfish and awful and I hurt innocent people. Oh my God, what if Grandma *does* find out?" I crumbled at the thought.

Mom wrapped her arms around me, pulling me into a tight hug. "It'll be okay," she whispered soothingly, changing her demeanor entirely. She gently ran her hands through my hair. "Everything's going to be okay."

I inhaled sharply. "She wanted a relationship with me. She bought tickets to the Nutcracker. But now, if she hears this . . ."

Mom sighed heavily and pulled my hands down from my face. "Grandma knows that you're a good person. You're smart and sensible."

"But . . ."

"Look," Mom bit her lip slightly. "Hopefully you two can learn from our mistakes and not let one wrong decision alter your entire relationship."

"But it doesn't seem that easy," I whispered.

"Willow!" Georgia's shrill cry interrupted my protest.

We looked up and saw her standing by the sliding doors.

"The doctor just came out," she yelled, running toward us. She came up beside us, breathy and eager. "Mia's going to be okay," she panted. "She broke a leg and dislocated her elbow, but the doctor said she's going to be fine."

A fresh burst of tears sprouted, but this time from relief.

Mom squeezed me. "She's going to be fine. Everything's going to be fine," she repeated, comforting me and, I think, herself.

31

Inside the hospital waiting room everyone chirped excitedly at the news of Mia's prognosis. Everyone stopped talking when they saw me enter but Mom and I just nestled ourselves next to the admissions desk. Mia's mother appeared, looking haggard and worn. As she scanned the crowd, Jake walked over to her. Mrs. Palmer smiled weakly at him. He asked her something and she nodded. "Yes," she said. "She does want to see you, but first she's asked to see Willow." She craned her neck around. "Willow?"

Everyone within earshot turned and looked at me again.

"Mia would like to see you." The look Mrs. Palmer gave me was slightly accusatory, and I knew she had heard the circulating rumors. I wanted to blurt out that I was sorry, that I didn't mean any harm, I'd do anything to help, to make it up to all of them, but before I could say a word, Mrs. Palmer turned and walked out of the waiting area and down a long sterile corridor.

I followed her quickly, feeling the same queasy feeling I had at the principal's office. I clasped Mom's hand like she was my security blanket and dragged her along. "Wait," I said as we passed by the gift shop. "Can I . . . can I grab something quickly?"

Mrs. Palmer looked at me then nodded curtly.

Five minutes later I emerged holding a big bouquet of fresh white roses. Mrs. Palmer was talking politely to Mom about hayrides at some pumpkin patch, and I smiled at Mia's mom gratefully. She didn't smile back. My insides tightened.

We walked down the hallway and opened the hospital room door. Mia was propped up on the narrow bed, one leg wrapped in a thick white cast. Her left arm hung from a sling and was pressed to her chest. Her father sat in a plastic chair beside her, drinking steaming coffee from a small Styrofoam cup. Coach Graham stood at the foot of the bed, nervously drumming her hand against the metal rails. All three of them turned and saw us enter. We walked closer to the bed, leaving the door open behind us.

Mia smiled at me. We walked up to her bed and stood awkwardly, forming a semicircle. My hand was hot and sweaty, still clutching Mom's hand.

"Hey," Mia said casually. At first I was shocked at how calm she seemed. How relaxed. But then I saw something in her expression and I understood. She was off the hook. Lying in a hospital bed with a cast and a sling meant she wouldn't have to perform some perfect Mia move. *But what about me?*

She nodded slightly at me as if she could hear my thoughts. "I wanted to have Willow here in this room when I tell you guys something," Mia said, looking back and forth between her parents and Coach Graham. "I'm pretty sure you've heard some rumors about me and Willow and hypnosis. I can tell by the look on your face, Mom."

Mrs. Palmer shifted, tried to change her expression from anger to just concern.

"It's true," Mia continued, and Mrs. Palmer gasped slightly. "Well, partly true. I did ask Willow to use hypnosis to help me do more advanced moves for the competition."

Mom didn't move a muscle. Didn't sigh or slump, but I could feel the energy around us change. There was tension—a force field of anxiety swelling from her pores.

"But Willow said no," Mia said.

Mrs. Palmer's brow furrowed. "Huh?" she asked.

"She said no," Mia repeated. "Many times. She said she didn't feel comfortable doing it. She said the flips looked too dangerous. She said I was getting too reckless." Mia's face contorted as she tried not to cry. "She was such a good friend—concerned for me. But I pushed her. I was emphatic. I forced her to do it because I thought it was the only way I could deliver what people expected from me—a big show. And now everyone is saying Willow did something wrong, but it was me. I was the bad friend." Her emotions won out and tears spilled down her flushed cheeks. "It's just so hard," she whispered. "Everybody looks at our family and thinks we're perfect. Dad's a successful doctor. Mom's so pretty and peppy. We live in a nice house with nice things and everybody just assumes life at the Palmer house is perfect. They expect *me* to be perfect—to get straight A's, to date the hot quarterback, to be the cheerleader that wins the competitions."

The room was stone silent—just the soft whirl of air rushing from the vent above Mia's bed and the drone of a laundry detergent commercial on the small TV propped in the corner of the room.

Coach Graham leaned over the bed rail, placed her hand gently on Mia's thick white cast. "Nobody's perfect, sweetie."

Mia's eyes filled again and the look on her face was crushingly transparent. She was waiting for her parents to agree.

Mom tightened her grip on my hand. I could feel that force field of energy swell again. I looked at her and saw thirty-three years of smothering expectation swirl in her eyes. I could anticipate the showdown. It would be so much easier to say the pent-up words to these people she hardly knew than to her own parents.

I squeezed her hand tighter. "Nobody is perfect," I whispered. I leaned over and gave Mia a hug.

"Thanks for the white roses," Mia said with a smile. "You remembered."

"Thank you," I said, "for explaining things."

She nodded.

I took Mom's hand and we exited quietly out of the room. When we walked through the lobby, everyone's conversation came screeching to a halt. The harsh beams of light from the fluorescent bulbs above hurt my eyes. I looked down toward the tiled floor.

Quinton raced over toward me and tried to hug me. I remained limp with my arms at my sides. "Quinton," I said, sounding a little desperate. "Thank you but I just need to go home."

He released me obediently. "Of course. I'll call you. Everything's okay," he reassured me.

Mom took my hand again and we walked toward the exit. Just as the sliding glass doors opened I felt a hand on my shoulder. I turned and saw Max. My eyes welled and my lip trembled. I couldn't face him. Not like this. Not after he had warned me about using hypnosis. Not after I had refused to listen. Not when my entire world was crashing in on me.

Without saying a word, he pulled his hand away. He gave me the saddest smile I'd ever seen. Then he turned and walked away.

When Mom and I got home I slumped onto the couch feeling depressed, like everything I wanted I had managed to destroy. Max. Grandma and Grandpa. I thought back to our first day here when Max and I were on the porch. There was a moment between us, I was sure of it. If only I had grabbed that opportunity and said how I felt, maybe everything could have turned out differently.

But maybe with Grandma there was still an opportunity to say what I really needed to say. I picked up the phone and dialed the numbers before I could change my mind. She answered on the first ring.

"Grandma," I said a little breathlessly. "I want you to come here—to our house—for dinner tonight."

Mom craned her neck from the kitchen and gave me an inquisitive look.

"Oh," Grandma replied. "Now? I could just pick you up and we could go to the steak house in town?"

"No," I answered. "I want you to come here." I felt a small burst of satisfaction.

Mom walked over. She had a small smile on her face. "Tell her to bring Grandpa."

I raised my eyebrows. She nodded. "I'd like you to bring Grandpa," I said into the phone. "If he's up to it."

Grandma agreed, sounding a little taken aback.

We hung up and I walked into the kitchen. "Where's the phone-book?" I asked. "I'm ordering Chinese food."

One hour later our doorbell rang. I thought Mom would be nervous but she wasn't. Instead she shuffled around, opening up the cartons of Chinese food with an intrigued look on her face. I opened the front door. Grandma was stiff backed and tentative, tightly clutching the crook of Grandpa's elbow.

"Grandpa!" I exclaimed, excited to see him up and walking. "You look fantastic!"

"I feel fantastic!" he bellowed.

I led them through the foyer and gestured for them to sit at the table.

"What's that smell?" Grandma asked as she helped Grandpa set his cane down.

"Hunan beef," I answered.

Grandma's eyes widened slightly.

"And sesame shrimp," Mom added, emerging from the kitchen with white cartons of food. She placed them down on the table with four glasses water.

I passed out napkins and utensils. For a moment Grandma

and Grandpa were motionless so I propped open the cartons, stuck spoons inside and said, "Dig in!"

Mom reached over and started dishing out the food.

"Look," I said before I lost my nerve. "I asked you here tonight because I wanted you to see me." I looked over at Mom. "I wanted you to see us—in our world. We don't eat on fine china. We don't have a lot of home-cooked meals. We didn't use an interior designer."

"You barely have furniture," Grandma said, looking around.

"But it's fine," I said. "It's not perfect, but this is us." My eyes started to feel glassy and the back of my throat burned. "We are not perfect. Mom's made some mistakes and I've made mistakes."

"Willow," Grandma tried to interrupt.

"No, let me finish." Through teary eyes I told them about using hypnosis on Mia. "I'm sorry if I've disappointed you. I'm sorry if you think I'm a terrible person, but I'm still the same girl who planted tulips with you last month. I'm still the same one who wants to go see *The Nutcracker* with you. I'm still the same girl who just wants my family to be whole again."

Grandma's lip trembled. "I want us to be a whole family, too."

"Well then you have to accept us the way we are," I said. "Mistakes and all."

"Of course I do," she said.

"No, you haven't." I started to cry. "Mom's tried really hard to change her life but you won't give her a chance. You didn't even ask about her new job; you just called it nonsense. That's not fair."

Mom reached over and put her hand on top of mine.

Grandma's forehead furrowed. She looked from me to Mom. "I'm sorry, it's just such a foreign thing for me and hard to understand."

Mom looked across the table at Grandpa. "Tell her, Dad."

"What?" I asked, confused.

Grandpa looked at Grandma. "Vicki's been coming over every week when you're at your Junior League meetings. She's been doing hypnosis on me to help me with my pain."

"What?" I asked breathlessly, thinking how I'd counted on Mom's late nights to allow Georgia and me to do our crazy potions and spells. I'd never stopped to question what she was doing.

"What are you talking about?" Grandma asked, swiveling her head back and forth between them.

"Vicki's helped me so now I can move my right side without the shooting pain. Not only can I walk, but Vicki has helped me with another important life skill. Now I can flip the channels on my remote." He laughed heartily, the sound ricocheting off the walls.

The sound of his laughter rang in my ears, resurrecting old memories from my childhood—of us playing checkers on the porch, him teaching me to bait a hook.

"But that's a result of your physical therapy," Grandma insisted, clenching her pearl necklace.

"Earlier in the summer I quit therapy," Grandpa grumbled.

"What?" Grandma exclaimed, throwing her hand to her chest.

"It just hurt too damn much," Grandpa said, grimacing at the memory. "Vicki suggested I give her pain control a try and I thought, *What have I got to lose?* After a few sessions of hypnosis, when the pain was less, I went back to physical therapy to help with mobility. This time I actually made some progress." He smiled over at Mom. And she smiled back at him with appreciation for his honesty. His acceptance.

"So all this improvement you've made?" Grandma's face scrunched up in disbelief.

Grandpa nodded. "Vicki's doing."

"But . . . but," Grandma finally said, flustered and confused.

"Yes, Mom, hypnosis can be used to help people," Mom said softly.

"Vicki's been taking online courses and she got a big fancy certificate and a pay raise," Grandpa said with pride. "And she's started an online business selling instructional hypnosis videos to help people stop smoking, lose weight and lots of other things."

"Well," Grandma said. "Well." She leaned her elbows on the table as if all this new information knocked the wind out of her.

I was overwhelmed too. I looked over at my mom and for the first time I didn't just see her purple heels or her short black skirt. When I looked in her eyes I didn't just see her enticing beauty. I saw something different. I think what I saw was contentment. Pride. Accomplishment.

"I came back to Georgia with the idea that I had to prove something to you," Mom said to Grandma. She tucked her long hair behind her ears. "But after our fight"—she bit her lip slightly—"I realized I have no control over how you think or what you feel. Only you can change your mind."

"Victoria . . ." Grandma said, but Mom interrupted her.

"But I realized I needed to prove something to myself. I needed to prove that what I was doing with my life was valued. Respectable. Meaningful." She turned toward me. "And I wanted to take better care of us."

"You take great care of me," I said. And I meant it. For the first time I realized that while all this time I wanted to have the perfect family, what Mom and I had was already pretty perfect. We took care of each other.

I leaned over and hugged Mom. Then I realized that while I was hiding my secrets of deception, her secrets were about making a better life for us. I swallowed the lump in my throat. "I'm so proud of you," I said softly.

Mom hugged me tightly.

The room was filled with the same silence that had penetrated Mia's hospital room earlier—the waiting for affirmation.

I looked over at Grandma. She was still leaning against the table looking completely staggered. "I'm so sorry, Victoria," she whispered. "I've been so"—she struggled not to cry—"unfair."

Mom broke free from my hug and reached across the table toward Grandma. "The thing is—I still may not be the ideal version of the daughter you always wanted. I'm never going to be a country club member or want to garden or go to the ballet. But"—Mom got a little teary—"I'm finding the ideal version of who *I* want to be. And you just have to decide whether that's good enough for you."

"We're flawed," I said. "We make mistakes. The best thing we can do is try and learn from our mistakes and move on. But we're never going to be perfect. But that's who we are. Take it or leave it."

"Oh, I've made so many mistakes, too," Grandma cried. She looked over at Mom. "All I ever wanted was to give you the perfect life."

"Maybe your perfect life wasn't perfect for me," Mom said quietly.

I thought about Mia's beach photo and realized that maybe there was no perfect model family. Maybe the more you try to mold and create something, the more likely it is to crack. Maybe, instead, we all had to find our individual best selves and that happiness would bond us together as a whole.

"Well," Mom said, spooning a heaping serving of sesame shrimp onto Grandma's plate, "if we're really going to make this thing work, you can start by calling me Vicki. I hate Victoria."

"But Victoria is such a beautiful name," Grandma insisted, smiling.

Mom huffed.

Grandpa shook his head. "Women," he grumbled, and we all laughed.

Grandma smirked then gave in. "Okay, *Vicki*." She took a tentative bite of her food. She raised her eyebrows in surprise. "Hey," she said. "That's not bad."

"In this house," I said, teasingly, "I was taught not to talk with my mouth full."

We all burst out laughing.

"Well," Grandma said after swallowing her food. She smiled. "Your mom taught you well."

33

For the remainder of the night, Mom and I smiled and joked around—happy to be accepted, happy to be part of Grandma and Grandpa's life again. After we cleaned the dishes and Grandma and Grandpa left, I plopped down on the couch, exhausted from the very long day. Mom sat down next to me with a more serious look on her face. "Do you understand now why I didn't want you fooling around with hypnosis?" she asked. "It can be fun, sure, and it can be very useful, but it's also very powerful and not something to be taken lightly."

I nodded. "I understand."

She sunk further into the couch and flipped through the channels until she found *Love Actually* just starting on a movie channel. And for a minute I thought it was all over. That all the chaos from my bad decisions was rectified—forgiven—but I couldn't rid myself of the lingering situation: Quinton. I wanted to think that Mom would forgive me for that, too. That she would help me out of the mess. But it was so hard to say the words, to admit more mistakes, to acknowledge my desperate need for her help. Would she think of me differently—not just because I'd done the hypnosis, but because I'd looked her in the eye and lied about it?

On TV, Hugh Grant's familiar voice narrated in his comfortable British accent: *It seems to me that love is everywhere. Often it's not particularly dignified or newsworthy, but it's always there—fathers and sons, mothers and daughters . . .*

And suddenly I was crying. I needed her help. But mostly, I needed to know she still loved me. Through heaving gulps, I told her everything about the love spell from the innocent start to Quinton's spiraling obsession. I told her how I tried everything to undo the hypnosis to no avail.

Mom sat stone still but put her hand on top of mine. And that was all I needed. "It's okay," she said reassuringly. "We'll figure it out. Tell me everything."

I calmed my tears and told her about Georgia's and my escapades in attempting to break the love spell.

Mom sat frozen. "You did *what*?" she asked, troubled.

I repeated the list of things we had tried—the cleansing potion, voodoo, banishment, and the Cut the Mojo love charm. "We tried everything to break the love spell," I repeated slowly, watching her mouth pop open in surprise.

"*Break the love spell?*" Mom stood up, putting her hand to her temples like she was in pain. "Willow, you didn't *cast a spell*. You're not a witch! You did hypnosis! It's totally different! There's science behind hypnosis—why do you think I've been studying so much? Why do you think it bothered me so much when Grandma called it 'new age voodoo'? You didn't cast a spell; you gave him a hypnotic suggestion!"

"Okay, okay," I said, cowering back a little. I had never seen her so worked up. "Well, what do I do then? How do I stop it?"

Mom inhaled deeply and ran her fingers through her hair, massaging her scalp. "You need to put Quinton under hypnosis and de-suggest the attraction."

I nodded. "I read that." I explained how Quinton didn't think he needed any more hypnosis because his sleepwalking had stopped.

Mom sat down next to me. "There is a method called rapid induction where you use a quick-jerk handshake and if the person has previously been hypnotized the handshake method will put them under almost instantaneously."

I nodded and told her I'd read that in her textbooks but that I had tried it to no avail.

"I'll teach you," she said. "So invite Quinton over tomorrow. And let's fix this mess once and for all."

And as I watched her, a feeling of reassurance washed over me. Mia had survived crashing out of a triple flip with a few broken bones. We had survived our reconciliation with Grandma and Grandpa, and were on the path to mending our family. Surely we could undo my control on Quinton's mind as well.

Sunday I invited Quinton over for lunch. He showed up promptly on time with a batch of brownies he made for me. We ate turkey sandwiches and talked about Mia's recovery, then ventured over to the couch with the brownies to watch a movie. I sat stiffly next to him, knowing this was my opportunity.

My heart beat nervously and I swallowed my fear. I reached for Quinton's hand and he looked over and smiled at me adoringly. With a quick, jerky flick of the wrist, a move that I had practiced a hundred times the night before on the enormous stuffed teddy bear Quinton gave me, I wrenched his hand, leaned in close to his ear, and spit out, "Sleep!"

Honestly, I hadn't fully believed that it would work, although Mom insisted. But sure enough, Quinton's head flopped over to the side like a scoop of ice cream tipping off its cone.

Mom leaned her head around the corner eagerly. "Progress?" she asked.

"He's under," I said.

She nodded. "Get to it, then."

So I turned back to Quinton and looked at his beautiful face. I tried to create a perfect boyfriend, a perfect relationship. But sometimes when you try to get everything, you walk away with nothing. I took a breath and tried my best to keep my voice steady. "Quinton Dillinger, when you see me, Willow Grey, you will think, *Willow is a nice girl. We had a nice relationship. But I need to move on. I need to focus on my academics and football. If someone else comes along, I've learned that too much obsession is unhealthy.*" I took another breath and brought him back.

He stretched out lazily on the couch. "Oh man, I think I dozed off," he said apologetically.

"It's okay," I said. "Boring movie."

He smiled and looked at his watch. "I better run," he said, and I walked him to the door. He gave me a funny look, but then shook it off, kissed me good-bye, and left.

Monday morning Quinton picked me up as usual and held my hand as we walked from the parking lot into school, but he seemed a little distracted. Something looked different in his eyes. We reached my locker. He kissed me good-bye and left.

Georgia scurried up next to me. "Any evidence that it's working?" she asked.

"Hard to tell," I said, grabbing my books and slamming the metal locker door.

"Did you hear?" Georgia asked.

"Hear what?" I asked tentatively, thinking, *Please don't make it be another Facebook fan page or some other insane display of Quinton's love.*

"Max broke up with Minnie." She raised her eyebrows suggestively.

"Really?" I asked, surprised.

We stated to walk down the hallway. I thought about the look on Max's face at the hospital—disappointment. And he hadn't called or texted me since. I wanted to talk to him, ask him what had happened, but I felt so unsure of what our relationship even was anymore.

The bell rang and Georgia and I darted into our respective classrooms.

Later, in English class, it was my turn to do my oral report. I walked up to the front of the room and everyone's eyes found me. I felt so exposed, like people had too much insight into my life lately and this report would be just another eyeful. I shuffled my stack of index cards and cleared my throat. "The topic for my oral report was to discuss three themes from *A Midsummer Night's Dream.*" I glanced over at Mrs. Stabile and she smiled at me, indicating that I should start. "*The course of love never did run smooth,* the character Lysander said." I flushed a little. Truer words were never spoken. "This highlights one of the play's most prominent themes: the difficulty of love and romance. Although the tone of the play is lighthearted, poking fun at the troubles the lovesick suffer, it demonstrates that when love is out of balance—when one person loves the other more—there can never be harmony in the relationship." I looked up from my notes and caught Quinton's stare. He was fixed on me, but not with a look of enchantment—rather, with a look of curiosity and interest.

"A tangled love affair," I continued, locking eyes with Quinton, "can only be resolved when symmetry in love is achieved. True love will always triumph in the end—but only if you've found the right person. And it's never an easy road to find them."

There was a romantic sigh from somewhere in the classroom. I looked up, half expecting it to be Mia, but her chair was vacant and obvious—like a missing tooth.

"Of course Shakespeare also touches on a theme of magic," I continued. "The fairies' magic brings about hilarious and entertaining situations, but the misuse of magic creates . . . chaos." I choked a little on the last word, unable to stop looking at Mia's chair or feeling Quinton's stare on me.

"Finally," I said, "appearances are deceiving. Thanks to Puck's pranks, reality wore a deceptive mask. Things were not always as perfect as they seemed."

I stacked my cards together, smiled one quick smile at Mrs. Stabile, then found my way back to my desk, putting love triangles and magical control behind me. All this time, Mia and I were both looking for something we thought we wanted, but maybe we underestimated what we already had. All the controlling and plotting toward what we thought we wanted left us only with broken bones and broken dreams. What's funny is that even though Mia was laid up with a cast on her leg and no cheerleading scholarship and I was alone with no perfect boyfriend and no spotlight, maybe what we found—families that loved us for the very things we were trying to change—was really what we needed all along.

The next morning I had an idea. Instead of using all my anti-frizz serums and sprays, I went into Mom's bathroom. I raided her cabinet and found something to add volume and enhance curl. I shrugged and gave it a try. As I blew my hair dry, something incredible happened. My hair fell into cascading soft waves.

When I walked out of my bedroom, Mom's mouth dropped. "You look fantastic," she smiled.

I smiled.

When Quinton picked me up for school, I noticed the dough love charm necklace he'd been wearing since Saturday was not around his neck. I was about to ask him where it was when Quinton stopped short at a light and turned to face me.

"Do you think I can stop by after football practice this afternoon? I kind of think we need to have a talk."

In all of romantic history, I don't think there's ever been a girl more excited to hear the dreaded *we need to have a talk.*

"Sure," I said. "Come over whenever you're done."

The whole day I fidgeted. Georgia and I placed bets on what he would say, whether the second round of hypnosis had worked. When we walked out of lunch, I passed Max in the hallway and my heart thundered. I wanted to rush over to him, tell him that I was so close to fixing my messes, that my life would be back to normal. *Could we go back to normal? Back to the way it was when Max was the first person I turned to for everything in my life?* But when I finally got the nerve to cross the hallway toward him, Trent walked over to him and devoured his attention.

After school, the minutes crept by so slowly it was painful. When the doorbell finally rang, I popped up off the couch like a jack-in-the-box springing out of captivity. I raced to the door.

Quinton stood on the threshold. Across the family room, Oompa raised his head from his slumber. He glanced over at Quinton, then dropped his fat head back onto his paws, not even making the effort to walk over to him.

Quinton suggested we take a ride to the park. He was torturously quiet as we drove the mile and a half to the entrance of Poplinger Park. He parked next to the swings, and for a moment of agony I shuddered at the thought of another meaningful reenactment of our initial encounter. He sat on the same swing Max had sat on just weeks before and began to sway back and forth.

"I got my midterm grades," he said.

I nodded, sitting on the swing next to him. "Me too."

Quinton looked up at a bird flying overhead. "I can't believe how bad my grades were."

My stomach churned with guilt.

He sighed loudly, his long bangs blowing a little in the breeze of his breath. "I've never blown off my studies or football before." He shook his head as if reprimanding himself.

"Let me help you," I offered. "Maybe Mrs. Stabile will let you make up your oral report and I can help you with it. Or I'm pretty good at math. . . ."

He used his foot to stop the swing, then looked over at me. "That's so nice, Willow. I feel bad, but I think that maybe . . . maybe you and

I should actually spend a little less time together. Maybe cool things off a bit. I'm really sorry. It's not that I don't like you . . ."

"I understand," I said. "Quinton, you are so smart and your grades have always been good. You'll be able to pull your GPA back up in no time. Everything will be okay, I promise. And I'll help you in any way I can if you need it. I don't want to be the cause of any stress for you."

"No, you've never been a stress," he said, smiling. "I really enjoyed our time together. It felt like . . . like a whole different me. It was fun—it felt liberating. But I think it's time to get back to the old me."

I nodded. I knew exactly what he meant. "It's been great," I agreed. Relief coursed through my body.

Tension released in his face. "It was the best."

"We'll always have Oompa," I said.

He grinned. "Yeah. Do you think I have to break up with him too?" He was smiling, but I could tell he was restless, anxious to get home and re-find himself, so I told him to go on—I'd just walk home. It was a nice night anyway.

He gave me a hug and we parted as friends—the way we had met back on that fateful day in August, when Oompa had sparked our very first encounter.

34

When I walked through the door, Mom was home from work and sitting at the table paying bills. "So," she asked. "Success?"

I nodded. "He dumped me."

"Great," Mom said. We both laughed at how strange that sounded.

I walked back to my room and sat at my desk. I pulled out a sheet of paper and a pen. I had so many things I wanted to say to Max. I wanted to tell him that Quinton was just a plot to make him jealous; that I'd loved him for so long. I had found the courage with Grandma, why was it so much harder to be honest with Max?

I looked out the window at the maple tree. All the leaves had changed into bursts of oranges and reds. It was like the tree sprouted into a brighter, prettier version of itself. It made it seem like anything was possible—like flaws could morph into something beautiful. I thought of how Max loved Oompa in spite of his squished face and moody disposition. He loved his truck regardless of its loud, rumbling motor and messy interior. I needed to see if Max could love the real me—the me he bonded to all those years ago. Was there any way he could love that girl again?

My phone rang. The caller ID flashed Georgia's name. I answered.

"I GOT THE PART!" She screamed over the swooshing wind. She must have been driving with her top down.

"Congratulations!" I yelled. "You're going to be a much better spiritual advisor than Silver Rain!"

"No doubt!" she yelled. "So how did it go with Quinton?"

I told her about our break-up.

"Good," she said. "Did you hear—Mia broke up with Jake today."

"Really?"

"Yup."

Good for her, I thought. She deserves so much more.

"So, when are you going to talk to Max? Wait, hold on, I need to put the top up so I can hear you better."

Suddenly her radio blasted at full volume.

I jumped and flailed my arm into a stack of books and CDs. They tumbled across my desk and a few fell to the floor.

"Sorry, sorry," Georgia said. "I hit the volume knob by mistake." She adjusted the stereo volume lower. I heard a mechanical hum and then the rushing wind died down. "Okay, so what are you going to say to him?"

"I don't know," I said as I straightened the mess of books. I reached down to retrieve the fallen things and there, on my carpet, was the clear, plastic case with an unmarked CD inside. It was the

CD Max had given me so long ago. I had never listened to it because my stereo was broken. On the phone, Georgia droned on about seizing this opportunity but I wasn't paying attention.

I held the CD case in my hand and thought of the music sheets resting on Max's drums. The way I teased him about a love song. How he got so secretive and stashed the music sheets away. How a few days later he gave me a CD. How at Quinton's party when we talked about music he looked like he was going to say something. How when we sat on his couch and talked about broken hearts he held my hand. How he invited me to the concert with him. How we sat on the swings and it seemed like a moment passed between us. How he sat on the principal's bench and told me he liked me just the way I was.

Could the clue to Max's feelings be on the CD? Had I held it all along?

I had to listen to it before I talked to Max. I thought about Georgia's car stereo blasting and suddenly I had an idea. "I've got to go," I said to Georgia. "No time to explain!" I hung up and grabbed the CD. I sprinted out into the living room. "I need your keys," I said to Mom.

She pointed to the table. "Is everything okay?"

"I'll know soon," I said and found the keys. I raced outside to her car and flung open the door. I shoved the keys in the ignition and slid the silver CD into the stereo. I turned up the volume and waited, breathless.

A clicky noise echoed through the speakers; followed by some static. *Hi Willow.* It was Max's voice, and at the sound of it, my stomach fluttered. It wasn't songs on the CD—it was a message.

We've been friends for seventeen years now, and I've always been able to talk to you about anything—good or bad, funny or sad. I've been able to tell you how fun you are and how smart or how absolutely horrible your taste in music is. But there's one thing I never knew how to tell you.

Oh my God. My heart pulsed.

But then you know what? You kind of showed me how to tell you. Without even realizing it—you gave me my answer. Max cleared his throat; then there was a strum of a guitar in the background followed by a drumbeat. The tune sounded familiar but different. I couldn't exactly place it, but then it hit me. It was Taylor Swift. The song Pink Sundress sang at Jake's party. He had been listening. He had understood.

Dreaming of the day when you wake up and find that what you're looking for has been here the whole time . . . Why can't you see? You belong with me.

The drumbeat slowed down. The guitar softened. Then there was only static. Then there was none.

My heart was on fire.

I needed to go find him. I needed to see if I still had a chance.

I revved the engine and backed out of the driveway.

I was on a mission.

35

I sped across town to Max's house. I pulled up his driveway and saw his black truck parked in the garage. He was home. I ejected the CD, turned off the car and sprinted up the front steps before I could change my mind.

Mrs. Montgomery answered the door dressed in green scrubs, home from her nursing job at the hospital. "Willow!" she exclaimed. "How are you? Isn't it just *great* about your mom? I'm so proud of her. So proud. She told me she already has about fifty preorders for her video series. Isn't that just amazing? Good things are in store for her. And you. Good things." She held the door open and gestured for me to come inside.

"Um," I stammered. "Is Max here? I, um, need to show him something out here."

"Sure, sweetheart. One second." She smiled at me and disappeared inside the house.

My heart ticked and my whole body felt electric, like I'd just drunk a hundred Starbucks mochas. *Please don't make it be too late.*

Max walked out wearing his white karate uniform, tied with his black belt double knotted in front.

"Hi," I said tentatively.

"Hi." He sounded cautious. "What are you doing here?"

I held up the CD case. "Do you mean this?" I asked, my voice wobbly and my hands trembling. "Is it true?"

He froze, looking completely caught off guard.

I walked closer toward him. "I—I finally listened to it. My CD player was broken, and I had to listen to it in the car—anyway, it's not important. All those times I felt something—something between us—did you feel it too?"

He looked down, fiddled with his belt.

"Why didn't you just ask me if I liked you? Why didn't you just try and kiss me or something? Why did you have to go be all cryptic and give me a CD?"

He looked up at me. "Because I was scared, okay?"

"Scared? How could you be scared of me? You're the person I feel most comfortable around! You're my best friend!"

"That's the problem!" he said. He looked over his shoulder at the front door then he hopped down the front steps. He waved his hand for me to follow him. We walked across the front lawn toward the street. "Remember all those years ago before you moved and we were goofing off in that tree? You hypnotized me to always be your best friend! I thought that was all you wanted, Willow—friendship! Every time I got that feeling inside—like I wanted more, like I wanted to hold your hand and kiss you and tell you how much I liked you, how

I thought you were the most interesting person I've ever met—I'd hear your voice in my head saying, *you'll always be my best friend*. Not boyfriend. Not crush. Not soul mate. FRIEND. BEST FRIEND. I was HYPNOTIZED, Willow! It was like there was a brick wall between us. I saw the wall. I felt the wall. And I couldn't climb over it."

I stumbled back and inadvertently fell down on the curb. Again, my affair with hypnosis had botched everything up. No wonder he was so against me hypnotizing Mia.

We stared at each other for a minute. Then Max sat down next to me.

"So all along you wanted to like me, but my own mind control prevented it," I whispered.

Max turned to look at me. His eyes were soft and sincere. "But the more I was around you, the stronger my will grew." He took my hand. "I overcame it—the hypnosis—because I swear I heard that brick wall collapse. I saw the barrier crumble."

"You overcame the hypnosis?" I gasped.

He touched his chest. "The heart wants what the heart wants."

A lump formed at the back of my throat. It was impossible to control people's minds, and now I'd learned you couldn't sway the heart, either.

"Say something," he whispered.

"I've always liked you, Max. Ever since the day on the phone when you told me I was special."

"Incredible. I told you that you were incredible."

"You remember?"

"Of course I do." He said, his face breaking out in a slow grin. "Man, I didn't like another guy looking into your crazy eyes."

I took a breath. I didn't want to do it, but I knew I had to be honest. I told Max that I had hypnotized Quinton to like me. I told him I realized what a mistake it was and that I was never going to use hypnosis again.

Max looked stunned. "The song dedications, the locker pictures, the flowers—all of that was because of mind control?" he asked. "Is that the kind of relationship you want?"

"No," I whispered. "I want you."

And then Max did something amazing. Without my having to hypnotize him, or tell him what I wanted, or without trying to control the situation in any way, Max reached over, pulled my chin up, and pressed his lips to mine. I felt all shaky, like my whole body was turning into Jell-O. He pulled me closer, kissed me more passionately. I lit up like I'd just swallowed a light bulb and flicked the switch. *Max wanted me. All along Max has wanted me.*

"So you think we can try this?" I asked between kisses. "Try to date?" Another kiss. "You don't think I need to"—another kiss—"rehypnotize you and take away that stuff about always being my best friend?"

Max pulled away abruptly. "Um, NO. Whatever I feel for you is stronger than hypnosis. Remember, the wall crumbled? Besides, I thought you just said you weren't going to do hypnosis anymore?"

"No, no, I'm not," I said, leaning in to kiss his neck. "I just want to make sure there's nothing else standing in our way." I leaned in to kiss his lips, but he put his hand up and looked at me suspiciously.

"You can't use your little mind control games to make me into some perfect boyfriend, okay?" Max said. "You can't hypnotize me to want to take ballroom dancing classes or set personal ringtone love songs or skywrite *I love you*. You have to want to be with *me*—the same Max you've known forever. Not some idealized version of me, okay? We can be perfect just how we are."

"I know," I said, and we just looked at each other. "There's nothing wrong with a little *romance*, though," I mumbled, smiling.

He smiled back at me and I reached over for his hand. Suddenly he snatched his away. "What are you doing?" he asked, his eyes popping open. "I remember what you told me about that handshake method to hypnotize people!" He stood up, pointing his finger at me accusingly.

"What?" I asked innocently, standing up. "I have no idea what you're talking about! I just wanted to hold your hand!"

"Yeah, right!" He grinned at me, shaking his head. "And I'm not singing any more cheesy love songs!"

"Why not? That was so sweet! I love Taylor Swift!" I reached out for him. "Come here, Max. Hold my hand!"

He turned and started to run away, laughing.

"Come here!" I yelled, laughing. "There's nothing wrong with a little ROMANCE!" I grabbed his waist and spun him around to face me.

"You are crazy," he said.

"Incredible," I corrected.

"Incredibly crazy." He smiled. He leaned over and kissed me again. It was a passionate kiss, filled with so many years of friendship and longing and obstacles and finally—finally—connection.

As we kissed, I made a mental vow to never use hypnosis to get what I wanted again. Well, unless . . .

Acknowledgments

The first person I need to thank is the fabulous Mandy Hubbard. She listened to me when I knew I wanted to write a book about hypnosis but couldn't find the story. Thanks for helping me nail down the concept.

Huge debts of gratitude to Jocelyn Davies, who scooped up the idea and helped me build this book. I loved working with you from the ground up on this. Your smart and thoughtful editorial vision truly brought this story to the next level. Thanks to Ben Schrank and the entire team at Razorbill for wanting to work with me again and for giving me another gorgeous cover.

Thanks to my first-draft readers Kristen Groseclose, Jenny Moss, and Shelli Johannes Wells. Your frank comments and critiques pushed me forward. The online group of authors, The Debutantes of 2009, remain a huge source of information and camaraderie. You guys are amazing.

Many thanks to Cass Briggs for reconnecting after so many years and sharing her thoughtful notes and experiences on hypno-therapy. A huge smile and hug to Crystal Patriarche, who loved and promoted Crush Control long before she even read it.

I'm so grateful for the endless enthusiasm of my parents, in-laws, and friends (far, near, and online—a huge shout-out to all of my Alpha-Phis!) for their support of my first book and journey through publishing a second. Eternal thanks to my best friends Jackie Tomaro and Kristen Groseclose for championing me in all aspects of life.

I've been so overwhelmed by all the emails and Facebook notes from readers. Thank you all for taking the time to contact me. Your interest and passion mean the world to me!

I'm so blessed to have found such a caring, energetic, and smart agent, Tricia Davey. Thanks for all you do.

Finally, all my love and gratitude to my wonderful family: Chris, Sam, and Izzie.